Riot Kings

The Bedlam Boys

Ruby Vincent

Published by Ruby Vincent, 2021.

Prologue

The clock ticked down to nine. Ten. Eleven.

Dusting off my hands, I checked outside one last time. No one had arrived or approached the house. Once you got to the trees, you had cover. Otherwise, it was clear sight lines on the twelve acres of farm.

I'll go inside and stand with my back facing the fireplace. I'll have them if they come through the front door or from the back. If they attack me, I defend myself.

A simple plan without holes—except when I considered the possibility all they wanted to do was talk.

The question invaded my mind on the walk across the green.

If the death of Axel Verlice changed things and now they were willing to tell me the truth, how would the night end? Do I hope to get him to the police station with a bow and arrow at his back? Do I entertain the thought of killing him and ending his threat to my life once and for all?

I climbed the porch steps. *If I find out his name and who he is, I'll let him go. The police can mull over the dilemma of killing him in a shoot-out instead of—*

Pausing, I lit on a small, black envelope lying where the welcome mat used to be. When did he leave this? He couldn't have come while I was in the barn, so it must've been sometime before then and after Jeremy and I drove away from the farm.

I picked it off the porch.

Did you really think you could fool me, bitch?

I'll give it to you, you had me going for a second. That just makes the betrayal worse.

You're not who I thought you were.

You're a fake. A mistake. A waste.

Damaged garbage left in the discard bin, and you're too stupid to know it.

I bet you still don't know who's on the other side of this door.

I read the note once, twice, five times, palms slickening with each one.

Did I think I could fool him? What did that mean? Did he know about Verlice?

How?

Doesn't matter. I dropped the note, leveling my bow. I didn't know who was on the other side of this door, but I was going to find out.

"This ends tonight."

Grabbing the knob, I let the door swing open. It parted a crack and stopped.

"Hmm."

Planting my feet on the wood, I kicked it in, running inside.

"Hmmm!"

Bella screamed at me—eyes bulging and wetness soaking her gag. She thrashed in the chair she was tied to, banging the legs on the rotted living room floor.

"Hmm!"

Snap.

A tiny missile streaked across my vision. The arrow sunk in Bella's chest, and it wasn't mine.

"Bella!" I ran to her, dropping my bow and arrow at her feet. "Oh, Bella, no. No, I'm sorry. I'm so sorry."

Her head dropped to her chest, the light fading from her eyes.

"No!" I screamed. My lungs ripped with sobs.

It was a trap. A trap that I sprung.

The Letter Man found out I didn't kill Axel, and my friend paid the price as promised.

"No, p-please. Bella, no. It's my fault. This is all my fault."

I scrabbled at her zip ties. She couldn't be dead. I'd get her to the hospital. I'd call—

Eeeee.

A door creaking open pierced my mania. The Letter Man was here. He came to watch the final moments with Jennifer, and now my destruction.

A polished black shoe stepped over the threshold.

Snatching up my bow, I whipped around, a keening wail breaking the silence, and released my arrow.

It stuck in the wood—centimeters from his face.

"Ouch." He stepped out of the shadows, and every beautiful inch of Cairo Sharpe was revealed. "Not the welcome I was hoping for."

Chapter One

Cairo stepped inside. "What the fuck was that—" His expression changed, eyes falling on Bella. "Holy shit, Rain, what did you do?"

"Me?!" My heart rended in two—both pieces screaming agony as they died. I asked it not be Cairo. Let the Letter Man be anyone else but Cairo, Roan, Arsenio, Jacques, or Legend.

I scrambled for another bow, aiming for a dead-on strike.

"You did this! You— You—" Understanding dawned. "You knew I didn't kill Axel Verlice. Of course you fucking knew. So, you killed Bella."

That gorgeous, perfect face remained fixed in confusion. "What the hell are you talking about? Once again there's a body and you're standing there holding a bow. I figured the first time you had no choice, but this..." He shook his head at my dying friend. "You really do have a taste for killing."

Fury eroded my veins, spilling hot blood that rushed to my head and cheeks. "That's not going to work. You don't get to blame me for this— Don't move!" I drew back, narrowing on his heart.

He halted, though no trace of fear shone in his eyes.

"Why did you do this?" Brushing against Bella's shoulder, tears dripped down my chin. "You didn't have to do this to her. Bella was good. Kind. How could you?"

Cairo flicked from me to her. "Rain, let me make this clear: I did not kill this woman. I don't know her. Now why don't you make clear why you think otherwise?"

The arrow shook. "I said that's not going to work," I hissed. "Nice shoes, Sharpe."

"My shoes? What the fuck are you on about?"

"Those are the same black shoes the Letter Man wore— I said don't move."

Cairo kept coming, advancing on me, predator's glint in his green pools. He reached for me, and I fired.

"Fuck!" Diving out of the way, the arrow caught his shoulder, ripping a tear through fabric and skin. Cairo flashed and snatched my bow before I readied another to finish the job.

"I don't know who the fuck the Letter Man is, Rain!" He flung the bow behind him. "Tell me what's going on?"

"You tell me," I said, backing away. "What are you doing here?"

"You've been gone for hours. You didn't pick up your phone." Cairo pushed to his feet, clutching his bleeding shoulder. "I've long since learned when I can't find my pet, it means she ran back home."

Watching me backing away, Cairo probed Bella's neck. He cursed under his breath. "What happened here?" His gaze continued to the kitchen, and the setup rigged to kill Bella the moment I entered. "Explain. Now."

Chest heaving, I replied, "I was told to come here by the man who's been tormenting and fucking with my life for weeks, after he took over for his buddy Cavendish. He said we'd meet tonight... then you walked through the door."

"I am not the man you came here to meet. Or the man, I assume, who killed this woman."

I wasn't giving in that easily. Not while Bella's blood stained the floor. "Then why are you wearing those shoes, Sharpe? Why are you dressed like that?"

"I had an invitation to dinner. The boss has a dress code," he said simply. "You done interrogating me? Ready to share what the fuck is going on?"

"Promise me."

"What?"

"Promise me!" I cried. "Promise you had nothing to do with this. Swear you're not him."

"That's it? A promise is going to convince you after this!" He motioned to his bleeding wound. "Should've said that from the fucking beginning, woman. I promise." The furious oath was a dagger through me. "I did not do this, Rain. I don't play these games. Not with you.

"With you I don't have to."

I didn't want them to. I fought through my rage and grief to hold it back, but deep down, his words were penetrating.

"I came here to find you. No other reason," he said, "and as a result I'm getting my blood all over a crime scene. Tell me why."

"Bella," I rasped. "Bella, she—"

I broke down, collapsing sobbing on the floor. I think I went on trying to tell Cairo what happened, but he couldn't understand me, and I couldn't understand at all.

Why had the Letter Man done this? It wasn't enough he held her life over my head. It wasn't enough to torture me and demand more blood on my hands. In the end, he punished my deceit by making me what I refused to be.

It was me who loosed the arrow that ended her life. He forced me to kill her.

He made me watch her die.

Hands circled me, lifting me up.

"No." I was carried out. "We can't leave her. Cairo, we can't—"

"Shh," he crooned. "We're not going far. You need to tell me the whole story, and you can't do that next to her."

Cairo dropped the tailgate and set me on the truck bed. He walked away, making me cry out, but soon returned carrying a first aid kit. He dropped it on my lap.

"Fix your mess while you talk."

Cairo climbed in the back and tugged me sniffling after him. Leaning against the truck, he winced shoving the torn fabric down.

The gash wasn't too deep but still nasty. He waited, expecting me to care for him. It took some time for my shaky hands to pry off the lid, and take out the bandages and antiseptic.

A grimace was all he afforded me as the liquid bathed his wound. "Talk," he ordered.

It came slow, but it came. "Months ago, I started receiving these letters on my doorstep. Creepy, terrifying rants and riddles warning me that if I didn't find and kill them before Ruckus Royale, they'd choose someone to sacrifice that night."

I dabbed around the cut, cleaning the blood. Somehow, the task was calming me—giving me something to focus on.

"You know how that story ended," I whispered. "I discovered the man was Cavendish and his victim, Jennifer Wilson. He said either he died that night or Jennifer did. I chose Jennifer and a text with her location came less than twenty minutes after he died.

"I rescued her and got to believe for all of one night that it was over. That was until I came home and found another black letter on my porch."

"Black letter?" Cairo sat up straight. "He's been sending you black letters?"

"Yeah," I replied, stilling at the intense look on his face. "Why?"

Cairo drifted off, staring through the trees. "Black letters come to those wise enough to untangle the prose," he whispered. "Black letters come to men who remember who served them when. Black letters come with a price. Remember what you owe. Bow to the sacrifice."

A chill gripped my spine. "Cairo, what was that? Why did you say that?"

"Not me," he muttered, eyes glazing. "It's something my father used to say."

"Your father?" Hatred rose in me as it always did at the mention of Jack Sharpe. "The sheriff?"

"When he was drunk, I'd hear him mumbling it to himself. I asked him once what it meant and he said it was an old Bedlam nursery rhyme."

"A nursery rhyme? What kind of nursery rhyme tells children to worship a sacrifice?"

"The same kind that has children singing about the plague and babies in cradles falling out of trees," he said. "Most rhymes are fucked up, Rain, but they all mean something. I figured that one had to do with the revolt and haven't thought about it since," he said, focusing on me. "But you're saying that's what Cavendish and his friend have been sending you. Black letters."

I nodded slowly, thinking over the words. "Yes. And it's like the rhyme. Or it was with Cavendish. He gave me a riddle, forcing me to untangle the prose. And what else did it say? Men that remember who served them when. Who served who? Why have I never heard this before?"

Cairo guided my hands back to the cut. "We didn't exactly sing it every morning during preschool carpet time. It's just something he used to say. The real question is, are these fucks copying the rhyme, and why? Why did Cavendish choose you, Rain? The truth," he said to my headshake.

"I don't know. I never knew," I said. "I asked and he rambled like a nutcase, saying something about my ancestors abandoning the fight but this time I wouldn't. They both acted like they knew me."

"Did you know Cavendish?"

"I never even spoke to the fucking man. That day you picked us up outside his house was the first we met face-to-face."

"Do they think you're someone else? Or are they making you pay for someone else?"

I finished cleaning him and pressed the bandage to his skin. It was soaked through in seconds. Cairo needed a real doctor and stitches.

"They mentioned your ancestors. What if this was never really about you?" Cairo gripped my hand, stopping me reaching for another bandage. "You'd be surprised how many of us in this town are paying penance for our fathers' sins."

"Maybe I am," I said softly. "But it's not my father, or his mother, or his mother's mother who is receiving these letters. It's not them who got their friend killed. It's me. Whatever started this, it's about me now."

"Who was she?" Cairo was still holding my hand. I slid up his palm, linking fingers as slick with his blood as mine.

"Bella was the night manager at the motel. She was sweet, Cairo. She didn't deserve this. It's all my fault," I said so softly the wind took my confession.

"Why her? Did you get another riddle? You didn't kill him in time."

"It wasn't him I didn't kill. He ordered me to choose an innocent person at random and make their death trending news on Dante's show. So I told him that I killed—"

"—Axel Verlice." Cairo sat up straight. "And he killed her anyway?"

"He knew I tricked him."

His brows snapped together. "That's not possible. The only people who know who truly killed Verlice are the six of us."

"That's not true," I said, wiping my face. "There's also the person on the other end of the phone who told the Bedlam Boys to kill Axel Verlice."

Cairo's expression wiped blank. "You don't know anything about that person, and you're going to forget they exist. Forget them," he barked when I opened my mouth. "They didn't do this anyway. Trust me, they have nothing to gain by torturing you and murdering night managers. This is something else."

"Then, how did the Letter Man know?"

"Verlice's place was trashed and the man's skull was beaten in with a pool cue. Possibly, they found out the details of his death and figured you didn't jump from careful plans and containers in the sand to Arsenio," he said simply. "Whoever Cavendish and his friend really are, they're not stupid, or we would've found them out a long time ago."

I nodded, sinking down onto the bed. "You're right. The arrow in the heart was me, but they must have figured out the rest was someone else. I thought I was being clever, and Bella died for it. What do I do, C-Cairo?" The words stuck in my throat. "How do I tell her father what I've done?"

"You're not going to." Cairo climbed out of the truck. "No one is going to know you were involved."

"But—"

"Listen. You don't know who did this, but while they're playing this sick game with you, they're not trying to kill you," he said. "If the game ends, who knows what the fuck this psycho will do, and we don't know who he is to see him coming. You can't go to my dad talking about Letter Men and burning Cavendish alive. If he doesn't flatout arrest you, it'll get very dangerous for you in Bedlam, very fast."

"Bella," I whispered.

"We won't leave her like this. I'll tell the sheriff I came out to an abandoned farm to fuck around and interrupted Bella's murder. The guy attacked me." He gestured to his shoulder. "And got away. I didn't see his face, but going by the arrow, he's connected to Cavendish's death."

I was listening even if I couldn't move. "Do you think that will work?"

"Yes. The sheriff won't blink an eye. His officers will work the scene. They'll find any evidence if it's there and look into Cavendish's background on their own. She will have justice. By Judge Stone's hands, or ours."

"Okay."

My voice was small. I was small—curling in on myself, pressing my forehead to my knees. Bella's cries. Her bulging eyes begging me to stop played on a horrific loop in my mind.

"Let's go." Cairo lifted me up. He groaned in pain but kept up till he placed me on the passenger seat. "You can't be here when the sheriff arrives. I'm taking you back. The guys will take care of you while I handle this."

"I... should drive," I said, though I still didn't move.

"Sleep, Rain." He gently closed my eyes. They stayed close. "This won't happen again. The shit finally made the mistake that's going to end him. No one messes with what's mine."

His possessive kiss stole my lips—the final send-off pushing me off the cliff. I sank into the darkness, where the Letter Man waited.

JACQUES

"Cavendish ordered his own execution." I repeated it, and for the points stacked against my IQ, it made no damn sense. "He asked to be burned alive?"

"I don't know that he specified the how," Legend said, voice not carrying. He glanced in his room where Rainey was an unmoving mound beneath his sheets. "According to Cairo, it wasn't just that he threatened to kill Jennifer Wilson. He ordered Rainey to kill him to save her life. Afterward, another deranged fuck took over."

I softly shut the door, leaving her to sleep. Legend followed me down to the kitchen, silent and allowing me to think.

I can't imagine what he thought was going on in my head that was different than his. I had no obscure theories to recall. My mind wasn't a source for abnormal psychology.

This was new.

"How did it start?" I asked. "Why?"

"Cairo got as much out of her as he could. Rainey said she didn't know him. Cavendish was a stranger to her, and she can't begin to guess who this new guy is."

Legend pulled ingredients from the fridge, preparing to make a late-night meal. People marvel that a young wealthy man knew how to cook as well as Legend did. But then people were ignorant creatures who based their conclusions on stereotypes instead of reason and observation.

Learning to cook and become self-sufficient was the logical path for a person with absentee parents, who frequently lost nannies and housekeepers for refusing to pay them a salary suited to the amount of work they made them do. Legend spent a considerable amount of time in his formative years in this mansion alone. He had to learn to cook. No one else was doing it for him.

"That doesn't follow," I said. "If this is a personal vendetta, naturally they cannot be strangers. Their paths will have crossed at some point and set off the chain of events that led them here. If de Souza doesn't know the direct cause, then there must have been an indirect one. Example, she ran over Cavendish's little sister in a hit and run, and didn't know she had a brother. There must be something," I repeated.

"Only one fault in that logic." Legend brought out the cutting board. The onion reduced to mince under his knife. "A vengeful brother would light her on fire. He wouldn't give her a choice between killing him and a random woman. The plan clearly wasn't to have her arrested for his death either. His accomplice continued the sick game instead of turning her over to the cops."

"You're correct." I dug my palms into my temples, clenching my teeth as pressure built behind my eyes. "This does not correlate to the majority of revenge killings. Why are both of these people determined to make Rainey de Souza a killer?"

"What do we actually know about Rainey in the first place?" Legend's voice was growing small. "I remember the times she came to the distillery, rattling in the back of the truck with the corn delivery. She's not lying about the farm or the old woman who rode with her..."

Sound blotted out. I opened my eyes, and rising towers of cabinets met me.

Some called this a memory palace. I liked to think I wasn't that pretentious. It was a simple receptacle for that which must be stored. In all instances, that described a storage room. Not a palace.

Rainey de Souza.

Rainey: English girl name meaning queen. Uncommon.

I did not go deeper down the aisle connected to names and meanings. Irrelevant trivia. If any name was to be important, it was de Souza.

De Souza: name originated from Sousa River in northern Portugal. History of name in Bedlam...

I took five steps, passed smaller cabinets, and turned down an aisle housing the history and families of Bedlam, once Crystal Canyon.

My fingers twitched, moving with me as I flipped through the folders, searching, searching, searching—

Here.

I withdrew the first instance of their name, sinking into my four-year-old memory. Mother is sitting on the couch, laying my flashcards on the kitchen table. I kneel on the carpet, glancing up at the television in the interval.

"—local couple passed in the accident on Chaney Bridge. Hudson and Aria de Souza. They leave behind two little girls and a family that will love and miss them dearly—"

I pulled out of the memory, letting the flood of information it sparked pour in.

That accident was caused by a drunk driver swerving into the wrong lane. That driver was a wasted nineteen-year-old, and he wasn't killed, only Rainey's parents were. There was no logical or illogical way to look at that tragedy and find fault with Rainey or her family. That could not be the catalyst that started all of this sixteen years later.

But I have the correct file. This is the right family.

I scanned for something recent in connection with Rainey herself. I came up with nothing. Rainey's path may have crossed the person she called the Letter Man, but it did not cross mine.

I abandoned that and continued up the family tree. I unearthed a line in an old Dante byline of the Bedlam Journal:

This year's rulers of Ruckus are Gabriel Lopez, Lincoln Wilson, Anne Thompson, and Elias de Souza.

"Date," I hissed. The pressure built, bearing down on my skull as I forced the eighteen-year-old me to look up, see the date, remember. *Come on.*

He looked up, lighting on April 14, 1969.

"1969," I said to Legend. He was still in the middle of creating what I knew would become French bread pizza. "Dante named an Elias de Souza a Ruckus King."

"Interesting. What does that make him? Rainey's grandfather?"

"Or a great-uncle."

"Anything happen that year?"

I shook my head. "An event that could lead to what is happening now would be closer to the surface. Easy for us all to recall. Some Royales were broken up by the cops. One was hosed out in 1976 when revelers set a fire that got out of control. Nothing special happened that year."

"Nothing that we know about," he corrected. "Who were the sacrifices? Maybe Cavendish's grandpa ended up on a stake."

"A family member's humiliation is not enough to motivate a young member to give his life avenging them. None of the sacrifices died that night. We were first in Royale history to lose one."

"Again I say, that we know of. Something could've happened that night that no one knew about. Something they covered up," he said. "Rainey said she and her sister were never allowed to go to the Royales. Their grandmother kept them in. If her husband or brother was happy to take part and be a King, what caused her hatred of the party years later?"

I nodded, going down another aisle. "Your reasoning is sound. There is something going on that none of us knows about. Not even Rainey herself. But if she can't give us insight, we have no way of understanding who or why this man has targeted her. It is safe to assume Elias de Souza is either dead or incapacitated, otherwise Rainey would've had someone to reach out to when this began."

"Most likely," he agreed. "I'd like to say this isn't our problem, but—"

"—it will be if she finds out."

His clenched jaw and neck were visible from across the island. "Some freak-ass death cult press-ganging pretty farm girls into burning men alive. That's the kind of thing that gets a town noticed. She'll order us to put them down if she gets word."

"Or put down Rainey."

Legend's gaze drifted up, peering through two floors to where our pet slept. "Yes. Or her."

"I'd rather she not die," I said, and found I meant it.

"Same. The girl can take a paddle as good as Roan," he said. "Plus, I get hard just thinking of that hot little mouth. I've been lying through my fucking teeth saying she isn't good at blow jobs."

My pants tented. *I can imagine.*

And imagining was all I was doing. All logic and reason dictated there was no sight more delicious than Rainey de Souza on her knees, glaring defiantly even as those ivory cheeks readied for another slap. She said it would do me good to slip in a few treats amid my health shakes. What the hell else did you call my morning dates with her?

"I find out she isn't as inexperienced as she claimed," Legend continued, "I'm hunting down every bastard that got there before me." Legend made a harsh noise in his throat, tearing the bread in half harder than needed. "Listen to me. Roan and I have been in an open relationship for five years. He'd fuck people in front of me and I didn't give a shit. Now this chick shows up and I get all... possessive. How the hell does that happen?"

When you figure it out, let me know.

"She's ours now," I said simply. "She goes when we say, and some twisted, masked sociopath isn't about to change the rules. It can't get out what we're dealing with, but we may need her help all the same. My knowledge isn't sufficient. What I know of the de Souza family ends with a news report and a line in a paper. *She* knows everything about the history of Bedlam. She could have something to say about the letters."

"I'll do the asking," Legend replied. "I have to see her tomorrow anyway. She wants an update on the Crows."

"We don't have one to give her. Roan sowed doubt, but the cattle got a taste of freedom. They won't go back in the barn that easily."

"At this point, they can go wherever the hell they want as long as it's not to the Crows. Foundry's close to getting their way. Closer than we wanted to admit."

"Close is all they will ever be," I said, finding my way down another aisle in my mental sanctuary. "Roan has an accurate assessment of the situation. If we strike back at the Crows, Steven Ellis, or Foundry's board with violence, we'll be the main suspects. Riding out of town on a prison bus won't protect Bedlam if the information has gone wider than those people. We can't guess how many know at this point.

"Even so, I count five—make that six options for forcing them out and making the thought of setting foot in Bedlam again vacate their bowels. No violence required."

Legend gave me a look, grin twisting his lips. "Where's the fun in that?"

"Why do you think they weren't plan A?"

"Any way we could work it in?" His knife cleaved the pepperoni in two. "I've got workers threatening to strike. Jeremy Ellis will leave our town, and he'll be carried out."

"Three options allow for physical harm that won't be traced back to us."

"Those three," he said. "Tell me about them."

RAINEY

I woke up the next morning, head pounding and mouth stuffed with cotton. I glanced at the clock and grimaced. I both slept too long and woke too early. Sleep that was fitful and plagued with nightmares.

The sun wasn't up yet. Through the gloom, I made out Roan and Legend on either side of me. Roan lay on his stomach, bare ass exposed with my lifting the blankets. He slept naked as I'd come to learn with his joining me and Legend in bed. Legend opted for silk drawstring pants. There would always be something of the proper gentleman in him—even when I woke to him fisting his cock through the waistband.

I gazed at them unseeingly. I didn't wake to them climbing in with me. Usually, I fell asleep after them. As in, after they had their fun with me. What did it say that they couldn't bring themselves to bother me?

It says they all know about my one-sided battle with the Letter Man, and the coldest, most uncaring men in Bedlam pity me.

What did I tell Paris? Anyone who knows me for any length of time feels sorry for me.

I slipped out of bed and dressed silently in the dark. Shutting the door behind me, I padded downstairs, out the doors, and trudged past the grand fountain. I ended up on the sidewalk and kept going, heading toward the end of Bay Avenue.

I should look for Cairo. Find out what happened with his father and Bella. The thought floated through my mind, stirred no action, and dissipated.

The end of Bay Avenue tipped me out onto a grassy bank that led down and into the forest. Unlike most of the forest surrounding our town, this particular spot afforded a break in the trees that gifted a view of the canyon.

I sat down, resting my chin on my knees. Silent tears dripped down my legs.

I couldn't go and speak to Cairo. To ask him if he was successful covering up my role in Bella's death was a shame I couldn't think of facing without wanting to throw myself in the canyon.

Bella deserved so much more than a terrifying, brutal death at the hands of a man who saw her as no more than a pawn on a chessboard. Her father deserved to know the full truth of why his daughter died.

The truth.

Would any of this have happened if I had told the truth? If I gathered Paris, Frankie, and Bella together that night like I planned and told them their lives were in danger? If I spent the last bit of money I had and hired a private investigator? Jack Sharpe could not be trusted, but someone could've helped me. They could've staked out the farmhouse, traced the letters, dug into the backgrounds of everyone connected to Cavendish.

All things an orphaned farm girl with only a bow to her name couldn't do. *But no.* I ripped up a hank of grass and flung it. *I let them scare me with threats and promises to reveal the truth of the body at Black Widow Hill that even I was afraid to know.*

Bella was dead because of me. A truth so simple I couldn't escape it. This was my fault, and there was no punishment I could endure that would grant atonement.

"What are you doing out here?"

I jerked. Whirling around, I landed on Jeremy crossing the bank, heading for me. I quickly wiped my face.

"What are you doing here?" I returned.

"I always come out here." Jeremy stretched out next to me, propping back on his elbows. "I'll say something for Bedlam, you've got us beat on this view. It's nothing but bush and trees around Hunter's Crest."

I studied him. Was this what we did now? Small talk.

"You've got other things going for you," I said slowly. "You're three times as big as us. And you've got a zoo."

"Caged wild animals suffering for the enjoyment of pasty gawkers. You're right, I should run back to paradise."

I might've cracked a smile if it was two years, two Letter Men, and too many losses ago. "Agreed. I don't like zoos much either. Strange thing for a farmer to say," I admitted, "but every day and everything we did was to ensure our animals were happy. Gran would say our job was to serve them, not for them to serve us. In return, we were allowed to benefit from what they offered. Life isn't like that outside a farm," I said, gazing out over the beautiful, perilous drop. "Out here it's about nothing more or less than serving yourself."

"That's a dark worldview, de Souza. No wonder you're out here crying alone."

"Am I wrong, I ask the guy currently using me for his own ends."

Jeremy grinned. "Touché. I've got no room to talk."

We lapsed into an almost comfortable silence.

"It's not about you and me, you know," Jeremy spoke up. "We're both serving someone else's ends. We just happen to be caught in the middle."

"Are you saying you won't benefit when your father gets whatever he's after from this town?"

He shrugged. "I'm saying that's nothing to do with me or you, but this shit with the Bedlam Boys"—his tone changed—"that's personal. I hope you have something for me."

"What? Since we spoke less than twelve hours ago?" I spat. "No, I don't have any *verifiable information* for you right now, Ellis. For fuck's sake, you noticed I was crying. Does this really seem like the time for your vendetta?"

"I'm helping you." Jeremy threw an arm around my shoulder. "It's called a distraction. You said you're not contractually required to help teach Banks a lesson. You're right, but I'm hoping you can see your way to helping me out of the goodness of your heart. That guy told the world I was fucking my own brother," he hissed. "If anyone deserves what's coming to him, it's Roan Banks."

"Jeremy—" Something moved in the corner of my eye.

Cairo stalked around me, moving in front of us with a sneaking silence that would've impressed me if it wasn't for the ferality in his eyes matching the beast his mimicked. He narrowed on the hand resting on my shoulder.

"Cairo..." Words failed me.

Cairo knew I signed the contract. While I knew he was still questioning if he could trust me. What he didn't question was who I belonged to. I didn't have to ask how he felt about finding me in a cozy spot cuddled up with his enemy. It was written in the snarl peeling back his lips.

"Leave," he hissed.

"I would," Jeremy sang, pulling me closer. "But someone has to comfort your girl. Poor thing was crying out here all alone."

Rage welled up my throat, bitter and hot. "Don't." I shoved him off. "I've had enough of being caught in some soulless ass's game. I'm not serving anyone today."

"Whoa, easy. You're right. I'm sorry." He rubbed slow circles on my back. "I care about you, Rainey. I just want you to be—"

Cairo pounced. Jeremy was up and slashing his blade through the air before the cry was out of my mouth.

"You keep waving that toy like it's going to protect you." Cairo didn't spare a look at the thing. "I can promise you, Ellis, you come near her again, nothing will."

"Why wait, Sharpe?" He winked. "Might as well come at me now, because I'm *definitely* going to come near her again."

"Guys, stop." I shot between them, holding out my arms. "I cannot begin to describe how much I don't fucking need this right now! I just lost one of the few people left in my life and I came out here to bawl my eyes out in peace. Either you go, or I'll leave, but it does not get to be about you right now."

Cairo snagged my wrist, snapping me to his chest. "You heard. Your beating is delayed in honor of mourning. Get going before I remember I'm not this gracious."

"Fuck—"

"Jeremy," I sliced in, flashing him a pointed look. "Go. Please."

He lowered the knife. "I'll go. Give you a chance to look after this girlfriend better than you did the last one. When he fucks it up, I'll give you what you need, Rainey."

I tried to remember Jeremy was smarting from the Bedlam Boys' latest blow. It stayed me punching him in the face. So much for the both of us helpless in the middle of another's war. This guy was more than happy to throw me over.

Jeremy strode off.

"Good deal," Cairo said, "except you're too busy giving my bitter ex and your brother what they need."

Roaring, Jeremy charged him.

Cairo jumped out in front of me, squaring up, wicked grin lighting his features. They collided with an audible sound.

"Argh!" Jeremy's knife flashed.

My wolf blocked the hit—snatching his arm with the other hand and twisting. Jeremy dropped the knife with a cry, then Cairo dropped him, wincing to reveal his shoulder was still a wreck. He bodily lifted him up and slammed Jeremy in the dirt. It was the last thing I saw.

I walked away, leaving them to fight and not sparing a glance back.

Cairo must've seen me leave the mansion. He came out to bring me back where I belonged, or to sit with me and share the news I'd been waiting to hear. When he was ready to do either of those things, I'd be waiting.

I passed Legend's mansion and continued on, leaving Paris's house behind as well. Paris would let me in and give me all the space I asked for, and the more I learned about Cairo's relationship with his mother, I was almost certain those gates would stop him coming after me.

But it wasn't that I wanted away from Cairo or the Bedlam Boys. It wasn't about getting away at all. There was just somewhere I had to be.

Frankie wasn't her usual cheery self when I stepped on the bus.

"Oh, Rainey, sweetie." She squeezed my hand, halting me on the steps. "Don't bother sitting down. I can't take you out by the farm today. It's a crime scene."

Crime scene.

Sheriff Jack is there. Bella would be laid in peace and the authorities would search for her killer. I doubt the Letter Man was worried about me, but his ass should worry about that. He and his friend before him skulked around my farm for weeks, going on months. If there was a trace to be found, they'd find it. As far as I knew, Sheriff Fucking Jack didn't have a reason to conceal evidence in this case.

"What happened?"

"The sheriff wouldn't say. Just told me the stop was closed."

"I'll get off at the one before and walk. I have to go," I said over her coming protest. "It's my home, Frankie."

Sighing, she dropped my hand, reaching for the gear. "I understand. I'll drop you closer. Don't let anyone know how you got there."

"I won't."

It was a silent ride through town. Frankie's natural mothering energy broadcasted in the worried looks she sent me in the rearview. She wanted to cheer me up or possibly talk me out of going. She could do neither of those things.

Frankie opened the doors on the side of the road, a short walk from the farm where my approach was shielded by the trees. I think I said goodbye. I wasn't certain. The next thing I knew, I was skimming past the police car parked in front of my sign, heading into the copse that lined the long driveway.

My home rose on the hill, surrounded by police tape. I rested on the bark, observing Officers Davidson and Andres speaking to two crime scene techs, going by their white jumpsuits. Sheriff Jack stepped out onto the porch, and my jaw clenched as automatic as my grip on Roan's throat at the suggestion he cheated on me. I'd never be able to stop my reaction at the sight of that man. Forever I'd hear him ordering his officers to bar me from the station, ignoring my pleas to investigate Gran's death. Always I'd remember his blank, clueless stare as he denied receiving the autopsy report I placed directly in his hands—swearing on his badge he knew nothing of my grandmother's poisoning.

Jack hefted his belt up his gut, saying something to his subordinates.

My fingers scraped the bark, digging splinters in my nail bed. I had to come to assure myself everything was being done for Bella, however, I underestimated the impact of seeing him again, in the flesh.

When my mind collapsed under the weight of grief and I rode out to Andrew Clein's office, I made a stop along the way. At Jack Sharpe's home, where I knew he went every day for his lunch break—the five-minute drive from the station allowing him to enjoy his pastrami and Coke on the couch.

I can't say exactly what I planned to do to the armed elected officer of the law. I simply knew I wasn't walking out of that house until it was done.

I got there and banged on the door. No one answered my pounding, so I got in the car and made for Clein.

Afterward, it was a thirty-day stay in a facility and Doc Nash's drug cocktail for me. Sheriff Jack didn't get a taste of the retribution I owed him—that didn't mean he escaped it.

There was proof of what he'd done in the second autopsy I couldn't yet afford, and the missing medical examiner I was still searching for. Once I had the latter testifying she gave me the same results as the former, I'd strip Jack Sharpe of everything that mattered to him. His shiny badge, his respected position, his little bungalow paid for by the town, and whatever relationship he had with his son. Everyone would see him for the rotted filth he was and then he'd spend the rest of his days in a cage with the men he locked away.

With him gone, they'd open a real investigation into Gran's death. What happened to her will? Did Andrew Clein work alone, or did his bosses order him to acquire the farm by any lethal means necessary? Why did they choose our lives to destroy?

The sheriff made for my barn, Davidson on his heels. My phone buzzed, but I couldn't relax enough to take it out until the man was out of my sight.

Inhaling a shuddering breath, I fished out my cell and it slipped through my fingers. I bent to get it and froze.

Crushed cigarette butts peppered the bed of moss, dotting the earth like raisins in a salad. My mind raced ahead of me, stealing my breath and me unable to move for the scenes tumbling across my vision.

This spot, next to this tree, was a perfect unobstructed view of the farmhouse and barn. Someone could stand here watching me go in and out, and concealed in wood, I'd have no idea they were there. Someone *did* stand here—long enough to burn multiple cigarettes down to nothing, and what about an abandoned farm would interest them other than the young woman who couldn't stay away?

The Letter Man. This is how he knew when to leave his filth. He watched me come and go.

A shiver ran up my spine, making me physically convulse. Gagging, I clapped a hand over my mouth, forcing down the sounds. Forcing air into my lungs. The whole time he was here. Not Cavendish who gave no sign that he smoked during the days that I watched him. But my new tormentor—the beast who demanded I kill an innocent person and took Bella as the price.

He was here.

Calm down, Rainey. Think! I shoved myself up. *I can use this. I finally know something about him he doesn't want me to—*

A hand clamped my mouth, smothering my scream as I was snapped to a hard chest.

"Let me make something clear to you," hissed the deep, husky voice. "You don't walk away from me. You don't go anywhere without my permission."

Seizing his fingers, I peeled them off one by one. "I thought the rule was I don't go where you can't find me. Didn't look like you had that problem."

"Rules change, baby."

CAIRO

I dropped Rain in the dirt, tearing her panties off with the most satisfying sound. Through the trees, cops pleased to arrest us for disturbing their crime scene flitted about in their gloves and suits, looking important. I didn't care an iota more about their presence than I did the damp earth ruining my new jeans or the cut that split my cheek as my fiery Rain swiped at me.

She'd give me what I wanted. She always would. But I'd fight for it like I'd done for nothing else in my life.

The next blind swipe I caught. Slamming her hand on the ground, I curled between her fingers—lacing them through the moss and soil—our mark a part of the earth.

Rain freed her other hand and closed on mine covering her mouth, keeping me in place for what we knew was coming.

I scratched my cock ripping my zipper down. It thrummed a dizzying gush of blood, draining reason and control, rock hard at the mere sight of her hair splayed over the roots. Thong in tatters beside me. Bare ass high and unwilling to deny me.

I shoved in and caught her groan in my hand, but I couldn't catch mine. I couldn't even stifle it to prevent our discovery.

There was nothing like being in the tight, wet paradise that was Rainey de Souza's pussy. She mumbled smart-ass remarks about her ability to bathe herself when I carried her into the shower, but the fact was, it's my capabilities that were the problem.

I couldn't go more than twelve hours without being inside her. If I tried, I started to lose my sunny disposition.

My skin molded to hers—covering her body like the wolf she named me—mounting my mate.

"Fuck," I hissed, pumping faster than I could handle. I had to slow down. Savor the feel. Relish her cries. Delight in her body instinctively curling in to reject the pain while Rain, law, and nature bent to accept more.

I moved faster still, balls tightening, muscles clenching to explode. My hand slipped off her mouth, letting those sinful pleas spill out.

"Cairo, please, no," she moaned. "Not here. We c-can't... do this here."

I loosed a roar like a wild animal, both pleased and enraged at her denial. I slammed into her, lifting both our knees off the ground with each strike of the bull's eye.

She choked, covering her own mouth, penning in a cry. "Fucking beast," Rain spat. Defiance lit the single jeweled eye that found me. "I may be your cure... but you are definitely my curse."

My grin split my face. "Save your money on the witches and talismans, baby, because I'm not going anywhere—"

Rain probably only caught part of that. Her eye rolled up in her head—pussy clamping down as the orgasm claimed her. I tried to swear and couldn't even do that. My control surrendered to the same force that took her. I fell prostrate on top of Rain, biting her shoulder as a violent, mind-rending orgasm spilled its gift in her well.

She couldn't hold my weight, and we collapsed in a sweaty pile in the dirt—two heaving mounds.

"How," she breathed, "can you do these things with a hurt shoulder?"

Just mentioning the damn thing brought the pain flooding in. I winced, rolling off her to lie flat on my back. I wasn't surprised to see I ripped open the stitches I made Doc Nash do at three in the morning. Blood soaked through my bandage.

Rain rolled to my other side, resting her head in the crook of my arm. The woman liked a cuddle after she was ravaged. I should discourage this. Her being mine and me being her boyfriend were not ideas that necessarily connected.

I looped my arm under her instead, dropping my hand on her ass. There were benefits in keeping my pet happy. Such benefits decorated my cock and Rain's inner thighs.

"Did you see?" she asked softly.

I nodded. "Someone's been hiding here, watching my Rain."

"This is something, though, right? They put their mouth on those things. There's DNA. Plus, now I know the new Letter Man smokes. That eliminates a few people off the top."

"I'll direct the old man this way." I dragged us up. "We have to go. There might be footprints and other shit we're trampling over."

I dressed my girl, then scooped her into my arms, ignoring the pain as I carried her out. De Souza was a slippery one. Disappearing whenever I took my eyes off her. I'd have to do better at keeping her on the leash.

"Don't come here alone again." I was soundless moving through the brush, leaving my father and his officers behind. "I'm serious. Consider how often it was just the two of you out here alone, and you never knew."

Rain's shudder rippled over me. "I have," she said, laying her head on my chest. "Makes me sick thinking of it. And it pisses me off. The whole time, he was that close.

"I won't come out here alone, but I don't want to drag you guys into this either. Whatever sick game this guy is playing, it was meant for two. He, and Cavendish before him, warned me against telling anyone about the letters. You said it yourself. If he comes after you, we won't know who he is to see him coming."

"I can take care of myself," I dismissed.

"I can too and that didn't stop him snatching me in the middle of the brawl."

I jerked to a stop. "What? You said that shit stain Ellis took you."

"No, you did," she said, dropping down in sight of my truck. "The Letter Man drugged and hauled me away among dozens of witnesses."

"What did he do to you?" The growl that leaked through my teeth unnerved even me. I'd taken the job of protecting Bedlam at all costs out of obligation. But this... Killing the man who dared lay a hand on what's mine would add no weight on my conscience.

"Nothing. Nothing," she repeated at my look. "He brought me here and left a letter saying he was *proud* of me for killing Axel Ver-lice. He must've learned differently after that."

Rainey led me into the truck and took up work cleaning and changing my bandage. I paid it no mind under my racing thoughts.

This bastard took such a risk grabbing her in the middle of a crowd. Was it just to pat her on the head, or to prove he could get to her any-time, anywhere?

"How'd he know that was the time to do it?" I cast a glance back at the copse. "Is he always watching you? Home, school, here. The fight broke out and he saw a chance."

"That's the only thing that makes sense, but it doesn't change that he came prepared. Something pricked my neck and I was out in seconds. Was he waiting for his opportunity and the perfect one just fell into his lap?"

I shook my head. "That's too convenient. As convenient as another shady piece of garbage jumping on that chance to kill Roan."

Rainey finished with my shoulder, so I started the car, taking off before Dad saw us. I was due another trip to the doc anyway.

"Why would someone want Roan dead? Other than the obvious reasons," she muttered. "He gets off on riling people up, but who did he upset so much they rolled up on him with a knife?"

"Roan goes with me on collection runs. Like you said, he makes a tense situation worse. He also has access to the university's database and security systems. We've used the records he's dug up and the things he's seen on the cameras to our advantage many times. Knowledge prevails where threats fail, Rain. Every time."

"In other words, your enemies are too many to count and literally anyone in Bedlam could want to kill Roan for blackmailing and extorting them."

"Basically," I said mildly. I wasn't about to say it another way. This didn't bother me as much as my father and psych degree said it should. "But it still comes back to how oddly convenient it was you and Roan were presenting as easy targets the same day you were picked out for a knife and knockout juice."

"You think they knew there was going to be a fight?"

"I think they knew there was going to be a crowd."

Rain gasped, clamping down on my thigh. "Quinn and the New Boys. They were all geared up to ambush you on the deck, but when we didn't show up, they and all their buddies took the showdown to the Green. Jeremy gathered those people beforehand. Told them it was time to take down the Bedlam Boys."

"So Roan's guy and yours suited up. We'd be outnumbered. Bodies and fists flying everywhere, you wouldn't see it coming," I said. "And you didn't."

"But it's not like Jeremy hung a sign-up sheet in the quad," Rain cried. "They had to keep that quiet so you guys wouldn't find out."

I turned off the road for the farm and drove down Marigold, heading straight to the clinic. "I also doubt the cowards invited Holly, the soccer mom, and Billy, the cafeteria worker, to the party."

"That means—"

"—if this letter guy and Roan's attempted assassin got the signal to show up, they're both students."

I didn't need to see Rainey's face to know she was gaping at me.

"Or teaching assistants," I offered. "Possibly grad students. Either way, they're connected to Bedlam University in some way."

"You're right," Rain whispered.

I shot her a look. "Still think I shouldn't be involved?"

"All right, sheriff's son, I admit your deductive reasoning was helpful in this instance, but you being involved isn't up to me. H-he—" Her voice cracked. "The Letter Man said people I love would get hurt if I defied him, and I can't pretend that's a threat he won't carry out. Not after last night."

She gestured between us. "We can do this. Talk. You can steer your father in the right direction and let me know if he finds anything, but you can't get in the middle of me and the Letter Man, Cairo. Not you, Roan, Legend, Jacques, or Arsenio. I couldn't live with myself if another person died because of me."

It was on the tip of my tongue to say she didn't make the rules.

I held it back.

Rainey had proven she didn't bluff either. I walked in on her once, trying to kill herself. I wouldn't let the fucking thought enter her head a second time that everyone would be safer if she took herself out of the equation.

"I've done this for a long time, Rain. No one is going to know anything that we don't want them to know. This letter guy included."

She eased her grip on me, turning her attention to stroking my thigh. In spite of the serious conversation and the threats that went with them, my trouser snake reared its head, heeding her call. I didn't waste time with feelings like shame, so none of that accompanied his insatiable need. I did bite back a wave of anger at the fact I wouldn't be able to give the junkie another hit.

Between my fight with Jeremy and my *fight* with Rain, my shoulder was wrecked and the pain pills I forgot to take were reminding me why the doc said to down them first thing in the morning.

The road spun.

"You're going to have to drive," I said, pulling off the road. "And wake me up."

My head hurtled toward the dash—black blotting it out before I hit.

Chapter Two

Rainey

R I brushed Cairo's hair from his eyes, tracing the curves and angles of his sculpted perfection.

Doc Nash was out. The clinic's nurse practitioner helped me carry Cairo out of the car, sewed him up, and ordered me to make sure he took his meds. I brought him home, helped him up to one of the many guest rooms, and fed him chicken soup till he dropped his head and passed out.

Cairo was surprisingly mellow about my fussing. Turns out Vicodin soothes even the most savage of beasts.

He doesn't look like a savage beast now.

Light streamed through the slats in the blinds, playing in his golden crown. When you couldn't look in those unnerving eyes, Cairo Sharpe was all soft, full lips, slightly pointed ears, and the smell of the forest I grew up in. But if I was honest with myself, awake or sleeping, he was perfect.

He was mine.

"So don't charge around with open wounds, spilling your blood all over Bedlam, Sharpe." I pressed a gentle kiss to his lips. "I'm the one who's going to keep you."

I shut the door soundlessly behind me, leaving my wolf to sleep. There was another man of mine I needed to see.

Roan reclined on Legend's couch, messing around on his laptop while porn played loud and proud on the television screen. I flicked it off.

"Just when it was getting good." A hand crept under my dress and delighted to find me panty-free. Roan teased my lips open. "You'll have to take over entertaining me."

"Later," I replied, drawing away reluctantly.

Roan had been getting his kicks watching Legend punish me, which left him satisfied, but didn't indulge my growing Roan addiction. I knew what he wanted, and that was for me to *take* what I wanted. But a few weeks ago, I was a virgin. The jump from that to knife-wielding dominatrix was taking a minute to get my head around.

"I assume Cairo told you all the truth about... last night."

He nodded, adopting his rarely used serious expression. "Do you want to tell me the rest?"

I did, starting from the first letter I received to the fatal mistake that cost Bella her life.

"That's not all," I continued. "Cairo thinks the psychopath that took over for Cavendish is a student, or in some way connected to the university. He believes the same of the person who tried to kill you."

"The latter isn't that surprising," he said, setting his laptop on the coffee table and tugging me down to take its place. "The former is." Roan inclined his head. "Or maybe it isn't."

"What do you mean?"

"I've been looking through Cavendish's old school records. Mom requires every student involved in a traumatic incident to see the university therapist. Don't need any festering resentment boiling into a school shooting."

I sat up straight. "You can access the therapist's notes?"

"Yep."

"Can you access the notes on everyone who sees the therapist?"

"I can."

I massaged my temples. "And you use those deep, soul-baring secrets to keep people in line. I'm no longer asking why someone tried to kill you."

He winked. "I'm a very unlikeable guy, beautiful, but you feel free to whip me into shape."

I just might, I thought even as a blush painted my cheeks.

"But this time, I assume you'll forgive me."

Roan assumed correctly. "What was in the notes?"

"Stella didn't detail her fears that she was sitting across from the next Bundy. Actually, I'm leaning toward telling Dean Mom to fire her after what you've said. Stella wrote that Cavendish was handling the loss of his best friend well under the circumstances, and that his strong support system would help him through. I'd bet the guy was sleeping like a baby after getting away with murder."

It was hard to argue for the woman's job considering. I didn't bother to try, and instead latched on to something he said. "Strong support system? Who was she talking about? Nathan Wade and Sam Dillion?"

"And Blake Jensen."

"Blake Jensen," I repeated. "Who's that?"

Roan crossed his hands behind his head. I was sitting on his lap in no underwear, and his hands weren't all over me. This was the first time I'd witnessed Roan taken off his single-minded course for pain and pleasure.

"He's the guy Cavendish was mentoring around the time he killed his best friend," Roan said. "Stella specifically made a note of it, saying that focusing on Jensen and volunteering was a healthy outlet."

"Blake Jensen," I said again, rolling it around on my tongue and finding the taste unfamiliar. "This is the first I've heard that name. It didn't come up in connection with Cavendish at all. He's not even listed as one of his friends on social media. I looked up everyone when the new Letter Man came crashing in to continue destroying my life. I'm certain there wasn't a Blake Jensen."

"But there was." Roan laced his fingers through mine, bringing them to rest behind his head and tease those silky strands. "Stella wrote down that they met three times a week."

I stared at him, trying to connect what he was saying. "Three times a week. You don't spend that much time with someone you can't stand, or who can't stand you. Did he need service hours for his degree?"

Roan raised his brow. "Accounting?"

"Of course not," I said, mostly to myself. "He spent all that time with Jensen because he wanted to."

"We can safely guess he wasn't mentoring a fifty-year-old father of three. Jensen would've been younger than him, but now old enough to go to university with us."

I shot off his lap. "You think Blake Jensen is the Letter Man? He killed Bella!"

"I don't know what I think." Roan tugged me back down. "It crosses my mind that someone who spent that much one-on-one time with a sociopath might've gotten tangled up in his immoral charm. Young, needy, and desperate for someone to look up to, then Cavendish walks in.

"All that said, there is no Blake Jensen at Bedlam University."

His words popped my bubble. "What? How do you know?"

"I know everyone who attends or works in my school. No Blake Jensen. No Blakes. But there are two people whose last names are Jensen. I can search the database," he said to my look, "but it'll say the same thing. It wasn't going to be that easy. Nothing ever is. But that doesn't mean the guy Cavendish mentored doesn't go to our school. People change their names. Or others change it for them."

My head bobbed, hope returning. "Cavendish would have no reason to give the real name of his protégé. I can follow the two

Jensens that go to the university, but if he lied about the first name, why wouldn't he lie about the second?" I brought my fist down on the chair arm. "Still, it's a place to start. And if it's not them, I've got other smoking university students to sort through."

Roan picked me up and carried me into the shower. I still had blood, dirt, and Cairo on me after the morning's activities. "Did you ever find out the secret?" he asked.

"Secret?"

"Cavendish told you he killed Douglas Herbert because he found out something he shouldn't and was going to expose him. What did Herbert discover that no one else could know?"

Roan slid my dress over my hips.

"It has to be that Cavendish was a raving lunatic."

"Can't be." He flicked on the shower, filling the space with steam. "Why can't it be?"

"Because he would've just said that, sweet lips. '*I killed Douglas because he found out I get hard killing animals behind the frat house.*' But he didn't admit to Douglas's find. He didn't actually admit to anything." Something in Roan's voice stilled me. "Nothing more than what you already discovered, which is that he killed Douglas and sent you the letters. He never told you why."

"I..." Whatever I planned to say died on my tongue.

"Douglas Herbert knew Cavendish his whole life. They were best friends. For that bond to break, he must've discovered something not even the most loyal of friends could excuse. And because of that, Cavendish had to kill him before he could tell anyone else. A secret that important wouldn't suddenly become so trivial, he dangles it in a twisted game with a girl he doesn't know."

"But maybe it didn't matter anymore," I tried. "The guy had a death wish."

Roan shook his head, even as it disappeared behind his shirt. "Someone with nothing left to lose has nothing left to hide. He didn't tell you what Douglas found out. He didn't give a straight answer to why he chose you. Rambling on about your ancestors, sacrifices, and running away from the fight. I'd think he really was a lunatic if I didn't know better. That guy was too smart, Rainey. Everything he did was for a reason. Everything he said had a meaning."

His gaze pinned me to the spot. "Take it from another manipulator. Use the situation we're in now as the proof. Cavendish didn't tell you shit about what's truly going on here, Rainey. Not why he chose you, why Douglas had to die, or why this isn't over. You still don't know who the Letter Man is. Doesn't matter that Scott Cavendish is dead, and it may not matter if the new one is Blake Jensen. You need to discover the secret that started this all, because they've got the whip, baby, and that just may be your safe word."

Deep, abiding disgust filled me at the Letter Men's torture compared to a sex game, but the point had landed, and nothing survived in its wake.

Roan scooped me up. "Now, on to the entertainment you denied me. Ride me, cowgirl, and slap me if I don't buck when you roll."

It was frankly astonishing Roan's ability to flip the switch that fast. This was not an ability I had, although he taught me quickly.

"RAINEY, WHERE'S YOUR head at?"

I snapped to reality.

"You just lost half your breakfast," Paris said.

I narrowed on Amy, disappearing the last of my avocado toast in her mouth. "Sorry."

"You sound it," I said, laughing.

Amy, Paris, Zara, and I huddled around a table in the student union, downing breakfast and conversation before we split in four directions. Naturally, there was only one topic on the agenda.

"You don't think it's true, do you?" Zara asked. "Jeremy and Micah? That's just— Ugh."

"You saw the sexts," Amy threw in. "And the rest of it was just as horrible. Jonah carrying that girl into a room to *sleep it off*. That video should be forwarded to the dean. We shouldn't be expected to sit quietly in class next to a rapist."

"I don't know that Dean Banks can do much," I admitted, "but we definitely don't have to sit quietly." My grip tightened on my plate. "The rich and privileged don't get to fuck people over without consequences."

"Damn right," said Paris. "I said the Crows would regret moving in on our town. Now they got the attention of Dante."

Two gasps and a "really?" was her response.

It was hard for someone who wasn't Bedlam-born to understand why that was a big deal. Harder still if their first introduction to Dante was listening to him beg and plead with the Bedlam Boys to leave him alone.

The single byline Dante appeared decades ago in an unofficial paper of a technically unofficial town. From the beginning, he reported the news those in charge denied to their last breath. Scandals, leaked documents, the truth of where the money went that was earmarked to pave the outer farm dirt roads. Hint: it paved the driveway to Mayor Harrow's new summer escape, and it built the home on top of it.

Dante was a journalist before he became the crowner of the Ruckus Kings. This legacy lived on through the years, surviving the shift from print, to radio, to internet. When Dante chose a target, he wrung every secret from their life like water from a dishrag.

"He'll find out the truth of what Jonah did that night," Amy said, "and how close the Ellis brothers really are."

"Can I ask you guys something?" I turned to Amy and Zara. "Even if the Crows run back to Hunter's Crest, there were still a lot of people nodding their heads to what they had to say. If someone else is leading the pack, would you guys consider voting to split Bedlam in half? Bring back Crystal Canyon?"

"Of course they wouldn't," Paris cried.

Amy and Zara weren't as quick to answer. They shared a look.

"I don't want Bedlam to break up," Amy said firmly. "And if half of what we found out about the Crows is true, I for fuck sure don't want it split up to put more money in the pocket of a guy like Jonah. But a lot of what they said sounds nice."

"You hate living under the Bedlam Boys that much?"

"No," Zara said. "They weren't lying about using the money they take from people to give back to the town. My mom lost her job and couldn't pay the bills. The bank was threatening to take our house. She heard they helped another family on our street, and out of desperation, she asked me to speak to Cairo.

"He handed over six months' worth of mortgage payments just like that. Even said she didn't have to pay it back." Zara dropped her gaze. "It may be selfish. I know a lot of people are angry about the payments. But I've never seen my mom that scared. I don't care what people say about the Bedlam Boys. They helped my family when we needed it, and that's good enough for me."

I squeezed her hand. I knew that fear—the fear of losing everything. Hell, I was living that fear. If the Bedlam Boys had swooped in and saved me from losing the farm, I can't say I'd look unkindly on their extortion either.

"But you're still unsure of how you'd vote?" I asked, voice soft.

"That part is me not being selfish," Zara replied. "Bedlam is stuck in the past. Hunter's Crest has music venues, theaters, cafés, shops, hotels, everything. All stuff we could have here but the council won't allow developers to cut down a blade of grass or touch a single historical building."

"No one wants to live here," Amy said. "There are more students attending this school than there are people living in Bedlam. And most of them are going to leave after they graduate." Amy gestured at Paris, who flushed. "It wouldn't be such a bad thing if Bedlam changed. Dragged itself into the future and was more like an actual town than a fiefdom. That's all I'm saying."

I couldn't help myself. My head bobbed along to her speech. "I can't deny what you're saying. I've never wanted to be anywhere other than Bedlam and the farm, but I'm not blind to the things that drive people out. We could stand to shake things up around here—"

"Yeah, okay," Paris sliced in. "I can't play like I don't get what you're saying. I want something bigger than this life too." She leaned in, dropping her voice. "But can we agree that Bedlamites should do it? Not a bunch of rapists, dealers, and brother-lovers? Yes?"

"Yes," Zara said. "No doubt we can't trust the Crows."

"Agreed." Amy bold as ever helped herself to a slice of my bacon. "The Crows and their rich daddies won't have anything to do with it, but they have people thinking. If we can form a separate town, we can make it into a place people actually want to live in. The mayor and the town council won't keep us in the past, and we don't give up our home." She smiled that sweet Amy smile. "Best of both worlds, right?"

And that's the soup the Crows are selling. It's no wonder people are slurping it down. Although the message might be going down harder after Roan's little video.

It might not matter, another voice said. *Sounds like people still want this even if they're not doing it at the Crows' lead. But with Foundry buying up half the town, their new landlords get what they want either way.*

The Bedlam Boys' dilemma was all too clear for me. The town can't split while Foundry has an ounce of control here. The only way was to force them out at all costs.

To protect a secret they're hiding from me. From everyone.

"You need to discover the secret that started this all, because they've got the whip, baby, and that just may be your safe word."

Roan was right in more ways than one. While I was in the dark, I was everyone's plaything to be pushed around and manipulated.

No more.

We steered the conversation toward light topics and broke apart with most of my breakfast in Amy's belly, not mine. I grabbed a butterscotch muffin on the way to bankruptcy class. The lesson was as fun-filled and interesting as you'd expect. All the same, I noted every dry word out of Professor Stein's mouth. Midterms were coming up and they wouldn't stop for Letter Men, Crows, or my hot jailers.

"I love your hair today, Julie," I told the TA on the way out. "Blonde highlights work for you."

"Thanks, Rainey. But nothing looks as good as those Jimmy Choos." She whistled. "Let me know the next time you want to trade for an old sweatshirt. I've got a whole closet of them."

Laughing, I waved myself out, sticking my headphones in. I was starting to get a reputation as the girl trading designers for Target brands, i.e., I was every girl's new best friend. Let that reputation get back to the Bedlam Boys. Maybe then they'd let me wear regular clothes again. As long as it wasn't "farm girl chic." Cairo was serious about that hatred hard-on.

I headed out of the Communications building, one eye getting me through the crush of students, the other scrolling through recordings. I tapped on the one from the night before.

"Hello, hello, hello, Bedlam." Dante's too-deep-to-be-real voice filled my ears. "How're you all doing tonight?"

Dante did his shows live, but helpful people recorded and posted them on their sites. No one could miss a thing.

"I know what's on your minds. So should I do the song and dance? Talk about the murder and kidnapping investigations that are going nowhere— Get off those flabby asses, Bedlam PD!

"Or should I get into the name on everyone's lips? Crows."

Homer Green was a peaceful spot these days. It would be seeing as Dean Banks posted no less than five security guards patrolling the place. I stretched out on a patch of grass. My next class wasn't for two hours. I had nowhere else to be.

"None of us saw it happen. One second, we're sipping our frappés, noses buried in our own lives, then an ear-splitting crash yanks everyone's heads up. Are we mad those assholes ignored the stop sign? Or we just interested to see what would happen to the fools who dinged the Bedlam Boys' ride?"

I frowned. It was hard to be sure of a man behind a digitally altered voice, but the Dante I listened to weeks ago sounded different from the metaphor-dropper I was listening to now. Was there a new Dante?

"You can admit it," he teased. "We all sat back, interested to see what would happen. Was someone finally going to knock the Bedlam Boys off their pedestal? Did we get front-row seats to the coup? Seemed like it with those whispers of building a new town—freeing ourselves from our lords and masters.

"Who heeded the siren call?" Dante asked. "Don't bother lying. Dante knows all. He knows you went to that party to celebrate every hit the Bedlam Boys took on the way down, only to find out why the kings have ruled for so long. Arsenio, Cairo, Jacques, Legend, and Roan won't drop at the hundredth hit. They sure as hell won't go down on the first one.

"Now we've all got a decision to make and I'm here as I always will be, to help you make it. How much of what we saw in that video is true? Are Micah Ellis's doe eyes and brown curls so irresistible, even his brother wanted a taste? Is Jonah Hayes a rapist? Is Gael Stoll a drug dealer? Does Bentley Levine jump scrawny, sobbing guys during the day and fuck their moms for cash at night?"

I gazed at the gathering gray clouds, falling into Dante's world. I couldn't say I was a regular listener. His show was scandals about people I barely interacted with. The crowning of Kings of a party I wouldn't go to. The occasional songs I didn't listen to. The common trivia I didn't care about.

That said, the rare times I turned him on, I listened to the end. A power Dante and all the Dantes before him possessed. He held on and didn't let go until his signature sign-off music released you from the spell.

"I will find out," he whispered in my ear. "Everything there is to know about Jeremy, Micah, Gael, Bentley, and Jonah. All the secrets in their head. All the skeletons under their beds. It's the battle between two evils, and we will unmask the lesser.

"Have no fear that anyone—Crow or Bedlam Boy—will stop me or interfere. The torch has passed on. My location changed. My holes in security plugged. If you want me, you're going to have to fucking find me." He laughed. "And you can take that as a challenge.

"Goodbye, Bedlamites, and... good luck."

My expression melted—and icy surprise spread down my face to seep into my bones. The laugh in his voice changed and morphed into a high-pitched sound that was not his sign-off music.

It was a call I wouldn't forget for as long as I lived.

A kookaburra laughing.

ARSENIO

The harsh *whew, whew, whew* expelled with each contraction of my abs, bringing me up to my knees and dropping me back to the floor. The sound filled my ears and spread throughout the gym, and still wasn't as loud as Rainey standing in the doorway, her silent stare speaking volumes.

"Something I can do for you, de Souza?"

She rubbed her temples out of the corner of my eye, wincing. "Maybe I'm just enjoying the show."

I chuckled. Rainey de Souza was an interesting specimen. Hard to pin down. Impossible to categorize. She took orders but not without a side of defiance and a large cup of sass. None of us could deny she enjoyed her punishments a little more than anticipated. She wanted to be here more than anyone should.

I sat up, hanging my arms over my knees. Sweat ran down to chill in the frigid air-conditioning. It was as if she trailed each one. Following their path collecting as wetness soaking my wifebeater. Counting the hairs they touched on the way. Peeling the layers only they reached underneath.

Maybe that's what's wrong with this otherworldly beauty who emerged from nothing and plunged our lives in a fog we wouldn't escape? It's how she looks into your soul like she can see everything, while her eyes hold nothing.

That must be it, because it certainly wasn't Cavendish or the new information I learned about her in the last seventy-two hours. That man asked her to choose, and she did not back down from the fight. It may have looked as though Rainey did not have a choice. She and I knew better. She could've left Jennifer to her fate. She could've put Cavendish's in the hands of the police.

But instead, she set him on fire, pierced Verlice's heart with an arrow, and went to that farm the other night prepared to do it again.

I advanced on her, peering deep in those unblinking brown pools. They reflected me as I stroked her cheek.

"Perfection."

"I don't feel so perfect today," she whispered.

"Why is that?"

"I'm seeing serial killers everywhere I go. I looked twice at everyone who passed me today with a cigarette between their lips. I jumped when my professor called on Jake, thinking for a second that he said Blake. And Dante," she said. "At the end of the show I thought... I thought I heard..."

"What?" I pressed when she trailed off.

"I thought the laugh track was a kookaburra's call." She tipped her chin, resting on my fingers. "Who is Dante? Or who was he? It's another guy now, isn't it?"

"It is," I confirmed. "His predecessor was a guy named Lawrence Clark. He left town a few days after Ruckus Royale."

"He did?"

"His apartment cleared out. He didn't leave a forwarding."

"How did you guys find him?"

I continued my exploration, skimming the bumps on her throat, brushing her pebbled nipple poking beneath the thin fabric. Why shouldn't I? She was mine to touch and caress as I saw fit.

"It takes specialized equipment to broadcast his show. We figured he was smart enough not to walk into a Bedlam shop. Jacques set up a few fake seller accounts, and we got lucky. Someone with a Hunter's Crest PO Box contacted him for a windscreen and shock mount. We kept an eye on the place and ended up following some brown-haired guy in his twenties out of the post office and right back to an address in Bedlam."

"Smart," she said with a smile. "Very smart."

"We do have a genius in our crew."

"Did you ever find out why he was chosen, or how a new Dante is picked? If I tracked him down, do you think he could tell me who claimed his place?"

"Possibly." I slid her strap off her shoulder. "It's a family business. Passed down from grandfather to father to son and so on. Clark doesn't have kids or cousins, but that doesn't mean he didn't have someone picked out. Although, if you're going where I believe you're going with this, you'd have to consider the torch wasn't passed on, it was taken."

Rainey nodded, solemnity stealing the brief smile. "It was a quick sound at the end of a broadcast, but I know what I heard. It was a kookaburra, Arsenio, and I've been through too much to dismiss it as a coincidence."

"You shouldn't." A little tug and her nipple was free. Free from its cover. Free to receive my attention. "But what is it we're saying here, de Souza? This man helped Cavendish kidnap Jennifer Wilson, killed your friend, and then took over a radio show? What's the endgame?"

"Ugh, I have no idea," she cried, fisting her hair. "New Dante said he's going after the Crows, marking the tallies in both columns for people to decide who they're going to follow. That's something a real Dante would do. If this is the same psychopath that's been torturing me, why would he take over the show to do something like this? Why would he care?"

"Questions I cannot answer for you." I lightly nipped her, catching a gasp between her lips.

"Everything I think I'm finding out about him just confuses me further. Is he some leather-jacketed smoker hanging out in the quad? Is he some hapless guy who got hooked up with the wrong mentor? Is he Bedlam's new radio shock jock? Or is the Letter Man none of the above?"

"You may or may not find this comforting, but I have a feeling you'll discover who this guy is soon enough."

She frowned. "You do? Why?"

"The letters, Rainey. All these clues, hints, and games. You don't play hide-and-seek if you don't want to be found."

She was quiet for a while. Long enough for me to tease her other nub undisturbed. Her dress slid down her body and snagged on my erect cock.

Rainey smelled of fruit teas and vanilla. She shifted, and her soft strands brushed my forehead. She gave every appearance of a delicate, fragile creature of porcelain skin and breasts like two marshmallow pillows. Until you spotted the thick, corded muscles in those archer/farmer arms, or imagined her balancing her scales and delivering justice. That both women should exist in one enigma got my heart doing something I never knew it could.

Race.

Rainey slipped her hand under my tank, tracing the ridges of my overworked muscles. I let her. Touching me without permission would've gotten Quinn in trouble. But she was Legend's pick, not mine. I never quite took to her.

I told de Souza as much.

"Legend's pick?" She wiggled her ass out of her thong obediently. "What does that mean?"

"We trade off picking our next girlfriend." I kissed a trail from hip bone to hip bone, tasting her shiver on my tongue.

"Why do it like that? Why share?"

"Legend and Roan bring people in their bed all the time. A few of them assumed the rest of us were up for their sex games, and they weren't shy about coming on to us. The same was happening with our girlfriends. They kept floating threesomes, foursomes, orgies at us." I winked at her. "Someone who likes to be punished, loves to be owned."

"So, eventually you figured, if your girlfriends all wanted to be shared, why fight a good idea? What does that make me? Cairo's pick?"

I grinned. "And it wasn't even his turn."

Rainey brushed my hair from my eyes and sunk her fingers within my strands, breaking a rule even worse than the first. No one pets me like a fucking dog, cooing about how adorable the little biracial boy is while their dirty-ass, forgot-to-wash-after-using-the-bathroom hands roller coaster through my curls.

I broke two fingers of the first person who tried it. Wrenching them away from me so hard, I didn't realize what I'd done until they were on the floor screaming. Mother was horrified by this.

I was eleven after all.

She sent me to an "emotion coach" who taught me everything I needed to know to survive. Don't give anything away. Be in control, never controlled. Pick the right time, place, and situation to express the right emotion.

The next person who groped me didn't scream, and they didn't tell.

Reaching up, I drew her hand away, curling around her wrist. Rainey sighed as I kissed her palm.

"Just because Cairo picked me, doesn't mean you had to let go of Quinn, or that we had to be here now." She claimed another kiss on her fingertips. "You guys can admit you all want me, and none of you will let me go."

"We all want you, and you're not going anywhere. Go for a deep, dark confession next time."

She giggled, spinning in my hands. I nipped and kissed along her tailbone. Rainey had the tiniest, barely there beauty mark in the middle of her left cheek. It was a certainty I'd now become obsessed with the damn thing, seeing it in my dreams.

"You willing to go deep and dark? Good," she said. "That's why I came. There are a few too many secrets holding sway over my life, Arsenio. I want to know who gave you Axel Verlice's name, who you're working for, and what the secret is that's brought the Crows and Foundry down on us."

"Do you?" Amusement laced my tone. "That's quite a list of demands, but I'm afraid the confessional just closed up."

I released her, getting to my feet.

"The priest has gone home."

"Could the confessional open for one more?"

She faced me, secure in her nakedness, and it was no wonder. It was a crime worse than all I committed combined for this woman to walk around in clothes.

"When will I be ready for you?"

"You tell me."

"Surely that's for you to decide." Rainey draped my arms around her waist. "Not me. Tell me I'm ready now, Arsenio. Take what you want from me."

My heart thumped painfully against my rib cage, yanking a hiss through my teeth. This went against everything I learned in emotions management. It contravened years of hanging on to my cool—containing the slightest slip of anger or lust.

Ask the forgiveness of an actual priest, I was getting impatient.

I backed away and stretched out on the loveseat parked in the home gym. "You say you know what I want and you're ready to give it to me. Prove it," I said. "Tease me. Seduce me. Be my whore." I flicked my painfully hard erection. "Get this guy to come and you won't have to ask, because I'll never stop giving."

"S-seduce you?" Her voice hitched, widening my grin.

Rainey had gotten too used to us telling her when to sit, stay, beg, and come. Time to see how she behaved off the leash.

Face fire-engine red, Rainey slinked across the room, grabbing hold of my thighs. She trapped my gaze as she spread them apart, wining her hips to the ground—beginning her dance.

Rainey bobbed, dipped, and ground to music only she could hear. A slow, sultry tune if her lazy sway was anything to go by. She lay back flat to my chest, hair falling over my shoulder, and pressed my hands to her stomach as she slid down. I was passed over her mounds, indulging a squeeze. Legend was right. They were the perfect size.

De Souza continued down while I continued up. She swallowed my ring finger to the knuckle, lightly scraping me between her teeth drawing out.

My jaw clenched. On the scale of my sexual experiences, this was after-school Barney-special tame. So why was my cock throbbing so hard my eyes crossed?

She flipped over and straddled me, rocking unhurriedly on my lap, and bouncing those cherry-topped lovelies in my face. Rainey wiggled, lightly slapping them on my cheek, and the control I honed for ten years snapped.

"Fuuuuccckkk."

"If this is what you were after, you shouldn't have tortured yourself waiting." The woman dared kiss me on the lips. "I was made to give you what you need."

She picked up my hand and looked me in the eye as she pushed two fingers inside herself. A flush that glazed her eyes chased away the last of the embarrassment. "Feel that?"

Course I felt it. Her impossibly tight hole was wetter than a Slip 'N Slide.

"That's for you, Arsenio. It's only for you."

My fingers dug grooves in her hip that would be marks in the morning.

Snap, snap, snap. My self-control was tangible, living twine breaking to each kiss dotted down my chest. What was this woman doing to me?

Rainey freed my cock from its flimsy cloth prison and sheathed it between her lips. That Legend was her teacher was obvious. The guy didn't believe in slow, soft, or easy. A trait he rubbed off on a woman who began giving blow jobs about a week ago. She bobbed her head like a hummingbird, sucking so hard her cheeks caved in.

My nails pierced the couch. If I thought I was sweating and exerting myself before, it was nothing compared to the fevered grunts pouring in her ears, spurring her on.

Let her ride the high of turning me on. I never denied that I wanted her or that I fully intended to have her. One day. On my terms.

Today wouldn't be that day. I was always in control, and when I come inside Rainey de Souza, it'd be after I extracted half a dozen screaming orgasms by order and punishment. I hadn't lost myself so completely that I couldn't keep a tight rein on my dick. It wasn't allowed to come outside unless I allowed it. She wasn't going to—

"Shit." I bucked, ripping the leather, and ejaculated with the power of a hundred stifled orgasms. "Agh," I roared.

Rainey smirked at me, too smug for someone masked in cum.

She deserved to gloat. Didn't everyone who did the impossible?

"I'm not quite sure what I won." She snuggled up on my heaving chest. "But I'm looking forward to finding out from here on. No more holding back with me, Arsenio."

Rainey propped her chin on me, peering in my eyes. "And no more secrets."

"I'D SAY IT'S GOOD TO be home, but..." I trailed off, glaring at the doghouse.

Dean Banks gave the word that the Bedlam Boys' suspension was lifted. They were allowed back on campus, which of course meant the Crows were too.

Cairo directed me to the middle of the living room while he swept every inch of the downstairs. Arsenio, Legend, Jacques, and Roan spread out, checking upstairs and outside.

"You know I picked that out special for you, Rain." He flipped the cushions off the couch. "Don't tell me you don't like it?"

I didn't bother giving that a response.

"Anything yet?"

"No," he replied. "I'm surprised. The Crows got someone in here once before. We figured they'd take their shot while we were forced out."

"Take their shot to do what? Jeremy already believes he has a mole."

Cairo flashed me a look I couldn't identify. "Does he?"

"How many times, Cairo? I'm only passing on the information you give me. No more, no less."

"That's not what gets me."

"What is?" I asked, moving into the kitchen. Cairo already checked in there and I was overdue for breakfast. We all were. I'd whip up some breakfast burritos, herbal tea, and quinoa breakfast bowls to introduce Shake Boy to healthy food with flavor.

"That Ellis chose you in the first place. What deep, dark secrets did he think you were going to find out that Quinn didn't?"

"You know, I thought the same thing." I pulled out the cinnamon, quinoa, and chocolate hazelnut almond milk. "Then I read the contract. I'm pretty sure Jeremy would've made the same offer to Quinn if you guys were still with her. They're most interested in your retaliation against the town splitting. Whatever you plan to stop it, I pass on to the Crows."

"Interesting. They're counting on a few slips of the tongue. Assuming that we won't hide plans to defend the town from someone who wants the same thing. Ellis isn't as stupid as he acts." Cairo inclined his head. "Though in this case, credit likely goes to Ellis Senior."

"He texted me to meet him tomorrow afternoon." Cairo's lips peeled back from his teeth. "He'll want his first update."

"You're not meeting him alone."

"You can hardly be there, Sharpe. Besides, we're meeting in the arboretum. Not so quiet but not empty either."

"We'll see," he gruffed.

I left it alone. Cairo didn't appreciate the idea of me meeting any man alone who wasn't a Bedlam Boy. Even if he understood it had to happen, he wasn't about to kiss my cheek and send me off with a parade.

"We're good down here. I'll take you to class after I check my room. Bring my breakfast in the bath."

I saluted with my quinoa-covered spoon. "Yes, sir."

Jacques came in, passing Cairo in the entrance. They nodded at each other, and that was the only sign of supposed closeness between best friends since childhood.

"I'm making quinoa breakfast bowls," I told him. "I checked and it's packed with all the nutrients a genius needs. Will you try it?"

To my surprise, he nodded. "I see no reason why not."

"Can I ask you something?"

Jacques claimed a seat on the barstool. "Reason follows you will anyway."

I laughed. "Fair enough. I'll skip the asking to ask and get right to it. What does my punishment entail?"

Jacques crooked a brow. The single request for me to expound.

"You said I could have some of your smoothie because starvation wasn't a part of my punishment. You guys have set limits. I'd like to know what they are."

"I gave you that information that day in Cairo's room."

"I must obey, but can I question?"

"No."

I quieted, carefully considering the next thing out of my mouth. "Is my punishment to remain in ignorance?"

"Meaning?"

"Do you five not want me to know you? Do we stay in this cycle of sex and punishment until you grow tired of me, and Legend takes his turn to pick the new girlfriend?" The words tumbled out one after the other—too fast for me to stop. "Am I supposed to be kept at arm's length, falling for men who won't tell me anything about their lives, families, plans, or dreams? Is that my punishment, Jacques?"

His expression didn't change during my speech. "No, de Souza." His voice was low. "That is not your punishment."

"So, one day, I'll know everything." I wasn't sure if I was asking him or telling him. "About you, how you guys came together to do what, who gave Arsenio a job like Axel Verlice, and the secret this town is hiding that you'd kill to protect."

Never let it be said I had Jacques Stone figured out.

Holding my gaze, he tipped his chin. "One day, you will."

I loosened my grip on the spoon. "Okay, then... I can wait."

We were quiet while I filled the kettle and set it to boil. There was likely more I could've, should have, said after finally receiving my answer. My guys weren't counting the days till they got bored of me and put me out on my ass. Soon, we'd share everything and I'd know all about them. Their lives. Their hearts. Their secrets.

Mine.

I finished making breakfast. The guys were all down by that time, their search for bugs and booby traps over. They ate with caveman grunts, saying it was good. Jacques finished his bowl. That done, my last guy to feed was Cairo. He waited upstairs for me in the bath.

We took off for class and went our separate ways in front of my lecture hall. I went in, sat down, set my pack at my feet, and took out my things with a single thought plaguing my mind. Why didn't Jeremy and the Crows try something?

The scuffle with Cairo didn't count because they both walked away from that. I heard the rage in his voice after Roan made him give up his phone. Who knew the thoughts going through his head, but I'd bet my life it wasn't to shake hands and cool off.

What are you going to do, Jeremy?

One side struck and the other rebounded. Back and forth they went till the Crows nearly wrestled control away from the guys, and the guys wrested their respect in retaliation. By my counting, both sides were even. They could sit on opposite ends of the aisle and wait for Bedlamites to decide where their loyalties lie.

But even as the thought passed through my head, I dismissed it. Neither side was going down that easily. That's why you don't put two alphas in the same pen.

"Hey, Rainey."

I snapped out of my reverie. Nelson smiled as he grabbed a seat next to me. He had a forehead riddled with acne scars and a black eye I was certain came with a story, but there was nothing to say against that bright, winning smile. "Did you get the notes from last class? Mind if I copy?"

"Not at all." I passed over my binder. "Go for it."

"Thanks."

I secretly thanked him for pulling my head out of those thoughts of Bedlam Boy versus Crow. It yanked me up and deposited me on the correct mental track: the Letter Man.

There was nothing sinister on the face about Cavendish volunteering for a mentor program. I assumed a fair amount of sociopaths filled their lives with good works, so no one would suspect inside they were empty. Who knew if he turned the kid he worked with, or how I'd prove he did, but either way, I was going to find Blake Jensen.

Or maybe who I was looking for was *Dante*. A shadowed figure behind a letter. A shadow voice behind a microphone. There was a certain symmetry in the name who patrolled this town for a hundred years, shedding light on its secrets, was also the dark counterpart making us pay the price for our sins.

Then there were the cigarettes. I didn't smoke, so they all just looked like crushed trash on the sidewalk. Only the cops would be able to tell if there was something special about them, and I'd have to rely on Cairo to pass on that information since I would go nowhere near Sheriff Sharpe. Still, I knew without a doubt he was watching me.

My gaze swept the bald, spiky, red, blonde, and raven-haired heads in front of me.

Somewhere on this campus, he was sitting in class, fetching research for a professor, running a field, or studying in the library. The image I built up in my head refined by meeting Cavendish, then it changed further with the truth he blended in the Homer Green mob. All I needed was to match the picture to someone looking at me too long, standing a little too near, crossing my path more than was coincidental.

I didn't know which route would lead me to him, so I'd go down all of them.

I start with Blake Jensen. There aren't that many youth mentor programs in a small town like this. It'll be easy to track down the one Cavendish worked for and find out who was cursed with him as their big brother.

I nodded to myself. Making a plan gave the illusion of control, but since I didn't have even that much a week ago, I'd take it.

"—de Souza. Miss de Souza."

"Ah, Rainey." Nelson nudged my shoulder. "Look."

Twisting around, I fell on my professor by the entrance, standing next to a guest. My jaw clenched hard enough to crack.

"Miss de Souza," said Sheriff Jack Sharpe. "Come with me, please. I need to ask you some questions."

A thousand emotions flooded my senses. Sound fled under the roaring in my ears. My muscles contracted, sending my pen skittering to the floor.

Sharpe hefted his belt higher up that gut. "Miss de Souza, come with me," he repeated.

"Am I under arrest?" I amazed myself. My voice was steady.

"Not at this time. It's just a few questions."

"Good," I replied, "then you can fuck off."

The room fell silent.

"Rainey," my professor scolded. "Who do you think you're speaking to? There's no need for that. Get up and go with the sheriff."

"Mind your own business."

Nelson goggled at me. The looks I was getting from my other classmates weren't much better.

I glared at Sharpe. "I've got nothing to say to a dirty cop, so you can turn right the hell around and leave."

Sheriff Sharpe was as expressionless as the day he told me he had no memory of receiving the autopsy results of Abigail de Souza.

"I'd rather we not have a problem," he said slowly. "I will ask you one more time, get up and come with me."

"Fuck. Off. I'd write it down for you, but I know how easily you misplace things."

Saying nothing, he stepped to the side, revealing two uniformed officers standing outside the door. "Looks like we will have a problem with this one. Arrest her."

"For what?"

The officers bore down on me—those two words their charge to action. Davidson grabbed under my arms and hauled me up and over the row.

"You're under arrest for trespass and vandalism." I did not imagine the satisfaction in his tone. "You know you're not allowed out at that farm, and I know that hasn't stopped you. You have the right to remain silent. Anything you say can and—"

"Get off me!"

I bucked, ripping an arm free from Davidson's partner. Sheriff Jack was there all too fast. A faint click was all the warning I got as the Taser jammed in my side.

Choking on a soundless scream, fifty thousand volts surged up my veins, drowning my mind in white light.

I was out before I hit the ground.

"CAN I GET YOU ANYTHING? Water? Soda?"

Davidson's voice barely registered. As far as I was concerned, he was the spectator. The unwanted guest. He didn't get to distract from the show.

Showdown.

Sheriff Jack and I locked gazes across the table.

I woke up in the back of his squad car, heading for the station. I hadn't said a word, barring one last shout at his balding head that he was a crooked piece of shit that tore his mother's anus when she shat him out. Davidson took particular offense to that and barked at me to shut up. The sheriff didn't say a word. Not then, not now.

Slow, measured blinks were our responses to one another during the last twenty minutes we sat in his run-down interrogation room. I wasn't certain what he was waiting for, but I was just counting the minutes till the yellow-faced bastard keeled over and died.

Jack came to life. Leaning forward, he pushed the open folder across the desk. It was the only thing on the table. That, and the recorder capturing the interview.

"Miss de Souza, do you recognize this woman?"

I flicked to the photo of Bella—dead on a mortuary slab. I didn't answer.

Davidson opened his mouth. "She was found dead—"

A raised hand from the sheriff silenced him.

"Do you know her?" Jack repeated.

I pushed down the flash of pain, holding my crossed arms tighter.

"I believe you do, seeing as she was the night manager at the motel you've been living in for months. How close were you and Miss Hope?" he asked. "Would you say you were friends?"

I cocked my head, studying the gray creeping into his mustache. What kind of justice was there in this world that men like Jack Sharpe got to live their life peaceful and undisturbed into old age, while kind, good people like Gran died alone in a field?

"A few days ago, we found her body in your old home on the farm. She was killed by an arrow. We also found this." Jack pushed her photo aside, revealing the one underneath. "You have quite the collection of bows and arrows, Rainey. How long have you been practicing archery?"

I schooled my face, though a flash of something else followed the heels of that question. *This is why he brought me down here? I'm a suspect.*

Breathing slow and even, I fought to let a rational word in. *Of course you're a suspect. It's your farm. They know I break in all the time. They know I practice archery. He'd be the terrible cop I said he was if they didn't bring me in for questioning.*

I knew all this, and it did nothing to quell the urge to shove the folder down his throat. Cairo told me the story he made up to his father. He walked in on Bella's murder and a *man* shot him and ran away. His own son told him to look for a guy, so why was I here?

"Ella Franklin, the estate agent," Jack continued, "told us you rescued these items in particular from the estate sale. Buying them back and then requesting permission to keep them in the barn until the farm was sold. Why was it so important that you hold on to these weapons out of the many things you could've retained from your childhood?"

I smiled mirthlessly at him. "My grandmother, the woman whose murder you covered up, scrimped and saved to buy me a new set for each birthday. I couldn't let her gifts—her being Abigail de Souza, you let her killer get away—be sold off to some stranger. My gran"—I leaned over the tape recorder—"died from poisoning and you buried the autopsy results. You remember my grandmother, Sheriff, once again, you covered up her death."

His face flushed a nasty purple.

"I'd never let the things she gave me end up in someone else's hands. Does that answer your question, Sheriff Accessory to Murder?"

"Yes," he gritted. "Thank you."

"No problem, rat-faced lying bastard."

"Hey!" Davidson shouted. "Watch your mouth—!"

"Leave us," Jack ordered.

"But, sir—"

"Now."

Davidson obeyed. The door shut on the click of the recorder shutting off.

"Let's try this again," he said, withdrawing his hand. "Where were you the night of the fifth?"

"I was certainly not trespassing or vandalizing, which are the trumped-up charges you brought me in for, so I guess that means we're done here." I rose from my seat.

"I can hold you for twenty-four hours and I intend to do so, but if you're that eager for a change of venue, I'll wake up Judge Stone and see how many days we can get you in lockup for resisting arrest and attacking an officer."

"Do it, then." I grabbed the knob.

"Gladly, but first I'd like to know where you were during Ruckus Royale?"

I halted. "Excuse me?"

"Crime scene techs recovered something in the sand beneath Scott Cavendish's body." There it was again—that smug smile. "Tell me, Rainey, does that look like the charred remains of an arrow to you? Expert like yourself, receiving a new set every year, I'm certain you're the one to ask."

I held still, mind racing. I didn't consider this. Not for a second did I consider this.

"Sit down, please."

"Not until you tell me what exactly you're asking," I said to the door.

"I'm asking where you were during Ruckus, Rainey. I wouldn't have thought that was a difficult question."

Slowly, I turned to him. "I was partying with my friends like everyone else. You can ask Amy, Zara, and your daughter— Oh, oops. Paris isn't your daughter, is she? Mom traded up for a handsome, rich daddy for that kid."

"Careful," he hissed.

"Why should I? I see what you're doing." I crossed in a bound, smacking my palms on the table. "I bet you wet yourself when the call came that Bella was killed in my home with an arrow. Finally, there was your chance to get rid of the one person who knew the truth of what you'd done.

"Get me tossed in prison as a murderer—and oh look, there's another unsolved death you can pin on me too. Wrap both those cases in a bow, stamp my name on them, and no one will believe a word I say against you for the rest of my life."

"That's absurd!" he roared.

"Is it? Then why am I here when I know Cairo told you the person who attacked him was a man?!"

Shock blew his rage to nothing. "How did you—?"

"Obviously, Cairo told me. So, I ask again, why am I here?"

He didn't hear the question. Snarl twisting his lips, Jack shoved in my face. "What do you have to do with my son?"

"I rather think that's between me and him," I sang.

"You stay away from him!"

"You turn yourself in," I whipped back. "No? Well then, I guess no one is getting what they want today."

His forehead knocked mine. "You're in way over your head, de Souza." Hot tequila breath filled my nose. "You think you know everything, but, little girl, you can't see even the corner of this blurred picture. You don't have the facts," he barked, "nor the capacity to understand them. Go home and be careful who you slander. Someone who allegedly did the things you accuse me of would have no trouble making a double homicide stick."

"Why did you do it?" His threat went in one ear and out the other. "Did AgriProspects pay you to cover up Gran's autopsy results? Did they make you botch the investigation in the first place?"

"Get out!"

"Your son tastes like cherries," I whispered. "He smells like earth, petrichor, and wind in your face as you run through the trees, but tasting him"—I licked my lips—"it's all sweetness."

Jack reeled back.

"He loves me, you know. Can't get e-fucking-nough of me, and isn't trying too hard to cure the obsession. He's surprisingly open to hearing the truth about you. I hope you weren't planning on dying with fond memories of you in your son's head, because I'll make sure that he and everyone in this town sees you for the monster you are, Jack Sharpe."

"I—"

The door swung open.

"Rain." His soft, cool voice doused the rage in our eyes. "Come to me."

I wasn't able to refuse Cairo the other times he called me. This time was no different.

He was tall, imposing, and perfect filling the entrance. His usual casual clothes of cotton hoodie and worn jeans hung on his sculpted frame. His hair was damp and curling at the temples—like he raced straight here from a shower. I curled into his side, feeling the heat of his father's glare as he put his arm around me.

"Dad," Cairo began, tone even. "I heard you pulled Rainey in for questioning, so I came down here to save you wasting your time. We all know how important the first few days are in a murder investigation. A guy killed that woman and attacked me. Didn't see his face, but I caught his polished black loafers as he was running out. Those aren't exactly my girl's style."

"She could still be involved."

"She's not."

Jack flushed an even darker shade of purple. "I will go where this investigation leads me, Cairo!"

"And I, as the witness, will have to tell the truth, whole truth, and nothing but the truth. Rainey didn't kill that woman."

He raised his chin, staring his nose down at us. "Are you... certain of what you saw, Cairo? Just how close are you two?"

Cairo held his father's gaze steadily. "I'm certain I've got a fucked-up shoulder and no reason to lie about the murder of an innocent night manager. You don't trust your son's word?"

Jack's jaw visibly ticced. The silence stretched past comfortable.

"Fine," he said. "You can go."

For the briefest second, Jack Sharpe changed. A figure claimed his space—less gray salting his pepper. Less girth lining his middle.

"*You can go.*"

I blinked and he was gone.

Cairo's firm grip on my shoulder led me out.

I glanced at him as we passed a watchful Davidson in the hall. I sensed a headache coming on. I massaged my temples, wishing my backpack and Advil wasn't still in class. "How much of that did you hear?"

"Enough," he replied.

I wonder if he expected an apology, because none would come where his father was concerned.

"How'd you know I was here?"

"Everyone knows you're here, baby. Your tasing is trending."

"Mmm. Camera phones, the number one worst invention of our lifetime."

"So," he drew out. "I taste like cherries?"

"Most days," I mused. "Others you're kinda lemony."

"Good to know. And when exactly did I fall in love with you?"

"That night in the woods." I brushed my fingers over his belt, and the dueling wolves tattoo. "You found your mate and claimed her."

He hummed.

If I expected more of a response, it wasn't coming. It was possible the idea of love hadn't crossed his mind till I put it there.

Cairo opened the truck for me to go in. Over his shoulder, I spotted Davidson, Officer Andres, and the sheriff peering through the glass door, watching us leave. Cairo climbed inside but didn't start the car. He followed my gaze to the man who gave him his height, chin, and eyes.

"What's this about your grandmother?"

I froze. Cairo truly had heard *enough*.

"Did Roan tell you about our conversation the night of the party?"

Cairo grasped my chin, turning me to face him. "He said he shared more of what we do than he should have. What did he leave out?"

"Wow. I wasn't expecting him to keep what I said to himself, but then, I should know by now not to underestimate Roan Banks."

He waited me out.

"My grandmother was poisoned." I almost turned to the station and stopped myself. I couldn't look in that man's face while I talked about her. "I had a feeling something was wrong when she suddenly died without a will. I knew it like I know my name, and I wouldn't let it go. I spent everything I saved up for college to get a private autopsy, and then I gave those results to your father. He said later that he never got them. Pretended he didn't know me or the name Abigail de Souza."

Again Cairo disappointed me. He showed not a lick of outward reaction. "Who did you think killed her?"

"A man named Andrew Clein. He worked for the company that constantly harassed her into selling."

"What happened to this Clein guy?"

"After AgriProspects folded up, he changed his name and fled further than I could reach. I even used the last bit of money I could spare to hire a private investigator and track him down. Nothing."

"Are you sure?"

I frowned. "What do you mean am I sure?"

"I mean, there are a couple of homicidal headcases who made you their single purpose in life. Is the answer staring us in the face, Rain? Is the Letter Man Andrew Clein?"

My head was shaking before he ended the sentence. "You'd have to have met him, and you'd have to read the letters, but the same thought crossed my mind and I dismissed it. The new Letter Man is rough and unhinged, but also enjoying himself. I can sense in his letters that this is a fun game for him.

"Andrew Clein was this nervous, twitchy person. His eyes were always darting around the room, and he spoke every sentence like a question. He's the kind of guy that takes orders, not action. Besides, he got away with what he did thanks to Sheriff Jack." I spat the name and title. "What reason would he have to come after me now?"

Cairo leaned against the door. "You really hate my father."

"I have good reason to!"

"Begs the question, why haven't you done something about it?" Cairo could've been talking about the weather for all his inflection. "I remember you saying you had proof."

"I do. I have— I have my grandmother," I said softly. "When I have the money, I'll have her exhumed and the second autopsy will say the same as the first. I'll put it in the right hands this time, and they'll hunt down Clein and the people who told him to kill her."

"How much money we talking?"

"Five thousand dollars."

He whistled. "Well, you're fucking a millionaire's son now. Let's say Legend writes you a check tomorrow. Would you do it, Rain? My love, my mate." A smirk twisted his lips. "Would you have my father thrown in jail?"

I gazed deep in those eerie green pools. "Without losing a wink of sleep."

Cairo laughed—hearty, rich guffaws pealing from his chest. "A wolf doesn't mate with a bunny, does he? I should expect no less."

"You're not going to stop me?"

"I am going to stop you," he said clearly. "Because you're making a mistake. Despite that gift of judging character, you missed that Andrew Clein and my father might as well be twins. Except Sheriff Jack invested in those acting lessons."

"What are you talking about?"

"He's a man who takes orders, not action. Actually, he's a man who drinks his shame while his son carries out those orders. He didn't one day get it into his head to cover up the murder of an old woman." Cairo drifted over my head. I wasn't sure if his father was still there. I didn't look to see. "He got that idea from someone else."

"AgriProspects must have paid him."

Cairo tossed his head. "He's got no use for money. Dad doesn't go anywhere. He doesn't do anything. He's been walking in boots he's had for six years ever since he handed over the keys to this truck. Hardly a man sitting on thousands in hush money."

"So what?" I snapped. "Someone *made* him cover up her death and that's supposed to be okay? He's the sheriff of this town. If he can be bullied into letting murderers free, then I'm doing everyone a favor seeing him thrown out."

"Did you not hear what I said? Someone made him cover up your grandmother's death, and it wasn't a bribe from a bankrupt company or threats from a nervous, twitchy businessman. You're not interested in finding out who is really behind this?"

My eyes narrowed. "Are you trying to manipulate me? Spin the facts to suit yourself and protect your father."

"Why would I do that when I just committed to finding out what happened to your grandmother?"

"I know what happened."

"And I know my father. He's not a good or a bad man, he's a weak one."

"He just threatened to pin a double homicide on me."

"Right, of course, you're only responsible for the one homicide."

I twisted away, turning my back on him. "I said Jack Sharpe was off-limits. We're done talking about him."

His grip was firm but gentle, making me face him. "This is serious, Rain. I'm not denying my father did what he did, I'm saying he couldn't have done it for the reasons you think. Maybe Andrew Clein isn't the one sending you letters, but could this guy now be the one giving *the orders*?"

My expression changed. Now I was listening. "The Letter Man? You're asking if Clein could've killed her on the instructions of another black letter? Why would he, or Cavendish, want to hurt my grandmother?"

"Why would he kill Bella Hope? Why would Cavendish twist you up in his sickness? Why did you wake up one day and find a let-

ter on your porch?" he asked. "You say you don't know what started this, what if that's because it didn't begin with you? It began with
her."

"But— But Cavendish had nothing to do with AgriProspects."

"Do you know that? He was an accountant and they were going
bankrupt."

Holy shit. Yes, Cairo definitely got my attention. I lurched across
the dash, gripping his arm.

"No one gained from her death," I said. "The company didn't get
the farm. They didn't have the money to buy it in the end. I've been
asking myself for two years why they ruined our lives to get a farm
they were forced to abandon."

"You're right, it doesn't make any sense. Something obviously
went wrong with the plan."

I looked back at the station. "Cairo, are we pretending your father isn't the one to ask? It's as simple as making him expose who put
him up to it." My grip on him tightened. "And are you pretending
that I'm not thinking of your father passing the orders off on his son?
Was this an order he got from the person on the other end of your
phone? One that he couldn't pass off to you because it's a sheriff who
buries evidence?"

"No," Cairo said clearly. "She's not behind this."

She?

"You can take the situation we're in as proof. The very last thing
she wants is a single piece of Bedlam in the hands of an outside company."

I accepted that—for now. "You said you're committed to helping
me find out the truth?"

"I am."

I eyed him. "Is this for me, or for Jack?"

He smiled. "Want the truth?"

"Yes."

"I've seen what you'll do when backed into a corner. If you lose all hope of getting her justice and exposing my father, I suspect you'll kill him, Rain."

The day I drove to his house came into sharp clarity.

Cairo's words reached me from far away. "If you try, I'll have to stop you, then you'll consider if this love goes both ways, and if it's stronger than your love for Abigail de Souza." Cairo lifted his shirt, revealing the tattoo in its intricate glory. "A wolf doesn't choose a bunny for its mate, and a man doesn't choose between his girl and his blood.

"I can't let you kill my father, Rain."

My voice was a low rasp. "I never said I would."

"You're not saying you won't."

I fell quiet.

Cairo trailed his fingers down my cheek, tipping my chin. "We're going to find out what really happened, baby, then you'll unleash that rage on the people who've earned it." He kissed me. "Agreed?"

My answer came slow, but it came.

"Agreed."

Cairo started the car. We drove out of the parking lot, watching the station grow small in the rearview.

It was Cairo's turn to wonder what I was thinking as I rested my head on the glass, eyes glazed on Bedlam going past. My thoughts should've been easy to guess.

I was thinking of the Letter Man, and how long he lurked out of sight.

Chapter Three

Legend flipped me over, smooshing me in the pillows. A move like that would break any kiss, but not the rolling-on-the-sheets, tearing-off-our-clothes, moaning make-out session we found ourselves in.

His tongue tangled with mine, as entrenched as his fingers woven in my hair. Our nightly blow job session ended with him saying I was "improving." I told him he was hooked on my tongue, and I'd start getting choosy if he didn't show some appreciation.

It'd been a stressful day and I was riding the agitation of being arrested, electrocuted, and interrogated by the person I hated as much as the Letter Man.

Legend said if my tongue was commanding respect, he'd have to see what else it could do. I wasn't sure who moved first. Next thing I knew, his palm was attached to my ass as he ground between my legs.

"Oh, Legend," I moaned. "Bet you love having a name like that during times like these."

His laugh rumbled his chest. "It was a prophecy, love, that I more than lived up to."

My hands were everywhere. Gliding down his chest, stroking him through the lining, scraping my nails along his back, bringing him down to me. All chatter ceased as his lips became mine again.

It amazed me how their personalities came through in their kiss. Legend was hidden passions and dual personas. He both kissed me sweet and thorough and rutted against my middle to produce a friction that was undoing me. It was not possible that I was about to come from that alone. But if Legend wished it so, I would.

He broke away, drawing a whine from me. "For heaven's sake, can we drop the Torture Rainey game for another five minutes?"

"I doubt you're going to find this torture."

My brows blew up my forehead. Legend draped my legs over his shoulders, flashing me a smirk as he dropped.

The last time one of the guys gave me head was when Cairo caught me in the farmhouse and had his way with me on the floor. Since then, the guys gave me a steady string of orgasms, but still, they were singularly focused on my punishments. Giving head did not fall in that category.

Legend nibbled on my clit.

I gasped—actually scooting back to flee the sudden lightning pulse.

He hooked around my legs, holding me in place as his tongue parted my folds, lazily exploring the secret they failed to defend.

"Fucking fucknuts," I cried. Arching off the bed, I fisted his hair, driving him and his tongue deeper. "Can we make this a part of the nightly routine?"

"Only when your blow jobs exceed expectations."

I felt each goose bump rippling over my skin, cresting on the surging pleasure spreading through me. Legend continued down and swirled his tongue around another hole entirely.

"Oh." *This is new.*

Gripping the headboard, rocking up to give him better access. My body was unsure of the new sensations, but if anyone was going to lead me on an enjoyable quest of new sexual explorations, it was the Bedlam Boys. There wasn't a single thing we'd done that I said no to inside, even if I said it out loud.

Legend pushed two fingers inside me, working one hole and teasing the other.

"Yes," I hissed. "Just like that, baby."

"Say my name."

"Legend. Legend." His name was sex and worship on my lips. "You are a legend."

He picked up the pace, bringing on what I couldn't hold back.

I came hard, jerking and flopping so wildly on the bed, I flopped myself off. I just lay there on the carpet, chest heaving.

Legend's room was smaller than his bedroom at the mansion, but it was no less decadent. The walls were painted black to match the midnight carpet. This should've made it cramped and gloomy, instead it felt like stepping into the secret passage behind a bookcase.

A dozen black-and-white framed prints covered his walls. Pops of red added color with his pillows and the single red chest locked at the foot of his bed. He opened it for me and removed all doubt of where he kept his twin set of paddles.

I decided I loved his room and the huge king-size bed that sat in the middle of it. Dragging myself up, I claimed another kiss and had to dance away giggling when he tried to drag me back in bed.

"Bathroom," I said.

I left Legend lying amid his kingdom and padded to the bathroom. This space had received a makeover from its original frathouse chic as well. The wall shower tiles were black, and the floor black and white. He went with a floating bathroom sink that I leaned over to wash my face and fixed up my hair.

Looking marginally less like a sex-drunk coed, I used the bathroom, then opened the door to leave.

Quickly I swung it closed, leaving a sliver for me to peek through.

Legend carded his fingers through Roan's hair, gently guiding him to his knees. "I've been dying to fuck that mouth."

"Really?" Roan licked his lips, tugging his zipper down. "Looked like you were getting your fill elsewhere."

"I'll never have my fill. You should know me better than that by now."

Their chuckling was drowned out by the loud *ca-thumps* banging in my chest. The pressure built between my legs, and they hadn't done anything yet.

Roan watched, and jacked off, while Legend paddled me, and so far, that was the closest we'd come to a threesome. I couldn't stop myself imagining what it'd be like to be the cheese between those slices of bread. I *didn't* stop myself picturing what they got up to when I wasn't around.

I low-key suspected it was more teasing and punishment that had them dangling this delicious treat just out of my reach. But I wanted it.

Bad.

Legend traced his lips, parting them as Roan's tongue darted through, licking his tip.

Heat exploded in my middle, weakening my knees and dropping me to the floor. It was fascinating watching the two of them together. Their open relationship had rules. They could hook up with other people as long as they knew about them, and the hookup was just a hookup. They didn't sleep with the same person more than twice, unless that person was their girlfriend—as in, me.

I have special privileges, so it's past time I claimed what I wanted.

"Rainey."

I jumped like I'd been caught stealing.

"Don't have to hide in there, love," said Roan. "This lesson is for you."

Giving up my failed game of peekaboo, I crawled out.

"Thought I'd give you some tips, bring you up to expert level on sucking our man's dick."

Roan swallowed him to the hilt. Hissing, Legend dropped his head back, reaching up to grab the beams of his canopy bed. My pulse picked up speed with each inch that brought me closer to them.

Roan drew back with a "pop" and reached for me. I breathed rough, shallow pants as Roan settled me between his legs. His touch was gentle—gentler than it'd ever been, teasing up my body, skimming my collarbone, brushing my hair over my shoulder. He leaned me against him and bent to drop kisses on my throat.

"Take him slow, baby," he whispered. "Give yourself time to adjust."

"Show me."

Roan did—taking him in inch by glorious inch. I bit my lip, penning in a moan as my hand traveled low. I was so wet, my fingers slicked to the touch, making their merry-go-rounding my clit easy.

Grasping my chin, Roan guided me to his place, parting my lips like Legend did to him. His thick, throbbing cock filled me, and I took Roan's advice—going slow, letting my gag reflex relax.

"Lots of tongue, beautiful." His words were heat in my ear. "He likes that. Don't you, Legend?"

"Fuck, yes," he bit off.

Roan replaced my fingers with his own, fucking me with two, then three fingers matching my increasing pace with Legend. I bobbed my head, cheeks caving, tongue worshiping him. Legend clung to the bed promising to do things to me I wasn't sure were all possible.

I came up for air and Roan was there before I spoke, nipping along the underside of his cock and licking his balls.

I spasmed, rocked by the first wave of my oncoming, violent orgasm. This is why they hadn't let me into their world right away. The inexperienced, newly de-virginized girl I was a few weeks ago would've died from the chain orgasms.

"Shit," Legend breathed. "You two are going to make me come so hard I'll be out of semen for a month." He tangled in my hair. "Who told you to stop?"

I didn't want to stop. Stop watching. Stop making them feel as wild and dangerous as they made me. Or stop to think what I'd do if what Jacques promised me didn't apply to all of them. Through all the girlfriends and boyfriends, Roan and Legend's bond remained. What if there wasn't room for me to stay?

That's not going to happen. I wouldn't be here if they didn't both want more. I was the one who gave them what they needed like Cairo, Arsenio, Jacques, Roan, and Legend each held a piece of what I needed.

I tugged Roan to me, crashing my lips on his. We kissed hungrily, sloppily, moaning to add a soundtrack over the *slap, slap, slap* sounding between my legs.

They were never getting rid of me.

Breaking apart, I dove between his legs, sucking Legend's balls the way I learned from my new teacher. Legend grunted and I felt the moment he tightened.

Hot spurts of cum decorated my hair and back.

"Fucking... fucknuts." Legend collapsed on his bed. "Damn. We're making some changes to our nightly routine."

I laughed as Roan peppered my face with kisses. "Fine with me."

"I believe I said you get a reward when your blow jobs exceed expectations."

My brows blew up my head. "Yes, I remember that agreement too."

"Get up here."

Roan tossed me shrieking on the bed. Giggling, I crawled up the pillows but didn't make it far. Legend snagged my ankle and flipped me on my ass. I melted into the sheets under his kiss, hissing as he scraped my bottom lip between his teeth.

"Roan," he said, and my red-haired devil imp was there.

Naked in record time, his hard, tanned body molded to mine. I sensed where this was going and held my breath lest I do or say a thing that'd make these infuriating men deny me. There was a time for punishment, and there was a time to get fucked.

Grinning, Roan swirled his tip around my entrance. "Should I?"

"You get me that knife and I'll show you what happens if you don't."

"Oooh, tempting."

"Ro—"

He pushed in with one hard, firm thrust. I broke a nail on his back.

"Ah, yes, faster. Roan, please."

The man took orders even better than I did. He bounced me on the springs, pogoing in and out of my pussy as my cries became unintelligible.

Roan grunted. Dropping his head on my shoulder, he slowed for a moment—hands tightening on my waist. Over his back, Legend rose like the fallen angel himself. His raven locks damp and shining in the low light. Lust darkening his mahogany eyes.

He winked at me as he thrust inside Roan, turning his pants to groans in my ear.

There was no saving me after that. I clenched around him, back bending in honor of my favorite bow, and came so hard I blacked out.

It was only a second. One moment Roan was licking my jaw, then my vision cleared on him towering over me, Legend's hand gripping his shoulder. I watched every expression of ecstasy cross his face, tracing them as they were stored in my mind forever. But I knew my Roan—

Traveling down, I clamped his nipple and twisted mercilessly.

—and what he really wanted.

"Ah!"

He came, jerking and spasming inside me. Legend followed right on his heels.

They both fell on top of me. I wrapped my arms around them, content to stay like that and never move.

I nuzzled Roan's forehead. "My treat isn't over yet, is it?"

"Fucking hell, Roan," Legend breathed. "We're definitely keeping this one."

Our sex games continued for hours. Roan and Legend were very kind to show me the many positions a throuple could bend themselves into.

Afterward, we lay on the tangled mess of sheets, sweat cooling on our bodies. Roan dozed, his arm keeping me safe and secure as he breathed softly on my neck.

Legend lay on his back, wide awake and gazing at the canopy beams, lost in his head. I skimmed the outline of a hummingbird tattoo on his chest.

"Why a hummingbird?" I whispered.

"One saved my life."

"Really? How?"

He shifted to smile at me, head resting on his arm. "I was playing in the woods one day when I was eight. Found a nice spot between the roots of a tree and sat down to read. Out of nowhere, a hummingbird flies up to me, pulling my head out of my book. A beautiful, tiny, wild thing that decided to visit me.

"I just sat there watching it fly. All of a sudden, it shot up and I bent my head to look, just as the branch snapped. I rolled out of the way in time because of that bird."

"Wow. Amazing how little things create big moments."

He nodded.

"Legend."

"Rainey."

I laughed. "Why do you live here instead of that big ole mansion twenty minutes away?"

"What grown man wants to live with his parents?"

"Good point, but you're used to private chefs, basement gyms, five garages, and a ninety-inch television in every room. Why trade that in for this place when you could at least get your own apartment off campus?"

"Trying to get rid of me so there'll be an extra room, de Souza?"

I flicked his nose. "I'm serious."

He caught my hand and dropped a kiss on my knuckles. "Roan's mom lets us all live here rent-free as long as Roan's here. And if Roan's here, I'm here."

"It's sweet how you two love each other. He's the only person you're nice to."

"Are you saying I'm not nice to you?"

"Yes."

His laugh rumbled from his chest. "Good thing you're into that."

"Do your parents like Roan?"

"Honey, very few people *like* Roan. Most of them wrestle between their loathing and lusting of him. Some flat-out hate him. One pushed him out and is biologically programmed to love him, but the list of people who like the guy deliberately pushing their buttons is short."

"Was he his naturally charming self with your folks?"

He smiled just thinking about it. "Roan wouldn't be any other way. Mom got over it quick, but Dad took some time accepting his only son's bisexuality. Roan helped the situation by flaunting it. Passionate kisses in front of him. Striding out the house in his clothes from the day before, and shouting bye to the old man's purpling face."

I heaved a sigh. "Oh, Roan. Did your dad give you a hard time because of it?"

"The half a dozen times he stopped to notice? Nah."

His hair fell over his eyes. I brushed it back, lingering, playing with his strands.

"I tell people that I'm not sure if Dad ever came around or if he just forgot. We're not close. We don't talk. We don't spend time together. We go through the routine at the distillery, but that's it. All those trips he takes out of Bedlam, I'm not invited along for the ride. The guy doesn't know shit about my life."

"I'm sorry," I whispered.

"You would be." The wry smile still hung on his lips. "All you folks with parents and grandparents that wrapped you up in hugs, kisses, and midnight cocoa feel bad for the rest of us. Just imagining your life without breaks you."

"I am living a life without, Legend, and I'd give anything to go back to the midnight cocoa. Of course it breaks my heart that it was never there for you." I stroked his cheek. "No wonder you hate sleeping alone."

Something flashed in his eyes.

"You never will again," I vowed.

"Are you going to make sure of it?"

"Yes."

He pulled my hand away and laced our fingers together. Nothing more, but the act said everything.

"There's still something I want to know," I spoke up.

"I seem to be in a sharing mood, so go for it."

"You and Roan could live here on your own. Jacques, Cairo, and Arsenio didn't have to move in, though I see the appeal of free rent. I guess I'm wondering why you all choose to live together. Some days, you five don't seem that close, and then others, it's like you're one mind split between you. How did you end up together?"

"We weren't given much of a choice." Facing me, he wound my strands around his free hand. "Small towns kind of pick your friends for you. No one else got what I was going through. Other boyfriends didn't want the same relationship that I did. So now, it's the five of us." He kissed me. "We all end up where we're supposed to be, Rainey. The trick is not to fight it."

I hummed. "You don't seem like the kind of guy that accepts the cards handed to him."

"Ah, well." A smirk split his face. "I'm probably eighteen percent that guy. But that eighteen percent put me in the right circumstances to claim my new toy. Sometimes you gotta be open to the gifts life hands you, baby. Stop reading, watch the hummingbird."

"Some wisdom buried in there."

Legend leaned in. His kiss skimmed my lips and caught the tender spot under my ear. "Reprieve is over, darling. You've got your own room."

I gaped at him. "You can't be serious. After everything, you're sending me back to the doghouse?"

"We haven't set an exact date for when your punishment is over, but I can tell you it's not tonight." He kissed me again. "We gave you a little treat before bedtime, don't get greedy."

"Legend, seriously, after being thoroughly fucked in both holes, you could at least give me one more night."

"I could..." That smirk widened. "But I won't. Get going. Close the door when you leave."

I might've argued some more, but the guy wasn't above picking me up and carrying me down himself. I credited his good mood that he at least sent me off with another kiss instead of the sore bottom I got most nights.

Standing in the silent hallway, I landed on Cairo's door. *Wonder if he's in there tonight.*

I knew he spent most of his nights away. When you slept by the front door, you notice people's comings and goings. It crossed my mind a few times to ask him where he went, but I let it go each time. I had a feeling he'd tell me on his own one day.

Sighing, I settled in the doghouse.

Legend liked me in his bed. He liked waking up with me sandwiched between him and Roan and his arms around both of us. They were getting as tired of this as me. Soon, he'd give in. Or Cairo would to keep his mate close. Arsenio would let me in to share the mysteries behind his eyes. Jacques would to indulge his time with one of the few people who didn't see him as someone to gawk and whisper about.

No matter what denials they voice, inside they said something else. Soon, I wouldn't be the pet. I wouldn't be another in a carousel of sex partners. I'd be their girlfriend, their love, their mate, their logical choice for the rest of their lives.

"I've seen what you'll do when backed into a corner. If you lose all hope of getting her justice and exposing my father, I suspect you'll kill him, Rain."

How could I be without these men? They see me like no one ever has.

CRASH!

I jerked up, banging my head on the roof of the doghouse.

Sticking my neck out, my mind struggled for a moment to make sense of what I was seeing.

Glittery pieces covered the floor, coffee table, couch—

My lips parted, breath stolen from my lungs before they uttered the scream.

Climbing out, my bare feet trod on the glass, stabbing pinpricks of pain that faded from register. Closer the dancing flames brought me—gorgeous in their reflection, deadly in their hunger.

"Ahh!"

"Call 911!"

"Is someone in there?"

I passed out of the living room, picking up the object lying beside the couch on autopilot. Outside, the cooling autumn air raised goose bumps on my exposed flesh. It was something for the spectacle before me that coeds spilling onto Greek Row paid no mind to the woman standing around in a lace bra and panties.

The 1957 Chevrolet Corvette wheezed its death. Metal groaned. Tires blew out in a gust that spat the fire at those who dared get too close.

I didn't see him first, I sensed him.

A presence spilling out of our home and standing the hairs on the back of my neck. Again, I did not need to see Arsenio Creed to know the expression on his face was terrible to behold.

Pristine leather. Polished surfaces. Not a scratch of chipped paint anywhere to be seen. Most afternoons, I sit at the window watching him in the driveway—shirtless and curls damp with sweat—while he worked on his car.

Arsenio stepped in front of me, veins stark and pulsing running up his back. The crowd parted for him, silence rippling through them like dominoes.

He spun, fixing on me, and I froze to the spot. Wild, blazing fire ten thousand times hotter than the inferno claiming the one thing he loved eroded away all color or emotion. I swear on my life, Arsenio's eyes bled black.

He flicked down and I realized I was still holding the gift sent hurtling through our window.

I peeled off the rubber band, opened the note, and dropped the rock. My jaw clenched.

"It says... get the fuck out of Bedlam."

Arsenio straightened. With the bursting of another tire, the blaze in his eyes was doused. The color returned. The handsome, smiling mayor's son stood before me. If I hadn't been looking at him,

I'd have missed the transformation. I *was* looking at him and honestly couldn't say which expression frightened me more.

Something dropped on my shoulders.

Roan draped the blanket around me. "Let's go," he said. "I'll take a look at your feet."

I didn't stop him lifting me in his arms or turning to carry me inside.

As Legend, Cairo, and Jacques streamed past, they let the door swing shut and I caught the barest glimpse. Standing in the crowd, watching the flames' desperate quest for more fuel, was Jeremy.

"THEY DID THIS."

Arsenio paced the living room, stomping a groove in the floor that stopped me voicing the half dozen comforting statements that floated in my head. I only had to look at him to see nothing I said would make this better. I didn't know the story behind his car, but if Jeremy wanted to hurt him, he succeeded.

"They did," I said, snapping that burning gaze to me. "I saw Jeremy in the crowd. Don't have to guess what brought him away from Bay Avenue in the middle of the night."

Arsenio spun on his heels, storming to the door. Jacques dropped the tape and moved in his path.

"You can't do what you're thinking."

Snarling, Arsenio got in his face. "You don't know what I'm thinking."

Jacques didn't flinch. "Yes, I do. Ellis will be tucked away in his mansion with the eight security cameras sweeping the property. They'll have you arriving on video and the sheriff—"

"I don't care!"

"Your old man would!"

My eyes went round. To hear Arsenio shout was shocking, if understandable in the situation, but Jacques too?

"He wouldn't want you going to prison for that car, and he sure as hell wouldn't want you there because of trash like Jeremy Ellis and the Crows." He gripped his friend's shoulders. "You know the plan. You know we can get rid of them for good, but we *can't* strike back."

"Jacques's right," Cairo said. He stayed at the window, carefully breaking the last of the jagged glass and covering the gaping hole in our home with cardboard. "Micah is telling everyone those photos are faked. He's dropping a sympathetic tune of trying to make peace with Roan and end the fighting, and then Roan used him and planted those nudes on the phone. This fire looks like victims striking back, and if we come at them, it'll solidify that martyr image they're painting.

"These fools came into our town, fucked with us, fucked with our people, and got what they deserved for using Bedlam for their own ends. That has to be the story on everyone's tongue when this is over, or Foundry and the Crows get exactly what they want, us out of Bedlam."

Arsenio bore into Jacques. "Get out of my way."

"I will, if you tell me the outcome of you going over there tonight." Jacques held out his arms. "You're a smart guy, Creed. Too smart to not know exactly where we'll find you in the morning. So, picture that ending, and then picture the one I've picked out for Jeremy Ellis and his boys. You tell me which one is more satisfying."

I held my breath, darting between them. No one clued me in to Jacques's plan, but I did know what would happen if Arsenio left this house. I'd seen that look in his eye only once before. Axel Verlice did too.

Arsenio sidestepped him and thundered upstairs. His door slam rattled the whole house.

No one spoke for a beat.

"What's the plan?" I asked.

"You don't need the details," Cairo replied.

"You're not seriously thinking I'll tell Jeremy, are you? Because if you are, I'll hit you over the head with another crossbow."

Cairo blew me a kiss.

"For real, I—" My fists balled. "I've never seen Arsenio like that. Tell me what to do."

"You don't need to do anything," Jacques said. "What matters is what you say."

I SHUFFLED ALONG THE path, walking a few feet, turning around, then claiming a bench only to get up again. I couldn't help my anxious energy. It took all the persuasive power I possessed to stop the guys from coming here in my place and beating Jeremy into the ground.

My phone buzzed. I fished it out of my backpack.

New Boy One: Keep walking past the memorial.

Me: What is this? Are we meeting up or not?

New Boy One: Past the memorial. Hurry up.

Blowing out a breath, I took off, leaving the arboretum and making my way to Douglas Herbert's memorial. I couldn't stop myself glancing at the kookaburra as I went past, or recalling the memories that would forever be attached to that blasted bird. How did my life become this?

I continued over a knoll and stopped, searching out Jeremy among the students crisscrossing branching paths to get to their different colleges. None of them wore a leather jacket or a crow on their neck.

Another message came through.

New Boy One: D Parking Lot. By the welcome sign.

I finally walked up to Jeremy's car idling by the back entrance onto campus. I gave him a look as I slid in.

"What's with the treasure hunt? I look like I got time to waste?"

He grinned. "Why so touchy? Just taking a few precautions."

I tugged off my heel and flashed him my bandaged foot. "Like you took these precautions? I was in the fucking living room when that rock came through the window. Don't tell me it wasn't you."

"It wasn't me, it was Micah," he said, wincing. "But fair enough, you should be pissed. I forgot they make you sleep in the living room like a literal dog."

"What was that about, Jeremy? Why did you do it?"

"Why do you think?"

He started the car, peeling out of campus and setting a course for who knew where.

"They told the world I was fucking my brother. I've got friends in HC giving me shit now, saying they always knew 'we were too close.' Fuck that!" He punched the dash. "They deserve everything they've got coming to them."

I grunted something.

"What's up with you? I thought you'd get off on watching the Bedlam Boys eat it for a change."

"Maybe I would if you weren't happy for me to get caught up in the process. You can't care all that much about what happens to me if you *forgot* I was sleeping under the window you shattered."

"Hey, I apologized for that." His voice softened. "We really weren't trying to hurt you. We just gotta make sure the message sinks in. A week ago, I was willing to go easy on them. That's over now. The Bedlam Boys are out. The Crows run this town now, and no one is going to hurt you when they're gone. I told you, Rainey, the Crows will worship you."

Jeremy felt up my thigh. My stomach heaved.

I'd do the rounds with a barroom full of unshowered, incontinent, flea-bitten randoms before I got naked with this guy. The Bedlam Boys spanked me, paddled me, fucked me raw and in the dirt, and not even they would disregard my safety as casually as the Crows did.

"Besides, if you think about it, your little cuts work in our favor. Sharpe wasn't supposed to see us together the other day. We can't have him thinking we're friendly, or he'll look to you when we start knowing things he doesn't want us to know. From here on, we'll make it look good. You want nothing to do with us."

"Fine. I've got no problem putting on the show." *None at all.*

"It was good though, right?" He laughed. "Creed shat himself when he saw that car."

I pushed down my nausea. Jeremy believed I hated the guys as much as he did. I couldn't play the spy if he guessed my allegiance wasn't with him.

"I've never seen Arsenio like that," I said honestly. "You broke him."

"Whoo! Nice."

He held up his hand for a high five. I smacked his palm and vowed to take three baths when I got home.

"I'm surprised you burned Arsenio's car and not Roan's." We passed the turn for Bay Avenue. "I thought he was at the top of your hit list."

"Banks has money. Not as much as his boyfriend, but enough that a little car fire wouldn't slow him down. He'll just get another or, like I said, ride around in one of the six St. James has parked in his driveway. Nah." An odd note crept into his voice. "I've got something special for all of them, and Roan... he's going to get it worst of all. When I'm through, they'll beat it out of Bedlam so fast, they'll leave the phone on the dresser and the shampoo still in their hair."

I observed him for a moment, saying nothing. "Where are we going?"

"Just driving around. Don't know how close an eye the Bedlam Boys and their buddies keep on you."

"I know they're having too much fun with this pet thing, but I haven't been chipped, Jeremy," I said. "But they do expect me home after class. Start driving back. This is a short conversation since all I've heard them say is Mayor Creed is planning to address the rumors of the town splitting at the next town hall."

"That's it?"

"Yeah. They're not talking to me about it, but I get the feeling they don't take you or the Crows seriously. Not after how easily Roan showed you up at the party." I admit it, I said that to wheedle him. "If it's between the devils they know, or the devils that screw their brothers, no one in Bedlam is going with you."

His white-knuckle grip tightened the wheel.

I shrugged. "Like I said, it's just a feeling, but they're not worried about the return of Crystal Canyon."

"They will be."

The air-conditioning blew frigid on me. I turned it off and was still cold. The atmosphere around Jeremy unnerved me. I mean, if someone convinced the town I was messing around with my sister, I'd want payback too. But even before Roan did what Roan does, the Crows were off.

They came in too fast and too hot. Jeremy stabbed Cavendish for the mere sake of proving he was big and bad. He organized a mob that put people in the hospital. He whipped out his knife like he was ready and willing anytime—just give him a reason.

It wasn't so much that I thought he was dangerous. It was that I was starting to think the Crows, Ellis, and Foundry were... desperate.

They wanted this town so badly, they were shelling out hundreds of thousands to buy homes out from under people. They were hiring college girls to spy and resorting to felonies to drive out the main op-position against them.

That's what made them frightening. There was no one more dan-gerous than a desperate man.

"If I ask you something," I began, "will you tell me the truth?"

"Depends on the question."

"How will driving Cairo and the guys out of Bedlam clear the way for you? Marjorie Creed is the mayor. Eileen Stone is the judge. Jack Sharpe is the one with the cuffs if they link you to the fire. I half expected the contract to say I had to get close to their parents, but no, you're focusing all your attention on the guys. Why? Whether they're here or not, it's not up to them how this goes."

Jeremy cuffed my chin. "You just keep looking pretty, de Souza."

"I'm going to punch your teeth in."

He barked a laugh. "Incredible the Bedwetters ever got you on a leash. What do they have on you?"

"I asked you first."

"Answer mine and I'll answer yours," he shot back.

I pressed my lips together. What they got me on is the burning death of a particularly disturbed accountant, but I'm hardly about to tell you that.

"I'm sure everyone already knows," I finally said. "I disrespected Jacques for the entire class and all of YouTube to see. They came after me and offered an exchange of services in place of punishment. The Bedlam Boys get unpaid help and a plaything, and my homeless ass gets a roof over her head. Believe it or not, the doghouse beats the motel."

"You'll have your farm back soon enough."

The spires of Bedlam Hall rose above the trees. My rendezvous with Jeremy Ellis was coming to an end.

"The place will need some serious work, but after those guys fuck off, you can stay with us until renovators make it livable. Although, it'll have to wait till the spot's not a crime scene. Did you hear about that?"

"Yeah," I said softly. "I heard."

"Two murders. This town is fucked."

"You haven't answered my question."

"Ah." Jeremy rounded the final corner, pulling up to the curb. "I guess it's understandable you don't see the hold those guys have on this town, you spent all your life living on the edge of it. It's the Bedlam Boys who got people locking their doors at night. It's the Bedlam Boys rolling up with a bat when Joe Corner Store is short on payments. It's the Bedlam Boys who'll carry out retribution against those who side with us.

"No one is afraid of the president, Rainey. They're afraid of the secret service. No one quakes in their boots thinking of flabby-bottom senators, but the armed forces our government commands have them reconsidering. It's the muscle behind the power that must be taken out first. Do that, you become the muscle, and watch how quickly they all fall in line.

"The town is scared of the Bedlam Boys. Imagine how they'll fear the guys who put them down—permanently."

"What are you going to do?"

"Can't get into it now, but hey"—he grasped my arm as I made to climb out—"remember whatever happens, it's not about you. It's about getting what we all want."

"I know." I tried to tug free.

"I gotta make it look good," he said, holding on. "They can't suspect you're on our side."

"So, I should probably get out of this car before someone notices us together." I gave the hand on my arm a pointed look. "Now."

Jeremy released me. "Bring me something I can use next week."

I followed his headlights around the corner, picturing the steaming hot bubble bath I was due with Cairo or Roan. Whoever was home right now and would wash my hair while I scrubbed every inch of me.

I shuddered. Some kind of fucking bold going on about me living with them after they drove the Bedlam Boys out. Not to mention the fantasy he's living in, playing like there was anything they could do to get the guys out of this town. There's a reason Bedlam is their name.

Turning around, I crashed into his chest.

"Fuck!"

"Arsenio?" I grabbed him, realizing immediately what he ran all this way to do. "What are you doing here? We said—"

"Fuck what we said!"

His shouting drew stares.

"I was waiting for him to show up at the arboretum. Smart little shit had you get in his car." He walked off like he was going to run after the long-gone Jeremy.

"Arsenio."

Spinning on me, he said, "You'll set up another meet tomorrow. Tell him it's important and you can't say it over the phone. Get him—"

"Easy." I reached for his temples.

Arsenio snatched my wrists, eyes flashing. "I'm not Cairo."

I flicked to those watching, lowering my voice. "You're not Cairo. He's impulsive, unpredictable, and as likely to shake a stranger's hand as he is to bite his ear off. But you..." Gently, I pulled free, sliding down his heaving chest. His heart banged wildly against my palm. "You're calm and patient, and always wait for your moment. The Crows won't get away with what they did, baby, but we both know this is not the moment."

The chilling ice in his eyes hadn't melted, but he was listening.

"We will get him back, I promise. Right now, you have to get your mind off it. I left campus between classes and got something to make you feel better." I touched my backpack. "Take me somewhere private, so I can give it to you."

"Unless you've got my father's 1957 Chevrolet Corvette in that bag, you've got nothing I want, de Souza."

I weathered the sting, facing him head-on. "You haven't seen it yet. Tell me where we're going."

We locked in a staredown. Even our audience wanted to know the outcome, which Arsenio finally noticed. Glaring at those watching, he strode off, the grip on my arm leading me behind.

"It's not far," he clipped.

I was quiet on our walk off campus. I could ask where we were going, but I'd find out soon enough.

We arrived at a crosswalk and veered left for the square. People were out like they were most days. At this time, it was couples basking in a stolen moment, sharing lunch and quick kisses by the fountain. I could almost imagine myself in that scene with Arsenio, Cairo, Jacques, Roan, or Legend, if a collar was around my neck.

This didn't stir the sadness some thought it should. That wasn't the kind of relationship that we were in, and with each day I spent with them, I was glad of it. It wasn't just anyone who could get Legend to open up like he did the night before. It wasn't anyone Arsenio would've taken with him the night he visited Verlice, and it wasn't just any girlfriend that put Cairo in a situation where he thought there was a choice between me and his father, and he admitted he couldn't make it.

What we had between us was twisted, raw, violent, and a little dangerous, but it was real. I'd take that over sushi in the square.

Arsenio took me down Clifton Street. I realized where we were going three houses down.

"The mayor's house?"

"Also known as my house."

"Is your mom home?"

"You asked for alone."

We stepped up the flower-lined drive and let ourselves in. I swept around as Arsenio tugged me along.

A bright, open-floor living room was done up by a tasteful hand. I could see the mayor entertaining guests huddled around the grand piano, or sharing appetizers on the plush white couches.

We turned a corner into the living room and I slowed down. This was where Arsenio Creed grew up. The photos of the chubby, curly-haired baby proved it. In a dozen pictures, he smiled or waved at me. Then, he grew, shedding the plump cheeks and onesies for little suits, bow ties, and the serious expression to match.

Farther down the wall we went, adding a young Roan and Cairo. Quickly the other photos added Legend and Jacques. A pic of the five of them in Bedlam High uniforms, smirking or grinning at the camera, made me glad I was farm-schooled. To have these guys dominating me during my formative years would've stolen the little time I had left with my innocence.

"It's so cute how your mom has a wall of you. Where are the photos of your parents?"

He motioned toward the stairs.

True enough, we climbed the steps and went on another journey through the years. The bottom showed the faces of a sweet young couple, beaming from faded photographs. The higher we climbed, the older they got, till they were married, then expecting their first child.

"You look just like your dad," I said.

His grip tightened on me, but he didn't reply.

Marjorie Creed was the mayor, which meant her past became an official backstory instead of her personal business. Everyone knew the daughter of a white mother and Black father left Bedlam to attend college in New York, where she met the Chinese international student who vowed he'd marry her on their second date.

A lot stood in their way. Visa issues, family drama, a forced return to China, and minimum wage jobs fighting to support big dreams. But they made it through all of that to marry and start a family, and one day, Marjorie woke up and her husband was unmoving beside her. He died of an aneurysm in his sleep at thirty-six years old.

Arsenio pushed inside what I assumed was his bedroom. All the family photos and personal touches were outside. This room was a bed, desk, couch, television, and white walls.

I moved to the bay window. "Nice view. I can see over the square and straight to the university from here."

He grunted. "You said you were packing something worth my time." Arsenio dropped on the couch—his long, powerful legs spread out as he reclined. "Let's see it."

"Any chance we'll be interrupted?" I drifted away from the window, stopping just in front of him.

"Our illustrious mayor is at the hall all day, then she's got a dinner with friends in Hunter's Crest." His brows rose up his forehead. "You trying to find out what happens if you make me ask again?"

The corner of my lip rose up. This was the Arsenio I knew. His beauty as sharply honed as his coldness.

"You don't have to ask." I shrugged my pack on the floor. "Just be patient while I do the prep work."

Holding his gaze, I tugged the halter strings of that day's short, slinky dress, and didn't miss his fingers flexing on the couch as my dress fell around my hips.

Legend told me often that my breasts were perfection. Actually, since I fell into the tender arms of the Bedlam Boys, I'd been assured of my beauty in many naughty ways. I wasn't sure if I saw myself as the silky-haired vixen they named me, tempting them by walking into a room.

That is until I watched Arsenio's carefully built walls crumble at the mere sight of me. I hope it didn't give me a big head to say I felt pretty beautiful then.

I wiggled out of my dress and kicked it over to him. He didn't react when it landed on his lap. Neither did he move to my thong dropping on top.

Bending over, I slowly unzipped my bag. The guy liked me teasing and seducing him. No matter what he said, this would take his mind off Jeremy and the Crows.

I pulled my latest buy out of my backpack. Credit to his expert control of his emotions, a slight twitch of his brow was all that gave him away.

"Turns out this is a real thing." I slid my new red butt plug tail between my breasts. Dangling from my fingertips were the matching ears. "Ordered them last night. Gotta love one-day delivery."

Arsenio could've been chipped from stone, he was rock hard, stiff, so nothing stopped me from straddling him. I smoothed my hands down his chest, dropping kisses on his nose, cheek, and lips.

"So," I purred. "My owner needs cheering up, and as his faithful pet, I'll do my job till I get it right." My tongue darted out, licking the tip of his nose. "Do you want to help me get into character? Or you can sit back and watch. The choice is yours... master."

A low, feral growl leaked through his teeth.

"Do not move."

I opened my mouth to ask what was wrong and found myself dropped on the couch and staring at his back till it walked out. If this was a good or bad reaction, I couldn't tell with Arsenio, but he told me to stay, so I'd stay.

My reflection caught my attention in the mirror across from his bed. I eyed the young woman naked and rocking sex gear, waiting for one of the inscrutable delinquents that were currently passing her around, and I tried to imagine her in boots and jeans, mucking around in the chicken coop.

Look at the images, tell me what doesn't belong.

I couldn't reconcile those two pictures. Not when I knew the twists, turns, and tragedies that brought that girl to me.

If I hadn't lost Gran, that seed of hatred wouldn't have taken root in my soul. If I hadn't chased Ivy away, bitterness and regret wouldn't have watered it. If the Letter Man hadn't crashed into my life, blood wouldn't have opened its leaves, transforming into a darkness that claimed half my soul, and called out to the Bedlam Boys.

This is who I am now.

I looked away from the mirror.

And I can never go back.

The hinges creaked.

Arsenio filled the entrance, holding a length of cloth in one hand. It looked like a belt for a bathrobe. I couldn't make out what he had in the other.

"You're impossible to categorize, Rainey de Souza. In anyone else, this would upset me." He stretched the belt out. "I'd feel the urge to fix them. Order them. Remind them their chaos would always be second under my command."

I rose up on my knees, holding my hands out for him. He stepped within them, cupping my cheeks and gifting me a searing kiss. I whimpered.

Arsenio was reserved in every aspect and area of his life, but not when he kissed. He nibbled my bottom lip, drawing a moan that was all the invitation he needed. Plunging inside, his tongue tangled with me, confusing its up and down, and me not giving a shit. I didn't need to know the right way up when I was with him.

We broke away, breathing hard. This was it: Arsenio losing control.

"But not you." He kissed the tip of my nose. "You intrigue me, Rainey. A part of me can't wait to see what you do next."

I turned around, slowly grinding my ass on his hardening ridge. "You won't have to wait long."

"On the floor. Ass up."

I dutifully did as I was told. Crossing my arms and resting my cheek on them, my butt was up and ready to go. I jumped as something cool squirted on me.

Arsenio steadied my hips, continuing his task. He was surprisingly gentle preparing me. My hole was stretched with one finger, then two, slowly dipping in and out.

My eyes fluttered shut, riding the rising warmth popping beads of sweat on my skin. My lids popped right open as the butt plug went in. The odd sensation took a minute getting used to. Arsenio helped me along by flicking my clit. The zinging, electric pleasure chased everything else away.

"Up. Sit."

I rocked back on my heels. He grasped my chin between two fingers and kissed me.

"Stay," he whispered.

Arsenio backed away, and it was my turn to sit mesmerized as his clothes peeled off, unveiling those thick arms, hard chest, defined V leading to a cock well above average.

"You put to shame every guy in the locker room with that thing, didn't you?" I licked my lips. "You were totally one of those guys strutting around with it all hanging out."

One half of his mouth quirked up. "Confidence isn't a character flaw now, is it? 'Cause it doesn't crack my top ten."

"I believe it's only a flaw when it veers into cockiness."

"And what are your flaws, Rainey?" He placed the ears on my head. "I'm afraid that if I don't bring you down to earth, make you real again, I'll do the unthinkable."

My lids grew heavy as he tortured my nipples, pebbling them under his touch. "What's that?" My voice was barely audible.

He shrugged. "Fall in love with you."

I opened my mouth and nothing came out. To be fair, I think the point was to leave me speechless.

"What tricks should I teach my pet first?" Arsenio traced something only he knew on my stomach. "You already know how to suck a cock."

I quivered under his seeking touch. "I've learned some new things since our last go."

"I'm not interested in Legend's secondhand sex tricks, baby. You're going to learn something new today."

"What's left for me to learn? You guys have been exhaustive in my education."

"You'll see."

Arsenio scooped me up and carried me out of the room. I was taken across the landing and down the hall to the door on the end.

"So, this is your room."

A floor-to-ceiling case of medals, awards, and books were first to greet me. Personality bled into these walls. Bled being the right word, seeing as that's what they were painted—red and gray. As he spun me to shut the door, I landed on the other case filled with dozens of model airplanes. They were beautiful in their differing sizes, designs, and little fine details that put them together.

Arsenio set me on the red cotton sheets—me secretly pleased at guessing his favorite color. I wagged my tail at him. "Why didn't we come in here first?"

"No one comes in here. That included you until I decided I liked your distraction." He was a deadly beast stalking toward me. "You're still going to bring me Ellis tomorrow. Noon. Behind the sports hall where it's quiet."

My smile dimmed.

"But I thank you for giving me this delicious hour or two where I'll think about something else but the things I'm going to do to him. I didn't know there was anything, or anyone, that could distract me when I get like... this." He kissed the soft underside of my thigh. "Keep surprising me, Rainey de Souza. I like it."

"Arsenio—"

"Shh," he crooned. "I know exactly what I'll do to my pet. First, I'm going to eat this tight little pussy out till I've had my fill. You'll come twice, not before I say, and no more than two seconds after. Then you will show me those sex tricks." He nipped that same tender spot. "What the hell, I'm curious. After, I'll flip you over, and... we'll see where this mood takes me."

He dropped flat on his back and drew me on top of him.

I was as helpless to resist as I was to come up with a reason he should sit back and choose pacifism. Jacques was adamant they do nothing and refuse to fuel the fire till the time was right, but Jeremy made a massive error in judgment going after a man like Arsenio Creed, and I didn't know if a woman like me could stop him.

Arsenio sat me on his face. A moan escaped me as his tongue began its exploration. I'd worry about saving Jeremy's undeserving ass later. Right then, I needed a distraction too. And Arsenio was just the guy to provide it.

I rocked up and down on him, gripping the pillows as bliss rippled beneath my skin. That's what I was calling the heady, addictive drug they injected in me with every touch—bliss.

Arsenio got his hands on my tail.

"Ah, the double attack," I cried.

He worked the plug in and out, double-teaming with his relentless tongue.

"That's not fair."

His laugh sent vibrations through my core. I wasn't allowed to come before he said, and if it wasn't soon, I was about to find out Arsenio's method of punishment.

The pressure built, making my knees shake on either side of him. "Now?"

"No." If anything, he picked up the pace, rolling my eyes up in my head.

"Baby, please... I can't..."

"Come."

I exploded on top of him, dropping in a heap against the headboard, and that was only round one.

Arsenio flipped me over and buried his head between my legs, not letting up on the tail for a minute. I finally understood why they were slow on giving me head. That was the next stage of exquisite torture that I had to reach by good, or bad, behavior.

"Come—"

"Ah!" I squeezed on his head, holding him captive as sunbursts exploded in my mind. He got himself free and slid up my body, claiming a kiss as I came down.

Arsenio had me teach him what I learned as promised. His cock plundered my throat, bringing tears to my eyes. I gripped his thighs. Relaxing my throat, I begged for more in unintelligible grunts.

"Fuck!" He broke a piece off his headboard, coming in my mouth.

I said I hadn't seen the same look I saw that Tuesday night till flames claimed his car. Now I could name the third time.

Arsenio gazed down at me, running his hands over my body like he was committing the touch and heat of me to memory. I finally understood that look wasn't bloodlust. It was just plain lust. It was the switch inside him that was usually turned off, coming to light and unleashing the pent-up living rage that was him. What did it mean that I brought out that lust?

I cupped his face in both hands, wondering what he saw in mine. Brows crumpling, his expression changed. "I..."

"I know," I whispered, smile stretching across my lips. "I know."

He shook his head, coming to. "On your stomach."

I flipped over on the sheets and found out what the belt was for.

Arsenio bound my wrists and feet together, bending me like a bow. I shivered as he trailed a finger up my spine.

"Why you?" he asked.

"I think you're supposed to tell m-me."

He dipped inside my folds, hitching my breath. "I would if I knew. You're the first."

I sobered, burying my face in his pillow. It overwhelmed me his confession. I couldn't fathom he, the most closed off of all, would be the one to tell me about their parade of girlfriends, and then admit I'd be their last.

"Don't ask yourself why," I said. "Just look up, and see the hummingbird."

I wasn't certain he understood me. He indulged himself another taste between my legs and I figured we'd get back to the discussion later.

Sweet, gentle lovemaking was not what the Bedlam Boys and I did, and Arsenio was no exception. I kicked a lamp off the nightstand. He bent my head back by the hair as he drilled me. All the pillows ended up on the floor and we did too.

Arsenio tossed the tail over his shoulder. Positioning my hips, I gripped the edge of the mattress for leverage, readying for—

He pushed in my newly used hole. Who was to blame for not going easy on me? Arsenio pounded me, shoulders rocking on the carpet and digging his heels for leverage. But I met thrust for thrust, screams ratcheting higher as I begged for harder, faster, and deeper.

Arsenio didn't have time to give an order. Our climaxes took hold of us both and dropped us on sparking live wires. The storm set off inside couldn't be controlled or held back.

I curled up on top of him—both of us huffing and puffing like we ran a three-second mile.

"Will you say it?" I asked, looping his damp curls around my finger.

"Nah. Not today."

"Well then, I'll have to keep surprising you."

"MY MOM LOVES OLD CARS." Arsenio's knife skills were quick and sure. He looked at me while his blade flashed on the cutting board. "The guy next door to their old place wanted to sell the Corvette, but he refused to let it go to some kid who'd fill it with cheap gas and have the interior reeking of weed within a month. Mom promised she'd save up to afford that car one day.

"When Dad was forced to go back to China to settle his visa issues, there was so much red tape and hoops to jump through, they almost gave up hope he'd make it back. When he finally got the notice his visa came through, the first thing he did was buy a plane ticket, grabbed a taxi to that old neighbor's house, and bought it on the spot. Mom walked out of work that afternoon and there they both were."

"That's so sweet."

Arsenio finished making his pineapple star and placed it over my right nipple. The guy said he was hungry. Apparently that meant lying on the kitchen island and playing the bowl to his fruit salad. I didn't mind. This was not the strangest after-sex activity the guys got me in.

"Grape, please."

Arsenio plucked one off the bushel placed strategically on my middle. He popped it between his lips and fed it to me.

"I'd fixed up that car with him since I was seven," he continued. "After Dad died, Mom couldn't sit in it without crying. She gave it to me when I was sixteen, and I kept it perfect... until yesterday."

"I understand, Arsenio. Everything of Gran's they took from me. You know what I've done to get even one thing back."

He arranged the strawberry slices on my belly in a pattern I couldn't see. His face was an unreadable mask once again.

"What did he say?"

"He said the car was just the beginning." I rested my hand on his. "He's got something picked out for all of you, and Roan worst of all."

He nodded slow. "Then we'll be ready."

"You're going to wait? Serve your revenge up cold?"

Another pineapple graced the left nipple. "You reminded me that's what I do. Besides, I'll give the analytical bastard something, Jacques is practical, but he isn't merciful. The retribution he has picked out for the Pigeons is more satisfying than the beating and jail time I picked out.

"In his version, there's fire."

Chapter Four

I tried not to smirk as the doghouse was dumped in the backyard.

"You're smug as shit."

Looks like I failed.

Cairo lifted me off the porch, wrapping my legs around him. I linked my fingers behind his neck as he pressed me against the door.

"Did you plan this with Ellis to upgrade your digs?"

"Nope," I said, grinning. "But I might've if I'd known that was all it took."

Waking up to find the doghouse covered in glass and my bloody footprints on the floor was enough to bring an end to that particular punishment. Cairo wanted me safe and tucked under a Bedlam Boy the next time someone came up on our house in the middle of the night.

"Will I sleep with you tonight?"

"You'll be in my bed. I'm going out tonight and want you where I can find you when I get back."

"Okay."

Arsenio and I got back from his place an hour before. After his snack, he bent me over the couch, pool table, and made me come twice in the shower. I thought I was sore after my marathon with Roan and Legend. The three of them back to back, and I had a noticeable hitch in my step. Arsenio was kind, or smug enough to carry me home.

When we walked in, the sun had set and the guys were finishing up dinner and talking in hushed tones that shifted to muted.

"What were you guys talking about?" I asked. "Your plan against the Crows?"

"Talking about you actually. Arsenio texted us that we have to be ready for the next hit. Any one of us could be next. We were also talking about you feeding him juicier info next time. Might get him to give you more in return."

"Makes sense," I agreed. "Are you really going to stand there and take the blows?"

"Jeremy has worse coming his way."

"What about Cavendish and AgriProspects? The investigation? Is there any news?"

Cairo popped my strap off my shoulder. I swear it was their mandate in life to ensure I was naked at all times.

"Sheriff sent the cigarettes out for testing. The lab is in Hunter's Crest. It'll be a few weeks before he gets the results."

Groaning, I dropped my head on the wood.

"Good news is he made the link between Cavendish and Hope on his own. He's digging deeper into both of them, figuring out what made them a target of a serial killer."

"He's digging to find out how they're connected to me and if I have a motive," I corrected.

"That's still good for us. If there is a link between Cavendish and your grandmother, he'll find it. And if he tries to bury it, that'll be all the proof we need about who had their boot on his neck."

"But how will you know if he finds something?"

"The old man brings his case files home. They make for decent reading."

I nodded, worrying my lip. "We can't rely on him to find everything for us. Correction: I *won't* rely on him. AgriProspects is gone, but Cavendish's accounting firm isn't. I'm—"

"We."

"*We* are going there tomorrow. Also, I'm stopping by the only two youth centers in town to see what they know of a Blake Jensen."

"Fine. We'll get it done before I go on a collection run."

He, and therefore I, headed inside.

"Shower," he stated. "You're going to do that thing you do."

Smiling, I kissed his cheek. "Happy to."

The next morning, I crawled out from under Cairo's arm and dressed in the dark. Paris and I had eight a.m. classes and were meeting for breakfast.

I stepped out on the porch and waved to the workers fixing our window.

"Morning."

"Morning. What do you got...?"

His friendly chatter faded as I landed on the mailbox. Poking out of the slot, tucked in with the supermarket coupons like another piece of junk mail, was a black letter.

I didn't recall telling my feet to move. The command to lift my hand did not come from me. All I knew was in the next breath, my fingers were running over the stamp.

It was a white rose.

The home you made a crime scene didn't slow you down at all. Of course, you just mailed it.

To the house, said a voice. *He wasn't worried about the Bedlam Boys getting their hands on this first. What does that mean?*

Hands shaking, I tore open the letter.

I'm very angry with you.

You lied to me and you gave away our secret. Why is Sharpe telling the cops he's a witness to the man in the shiny shoes who murdered Hope?

I've got friends everywhere. They let me know when a stupid little fool is trying to get one over on me.

When I found out what you did, I was so angry, I didn't want to talk to you anymore.

I saw you coming out of St. James's place the other day and decided to kill you right then. If you think you can trick me, or that you don't have to play the game properly, then you're not going to play at all.

I was about to end this shit for good, but I didn't because you don't get that gift.

It's you and me, bitch.

Forever. For always. Until I say you can go.

With that fact accepted, you'll have to make it up to me.

I don't know who killed Verlice, but it sure as hell wasn't you. Even though it should have been. That guy was nothing. He wasn't worth what we're building.

I'll make you see that.

The next one won't be so easy, but you'll do it because from you they'll have a peaceful death.

I won't be that nice.

Fuck you.

They left the creepy hugs and kisses off their sign-off this time. The new one didn't make me feel better.

I shoved the letter in my backpack, torn between going inside and telling the guys, or walking straight into a police station.

This was beyond me now. This psychopath was not playing around and I did not need to bury another friend for the message to sink in. The sooner I found out who he was, the sooner I could hand these letters over with a name and never think of the Letter Man again.

"Rainey."

I plastered a smile on my face as Paris climbed out of her car. She was gorgeous as ever. Paris loved raiding her mom's closet for outfits she could turn vintage. That day's look was a puffy top, brown leather skirt, and clunky boots.

"Hey, I've got your change of clothes here." Paris waggled her bag at me. In it would be jeans, a top, and maybe even a sweater if I was lucky. My days of bargaining for clothes were over.

"Oh, how I long for the days of sneakers," I called. "Remind me of what it's like. Is it glorious?"

"It's pretty glorious."

I ran up to her and we smooched cheeks. Pulling back, she gave me a funny look.

"Wow."

I squeezed my pack strap. "What is it?"

"Girl, you are sexed up. Are you getting any sleep at all?"

Fire licked my cheeks. "What? Where did you get that from?"

"Um, you practically galloped over to me, walking funny like you've been going cowgirl—bareback and bucking all night and day on that saddle."

"That's too many puns!"

"Plus, you're covered in hickeys and glowing like someone, or someones, broke your orgasm meter. Spill it. Tell me everything."

"Do you really want the details of my sex life with your brother?"

She scrunched her face. "Okay, spill four-fifths of it."

Laughing, I threw my arm around her, setting off for class.

"Okay, I will say things have progressed positively in that area. Except with Jacques." It was hard to hold my smile, thinking of the distance between us. "I know he feels something for me, but he won't take it as far as he can. Has he ever had a girlfriend that he didn't share with the guys? Just the two of them."

"He dated a couple girls in high school. Brainiacs like him. But it never lasted long," she said. "Going by the locker room talk, they couldn't figure out what was going on inside his head to give him what he wanted either."

I blew out a breath. "I have a theory that women are a super-species. We live longer. Carry the young. Aren't afflicted by testosterone poisoning. But the Lord created men for the same reason lions and antelopes share the same savanna. No one should have it too easy."

"Are you making another play to get in my pants? No doubt ladies-only would do wonders for our stress levels." She held up her hands. "But you must be this long to ride this roller coaster."

"I hate you," I said, cracking up.

She popped a kiss on my cheek. "Wouldn't have to keep giving you these reminders if that was true."

We strode along the sidewalk, taking the lazy way to the student union.

"I'll figure Jacques out." I tapped my fingers together, putting on my mad scientist voice. "Slowly but surely I'll lure them all into my web. Muahahaha."

Paris laughed so hard she snorted. "You are so adorable. My brother does not deserve you, Rainey. I hope Assface knows that."

"If he does, he does not care." I nudged her. "Don't let me dominate the conversation. I want to hear all about your latest playmate. Last text said he invited you to dinner with his mom."

"Ugh, I know. He said he was cool with casual and then he caught feelings like Corona at a Covid party. He's a nice guy, and he does this thing in bed that would set your ears on fire. Seriously, I can't tell you."

"But you will."

"I totally will. Tonight when you come over for the next season of our *Doctor Who* marathon. My parents took off this morning, so I'm inviting everyone."

"Okay, is this actually a party and you're trying to disguise it with *Doctor Who*?"

"Who throws a party in the middle of the week? I promise, it's fun, food, and—"

Squealing tires battered our eardrums.

The car jumped the curb, screeching to a halt in front of us. Six guys piled out—all decked out in black masks.

"Hey," Paris shouted. "What the hell is wrong with—?"

The lead guy punched her in the mouth.

"Paris!"

She flew back, crashing into me. We tripped over my feet and landed hard on the sidewalk. They hauled her off me, tossing her on the grass. Paris screamed as a slap snapped her head around.

"Stop!"

I jumped on Paris, trying to shield her from the kicks and blows. Pain exploded in my skull.

A filthy, meaty fist tangled in my hair, dragging me off her. Its pair sailed at my face.

My lip split on impact and filled my mouth with blood. Dazed, I rolled on the concrete. One of them ripped off Paris's shirt.

Shoving myself up, I leaped on the brute's back. Hooking my arm around their neck, I squeezed.

He gagged and clawed at my arm. My captive shot forward, bent, and slammed my head into the car window. It shattered in a shower of glass.

"Get this bitch off me!"

"Hey," someone shouted. "Hey, look! Over there! Get security!"

Two grabbed me, yanking me off. I whipped around and smashed one across the temple. His mask tugged up, revealing half a cheek and the corner of his mouth. I seized the mask to pull it the rest of the way.

A hard body tackled me, throwing me against the car.

"De Souza, stop."

I stiffened. I didn't know why I was surprised. It could only be him.

"You weren't supposed to be with her, but there's nothing we can do about that now," Jeremy said. He shoved me down, grip ironclad on my collar. "Sorry, we have to make it look good."

He punched me.

My skull banged off the metal, popping black spots in my vision.

"What are you doing? Leave them alone!"

"Let's go," Jeremy bellowed.

I was thrown to the side.

Our attackers jumped in the car, peeling out in a haze of burning rubber.

Crawling over the pavement, it scraped me raw, marking my path in blood. Finally, I made it to her.

I shielded Paris as our rescuers ran over much too late, holding her as she cried.

JACQUES

Rainey curled up on the cot, unmoving under the scratchy cotton blanket.

My arrival didn't awaken her, so I didn't either. Casting a shadow over her, I noted and cataloged Rainey's injuries.

Puffy lip. Swollen eye. Head wound.

The animals who did this would get the same pain and bruises multiplied by ten. My conclusions told me this would permanently maim or injure them. I was satisfied by that outcome.

What I couldn't conclude was why Rainey called me of all people when they were brought to the med center. Maybe she thought I would handle the information calmer than the other guys. It's true I didn't put my fist through the wall like Cairo did after receiving the same call from the sheriff, who responded to a dozen reports blowing up the station at once.

No, I did not put a fist through the wall, but calm...

I sifted through the six options for running the Crows out of Bedlam, and discarded each one.

There was only one option now, set in stone when Rainey stuttered on the other side of the phone, holding back tears.

They would be taken down in the harshest, cruelest manner I could plunder from the depths of my intellect, and everyone would know it was me. I'd proclaim it proud in the courtroom, smile as they gave me my sentence, and wear it as a badge of honor as I passed through the prison walls.

Of all the rewards, trophies, and recognition I garnered over the years, this would be my crowning achievement.

Her thin voice drew my attention.

"Jacques, you're here."

"I am."

We were in a small room in the back of the center. Efforts were made to brighten it up. Purple flower wallpaper matched her purple blanket. A small side table carried a fake rose in a vase, water bottle, and a bag of cookies.

"The nurse wouldn't release me on my own. I didn't know who else to call."

"You don't have to explain." I sat on the edge of the mattress, smoothing down her hair. "You're our girl. I'm the right person to call."

Her eyes welled. "Is Paris okay?"

"They wouldn't give me any information. Cairo is with her now, though. He'll take her home."

She nodded, sniffling softly. "It was Jeremy."

"I know."

"He was planning to get her alone, but he didn't let me being there stop him. Why would he do this?" she sobbed. "Roan hit them hard, but he only went for the Crows. No collateral damage. Paris never hurt anyone. Why would he do this?"

"I suspect..." I trailed off.

"Suspect what?" Her hand poked out of the blanket and slipped under mine. "Tell me, Jacques."

"They know threats and violence aren't going to work with us. They tried both and failed. Now, they're going after our weaknesses. Weaknesses we didn't know we had. Jumping Cairo wasn't going to do shit to get him out of this place. But jumping his little sister." I shook my head. "He'd leave to protect her."

"They're going after who you love."

"Looks that way," I replied. "Arsenio's dad's car, and you and Paris walking around campus were easy targets. It won't be so easy getting to a sheriff, judge, or the mayor. The same for Legend's parents behind their high gates, but we won't wait around to let them try. This ends."

"Please," she whispered. "Let's talk about something else. I can't cry any more today."

"What would you like to talk about?"

Rainey nuzzled her cheek against my palm. "Something good. Happy."

I didn't have to dig deep in the cabinets for this one. It was right at the entrance.

"My cousin had a baby. Brand new. Born a couple days ago." I fished out my phone. "An unattractive little thing, but I'm sure she'll be cute when she's not screaming."

Rainey smiled as she flipped through the pictures. "She's beautiful, Jacques. What's her name?"

"Fleur."

"You Stones have a thing for French names."

"It's a family tradition. Our last name used to be Perreault. That's French for stone. When my great-great-grandparents came here, they were pressured to strip everything foreign about them. They changed their last name and didn't teach their children French. So, we honor their sacrifices by taking a little piece of what they gave up back."

"I love that. I wish my name had a beautiful story. My mom read the name Rainey in a romance novel and liked it." She laughed and the cracked, bubbling pot of rage settled slightly. "The rest is history."

"Maybe you were meant to give this name your own story."

She smiled softly. "Maybe."

"Ready to go?"

"Yes."

I lifted her up despite her weak protests. We collected stares as I carried her across campus. Word of what happened would spread through the whole town by now, and her bruises confirmed the rumor.

I told the guys the Crows would hang themselves if we left them to it. They'd run out of sympathy and find themselves in a town that despised them. That day was today.

Rainey didn't remark on my bringing her home and taking her into my room. A neat, orderly space, the sheets were laundered and made up. My mini-fridge stocked, and my television remote placed beside her. I made to leave.

"Please, Jacques. Stay with me."

I turned around and climbed in next to her without a thought. Rainey buried her face in my neck, holding me tight.

"Why aren't we together?"

The question surprised me. "That's what you want to talk about right now?"

"That's the second-most asked question in my mind, Jacques. Right behind *who is the Letter Man*? I can't help but wonder why you don't want to be with me."

I frowned. "Did I say I didn't?"

"It's been weeks. We could do just about anything, just about any time you want. But you don't touch me outside of spankings. Is that where our relationship ends?"

"Do you think I'd tell you anything other than what you want to hear today?"

"I know you'll tell me the truth, Jacques. You always do."

"You're right, so here it is. The truth and all that you'll get from me today. This," I said, "is where we begin."

RAINEY

Jacques turned down Bay Avenue and parked in front of Paris's house. I followed his gaze down the street to the mansion on the end.

"It's awful she has to be this close to them. That there's even a risk she'll see them drive past in the morning or sit across from her on the deck, eating bagels." My nails dug half-moons in my palm. "I can end this right now. Tell the sheriff it was the Crows who attacked us."

"You can, and I won't stop you if that's what you want to do," Jacques said. "Just know the likelihood of his rich father getting them off by claiming the witness saw they were masked, so you couldn't be sure who it was. I respect whatever decision you and Paris make. Justice may not come from the legal system, but I can promise you, it will come from me."

I was quiet, turning the last twelve hours in my mind. Justice did come slowly to the wealthy. That's how it worked when the game is rigged in your favor. Whereas with the Bedlam Boys—

An image of the sex-trafficking rapist, Axel Verlice, lying in a pool of his own blood floated through my mind.

No one escaped their punishment.

"Does it help you guys that Jeremy thinks I'm on their side? Does your plan rely on it?"

He nodded.

"Then I won't file a report. But," I said, "I also won't lie to Paris about who did this to her, if she hasn't figured that out already."

"Bye."

I kissed his cheek and earned a crooked brow—his sign for *what does that mean? Explain.*

This was one of those things a genius could figure out.

"You don't have to wait for me." I flicked to the Crow house. "I'll find a way back."

Esteban opened the gates at the sight of me. That's the friends we were. Paris already trusted me. It wasn't just on the Bedlam Boys to see the Crows paid for what they did. Jeremy wanted to know where it hurt? He'd fucking find out.

I walked up the drive, unsurprised to see Cairo's truck.

The housekeeper sent me up. I went straight to Paris's room, knocked, and let myself in.

She huddled in the bed, swallowed in her oversized hoodie and three blankets. The mound shook as she sobbed into Cairo's chest.

I padded in, catching his attention.

My wolf was out of place in this soft pink setting. He even looked out of place with Paris. I didn't get the impression comforting was something he provided often. He leaned stiff against the headboard, the human-sized pillow she was clutching. He didn't say or do anything other than rest his hand on the back of her head.

That could be exactly what she needs. For him to just be there.

Nora came in holding a tray. "Paris, dear, I brought you some— Oh, hello, Rainey. Now isn't a good time..." The polite send-off died on her lips as I faced her. "You too?"

I just bobbed my head.

"Sweetie, I'm so sorry." Setting down the soup, she gathered me in her arms.

"R-Rainey tried to st-stop them," Paris whispered from her co-coon. "And paid for it."

Nora gasped.

"I paid for not making a difference. They still hurt you, Paris, and I was useless to stop them. I'm so sorry."

"Don't say that. You helped me while half the quad was standing around squawking about what to do." The smallest smile broke through the blankets. "Thank you."

"Yes, thank you, Rainey."

Nora squeezed me again, and the warmth of a mother's hug so rattled me, I think I rested my head on her shoulder. It had been years since someone just... hugged me.

"You get comfortable because you're staying with us until these animals are caught and I'm not changing my mind," she added as I opened my mouth. "Paris will take some time off. When you're both ready, our driver and guard will bring you to and from campus. Shouldn't be long before they're dragged out of that house in cuffs. Paris says she knows who attacked her."

"The Crows." She spat the name.

Yeah, I didn't need to fill her in. Paris knew exactly who was responsible.

Nora's lips pinched. "Those little shits will not lay a hand on you ever again."

I would've been surprised at such a statement coming from the refined woman before me, if she wasn't going easy on them. There were infinitely harsher things she could've said, and all would be appropriate.

"Go on, dear. Get off your feet." She nudged me toward the bed. "Cairo is staying too. My babies in one place. Your best friend with you," she told Paris. "You're safe. Everything's going to be okay."

"Is it okay?" I asked Paris after her mom shut the door. "I can give you space if you want."

"No, stay." Sniffling, she burrowed in the crook of Cairo's neck.

It was my first proper look at the cuts and purpling bruises covering her face.

"I want you both here. You'll stop me going over there and killing them."

"No."

"Wrong."

Cairo and I spoke at the same time.

"I won't stop you fucking up those bastards," Cairo said. "Actually, I'll be your alibi, saying you were here all night if you do, and you'll be mine when *I* do."

"I'm hardly going to stop you going over there," I added as I climbed in next to Cairo. "When I'm paying a visit myself."

"Guys..." Paris reached out and took my hand. She didn't have to say anything else.

Cairo got up and grabbed the tray. "Eat. You too," he told me. "I'll put on that alien show you guys like."

"*Doctor Who* is so much more than an alien show. You've now earned yourself the full in-depth lecture on the Whoverse."

"No good deed, right?"

We smiled at each other across the room.

Fucking right, he loves me.

THE NEXT MORNING, I stood outside the Crows' gate.

I didn't normally wear makeup and I hadn't changed that fact that morning. Let Jeremy see what he did to me.

I stood under the camera for a full fifteen minutes before someone buzzed me in. Jeremy waited for me at the door.

"Rainey, before you say anything—"

I decked him across the face.

His neck snapped, smashing his temple against the doorframe.

"Ow." Jeremy cracked his jaw. "You can throw a hit."

"It's how you take on a charging bull. Strike hard, fast, and without hesitation. You're half as smart and twice as aggressive."

He smirked, wiping the blood from the corner of his mouth. "Fair enough, I deserve that. Got it out of your system?"

"Not even close! She's my best friend!"

"She's Sharpe's sister and the only person in this godforsaken town he gives a shit about. I thought you understood that we couldn't do this by asking nicely."

"No, you didn't think I understood that, or you would've told me what you were going to do. You know I'd stop you. Warn Paris." I punched him again. "We're not on the same side, Ellis, so you can take your lies and manipulations, and shove them up the same amoral hole the Bedlam Boys keep their twisted justifications. You're no different from them."

"Rainey."

I spun on my heels, flipping him off over my shoulder. "Go fuck your brother up the ass."

"Rainey!" Footsteps sounded behind me. "If you walk out that gate, you'll watch the smoldering firepit that used to be your farm on the six o'clock news."

I ground to a stop.

"That's right." His self-satisfied tone grated on my ears. "Turn around. Come inside. And let's talk this out like adults."

Stiffly, I picked up one foot, then the other, forcing them to take me inside the lion's den.

Jeremy slung his arm over my shoulder—a grin riding his lips he didn't bother to hide. "That's better."

The door shut behind me.

Hanging out in the living room were five guys in various states of dress. Two in their boxers. Two missing their shirts. And Micah dressed and looking like he was on his way to class. I pictured him standing outside our window, lofting a rock.

"Who are you?" I asked the two unfamiliar faces. "And which one of you hairy cunts tore Paris's clothes off?"

They were stony-faced, glaring back at me.

"Who did it?!" I charged them.

Jeremy scooped me around the middle and hauled me upstairs. My threats, each more creative than the last, rained down on the silent crew.

He brought me into the same office where I signed the contract.

"You need to calm down."

"You need to not stand so close to me."

He backed up, hands held in surrender. Didn't stop me noticing he was between me and the door.

"I tried to warn you that it would get bad, and that whatever happened, it wasn't about you." He motioned to my face. "If you had walked away, none of that would've happened, but you kept coming at us and we didn't have a choice."

"Walked away? And let you beat on my best friend? Are you dead inside, Ellis? Because that's something I should know."

His raised hands balled into fists. "What I am is willing to do what has to be done. Think I wanted to beat up on some chick whose only crime was some unfortunate shared DNA? Think I liked having to hurt you?" he flung.

"Ask yourself this: would any of this have happened if those guys got out of our way the first or tenth time we told them? If they cared so much about their families and this town, they wouldn't have escalated this to a war. What else did they expect but casualties?"

I had to stop myself from punching him again. Of course he refused to take responsibility for his repulsive actions. Everything was the Bedlam Boys' fault.

"And those guys down there? Two more *soldiers*?"

"That's Asher and Zeke. Jonah transferred back to HC," he said. "All anyone wanted to talk about was that video and its made-up bullshit. Thought it was better he take himself out of the situation, and we get some friends up here in his place. Can't have the Bedlam Boys outnumbering us."

Folding my arms, I sat in the armchair by the window. "Has it ever occurred to you that there is no war? There's just a fight you picked on someone else's playground, and now you're throwing a tantrum because the bullies were too big for you."

He dropped in the seat next to me, chuckling. "You're mad. It's understandable, but around now is the time you should get over it. Keller's bruises will heal. Her embarrassment will fade. But Sharpe just learned a lesson he won't forget. Neither will Creed. If they don't want another one, they'll get out of here. If St. James and Stone don't want to find out what we've got in store for them, *they'll fuck off out of my town.*"

Someone was missing from that threat.

"What about Roan?"

His lips peeled back from his teeth. "He made his bed."

A chill climbed my spine. "And what if I want nothing to do with you anymore? I'll mail my weekly updates to your father."

"You talk to me, de Souza. You'll tell me everything—*everything* the Bedlam Boys do or say. I want reports on the frequency of their shits."

"That's not in the—"

"Contract." His grin only got wider. "Know what else isn't in the contract? The day we have to hand over the deed."

"The fuck it isn't. Ownership is transferred to me on close of sale."

"Sure, but we never specified *when* we'd close that sale. Dad's got no problem with continuing to bribe Ella Franklin to keep it off the market until we're good and ready to buy it." He held out his hands—a dangerous move seeing as he wasn't protecting his sensitive areas. "Who knows when that will be? Months? Years? Actually, I'll tell you when it'll be: the day after the Bedlam Boys leave for good and not a second before. So I'd worry less about my methods and more about giving me useful information."

My expression went blank. I didn't recognize the voice that left my lips. "You don't want to play with me, Ellis."

"I don't," he said. "I truly don't. I'd like us to move past this unfortunate incident and go back to how we were. We do that, and we don't have to threaten or punch each other in the face anymore. Deal?"

I eyed his outstretched hand.

"You don't ever lay a hand on Paris again. Ever. If she so much as trips on the wind and breaks a nail, that contract won't protect you."

"That's fair. Paris Keller is off-limits. We good?" He thrust his hand out farther.

"And," I continued, "since it seems I'll be waiting a while before I get anything out of this arrangement, you'll provide me a few things to keep me happy."

"What do you want? Money?"

"I do want money. Five thousand dollars— Actually, make that six. You can write me a check for the five thousand. The thousand I want in cash. Also," I said, "your car keys."

He pulled a face. "What for?"

"I don't have a car. I need to get around, and it's better the Bedlam Boys don't ask questions about where I'm going."

"If it's something that'll piss them off, you can drive it for as long as you want." He dropped the key on my palm. "Anything else?"

He's amused. He won't be laughing when I'm done.

"That's it. For now."

A half an hour later, I walked out with my check, cash, and keys.

Cairo and I had a list of stops we meant to make. The accounting office and the youth centers.

That was before Paris and I were attacked, and before the message from the Letter Man. He knew Cairo backed me up for Bella, so he knows I must've told him the truth. I wouldn't put him in more danger by dragging him deeper into this.

I'd find out without him if there was a connection between my grandmother and Cavendish. The same for the identity of Dante, or Blake Jensen, or whoever took up the pen.

I climbed in his car and drove out to Hunter's Crest. I looked up private investigators enough times, I knew which street to go down and how long to wait for him to open for the day.

Dropping my seat back, I nibbled on an egg sandwich I picked up at the drive-through.

I saw the appeal of Hunter's Crest. Bigger town, bigger parades on Founder's Day, more to do, more to see. Still, I wouldn't live anywhere other than my patch of grass on the dot too small to show on a map.

The clock hit nine, so I got out, making my way to Gold Investigations. A tall, raven-haired man with temples just beginning to gray looked up from the coffee machine. He was handsome in an easy, approachable way. He flashed me a smile that loosened my tension.

"Hello? I'm Henry Gold. How can I help you?"

I pulled a black letter from my backpack. "I'd like you to find the serial killer who's been stalking me."

He didn't blink. "I see. Sit down. I'll pour you a cup of coffee."

An hour later, we were both on our third cup.

"Who is this Axel Verlice they mentioned?"

"Local bar owner," I replied. "He happened to die shortly after the Letter Man ordered me to kill an innocent person. I thought I could save myself by claiming credit, but... he saw through me."

"And killed your friend, Bella."

I bit my lip, holding back tears.

"Have you shown the police this letter?"

"I can't." I jabbed the paper. "*I've got friends everywhere. They let me know when a stupid little fool is trying to get one over on me.* My boyfriend"—I dropped the word so casually—"gave a statement to the police about him and he found out in two days. I don't know who I can trust. Why do you think I'm here?"

"Alright, alright," he soothed. "I understand you're in a difficult and deadly situation. What matters is you have come for help. There's already been one innocent death. We don't need another."

Yes, one. I wasn't saying anything about Scott Cavendish. He'd have to get to him on his own.

He took a notepad out of his drawer and flipped to a clean page. "Start from the beginning. When did this start?"

"That's the thing, this may have started long before I thought," I told him. "Two years ago, a company was harassing my grandmother to sell her farm. She refused them, and I woke up one day and found her lying in the cornfield. She was poisoned."

"Goodness," he breathed.

"I used all the money I had to get a private autopsy, but the results, along with the medical examiner, disappeared. I didn't think any of that was connected to what is happening now, but she was killed and whoever planned to benefit from her death, didn't. The farm wasn't bought and soon it'll be mine again."

His head bobbed up and down as he scribbled. "Have any of the letters mentioned the farm?"

"No. It's been crazy stuff about stealing my soul and turning me into a monster. One did say something about my ancestors running from the fight, but I wouldn't."

"Interesting." *Scribble. Scribble.* "What's special about your farm that someone would kill for it?"

I shook my head. "If I understood any of this, I wouldn't be here. All I know is I've spent my whole life mucking around in pigpens. I was homeschooled. All my friends were feathered. I haven't done anything to anyone for them to hate me as much as this person does. So if I didn't start this, I have to believe it's connected to the other unexplained tragedy in my life."

"It's not an unreasonable assumption. I will certainly dig deeper into the circumstances of your grandmother's death. Is there anything else I should know?"

"A few little things that may add up to something bigger." I told him about the cigarettes and kookaburra laughing at the end of New Dante's show. "The first letter was a riddle about a kookaburra," I explained, keeping it short. "Kookaburras aren't such a common bird around here that I believe it's a coincidence."

"Indeed," he said. "You're not the first person to come up from Bedlam asking me to unveil Dante."

"Really?"

"Yes, and I turned those cases down. I don't do cheating spouses, setups, or unmask freelance journalists because people don't like what they have to say. But if you're saying someone new has taken over and they might be"—he looked at the letter in disgust—"this person. It's worth finding out if only to find out if the previous Dante gave up his post willingly, or it was taken from him.

"Contact me immediately if you receive another letter," he said. "I have a few buddies on the force. I trust them with my life."

"I won't have a choice if he tries again to force me to kill."

"It will not come to that. No one else is going to die."

"How much to hire you?"

"It's five hundred dollars for the retainer and forty dollars an hour at my rate, but don't worry about the bill. Pay what you can afford, Miss de Souza. It's more important that we catch this guy."

We talked a little more, then I left, making him take the thousand on the way out. It was Jeremy's money. Let it all go to something good.

It was a long drive back home to Bedlam. Made longer by the grim thoughts spinning in my head.

My first stop was to the accounting firm. The trip was quick. They never heard of the company AgriProspects. If Cavendish did business with them, he did it on his own time. With that settled, I set off for the youth centers, and arrived as volunteers began setting up for the after-school programs.

I went to the Eagle Track Center first and came away empty. My next stop was the Westchester Youth Center.

I walked up to the first official-looking person I saw. A woman in a green vest and smile lines around her mouth stood behind the desk, marking things on her clipboard.

"Excuse me."

She faced me and I read Grace on her name tag.

"Hello. Are you alright?"

"I am, thank you." For a second I forgot how frightening I was to look at. "My name is Emily. I was wondering if you could tell me if a volunteer used to work here, and if he did, could you give me his contact information?"

"What is this about?"

"It's um— I—" I dropped my head, lips trembling. "My half brother used to live in Bedlam with our father and his mother. Anyway, we didn't grow up together, but after he moved out, he'd told me about the program and his mentor, Sam Cavanaugh, who got him through a hard time and helped him turn his life around.

"My brother, he died," I cried. "I know it would've meant a lot to him if Sam could be at the funeral. I've been trying to find him, so I can send him the details. Can you help me?"

"Oh, sweetie." She clutched her chest. "I'm so sorry for your loss, and I'm afraid I have more bad news. I believe the man you're looking for is Scott Cavendish. He was one of our mentors but he passed a few weeks ago. Murdered."

"What? That's horrible." I was becoming quite the actress.

"It was terrible. And to go in that way." She shook herself. "But I shouldn't lay more grief on you."

"No, it's okay. At least now I know why I couldn't find him." I crossed my fingers behind my back. "I don't know if you have this, but is it possible I could have a photo of them? Activities they did together or something like that? I'd like to put it in the slideshow of his life."

"Of course."

Grace set down her clipboard and disappeared behind the desk. She popped up holding a box of folders.

"What was your brother's name?"

"David Holstead."

Her brows scrunched. "Holstead? I don't recognize that name. Are you sure he was with our program?"

"I'm sure. I got Mr. Cavendish's name wrong, but I do remember him saying Westchester Youth Center."

"Hmm. Well, we do get children who come after school for a snack and quiet place to do homework. It's possible your brother wasn't with us officially, but became close with Scott." She flipped through the folders and stopped at one with a purple tab. *S. Cavendish* scrawled on the label.

"Scott was only with us for a year, but— Ah. There we go." She plucked a photo from the file. "Here's a picture of Scott with the kids after a basketball game. Our kids and a few from the neighborhood came out. Do you see your brother?"

I bumped my hip on the desk, leaning in to see.

The Scott Cavendish as I didn't know him threw his head back mid-laugh, arms around two tall kids. Around them there were about a dozen more—eight of them rocking shirts with the center logo.

Blake Jensen, are you here?

"He's there," I said. "Thank you so much. You don't know what this means to me."

"I wish I could do more."

I clutched the photo, making fast for the exit like she might change her mind. In the car, I fought to pay attention to the road. Back and forth my gaze ping-ponged to the older teenagers in the photos. This was taken a few years ago, so Cavendish's protégé had to be at Bedlam University now.

I drove up to Jeremy's gate, parked, and scrutinized the photo. None of the faces stood out to me, but it was a group shot of people looking this way, that way, pulling faces, or covering her eyes from the sun in one girl's case. At the very least, I had the vague features of four guys—one blond, two brunette, and one green. I definitely wouldn't miss the last next time he crossed my path.

The Letter Man may not be in this photo, but it's a start.

I got out, stuck the photo in the Crows' mailbox, and pressed the buzzer to be let in. A beep sounded, letting me know the gate was about to open.

I drove up as Jeremy strolled out of the house shirtless and in a pair of sweats tied low. Quinn came out behind him.

Ah. There's his shirt.

It didn't stretch far enough to cover her cheeks. She didn't seem to care as she came skipping out after Jeremy, throwing her arms around him possessively.

"What the hell are you doing here, farm trash? The Crows aren't looking for an open-for-business slut with mad cow disease."

"I figured, since you've got that position locked up."

She flew at me.

"Whoa." Jeremy caught her around the middle, holding tight. "It's cool, baby. Rainey had to borrow my car to take care of some private business."

"Had to get a chlamydia shot and the clinic closes at six!"

Damn, she's quick with the clapbacks.

"Oh, shit. It closes at six? Better get your ass over there, then. I can see the love bumps on your cootch from here."

I'm quick too.

Quinn clapped her hands over her thong. "Fuck you!"

"Give it a rest," Jeremy snapped. "And give me my keys. I've got somewhere to be."

Jeremy stepped off the porch, and I hit the gas.

"Hey!"

I hit the lawn border and popped off, bouncing in the seat.

"What are you doing?!"

I jerked the wheel and whipped around the house, speeding to the backyard. Moving fast, I rolled all the windows down. The seat belt was next to go.

Jeremy's car careened through lawn chairs. I braced myself as I shot off the rim and drove into the pool.

Water rushed in the openings, swallowing the car to the six-feet depths.

I swam through the driver's window, grabbing on to the ladder in time for Jeremy to burst outside.

"What the fuck?! What did you do?!"

He skidded to a stop at the edge and dropped on his knees. Eyes huge, he clutched his head, jaw working and nothing coming out.

I strolled over to him, peeled his hand off, and shook. He was too dumbfounded to stop me.

He received the same shit-eating smirk he gave me while saying I should get over my and my best friend's beating.

"Now, we're good."

Chapter Five

Cairo

"Whoo, baby. Tell me about the look on his face one more time."

Laughing, she dug deeper in my temples, making my lids heavy.

This had become our routine. Day or night, I got my girl in a bath and treated myself to every soapy inch of her. Afterward, we stretched out in the tub while her fingers did their magic.

She was under the impression that our current incarceration in my mother's house changed the routine. Why she thought I wouldn't fuck her here was anyone's guess, but I rid her of that idea twice in a closet and once on the bathroom floor.

"I thought he was going to piss himself. So much for rich boys not caring about losing their cars."

"He still think you're on his side?"

"Yeah." She nestled my head between her breasts without stopping. "He'd know something was up if I was willing to forgive and forget that easily. He and the Crows knocked us around. The retribution had to communicate my displeasure."

I went rigid at the mention. Rain sensed it and massaged slower.

"He'll think this makes us even. Just tell me what to do to make us even for real."

"There's an event we used to throw in high school. Next time you meet up, tell him what he needs to hear to get him there. I'll take it from there."

"Okay."

Rainey's spider fingers crawled up my forehead. Even that was fucking soothing.

"Where'd you learn this stuff?"

"I had some epic tantrums when I was a kid. Screaming and carrying on for hours. Gran called them my thunderstorms," she said. "She went through all the parenting books till she stumbled on this. Don't know why it calmed me down when nothing else would, but it does. She'd do it whenever I had my *stormy face* on. It worked even when I didn't want it to."

I grunted something.

"I'm glad you like it." She wrapped her legs around me. "It's something else we have in common."

"What else is on the list?"

"Cinnamon sugar bagels."

That tugged a grin up my mouth.

"Sex," she added.

"That's a recipe for soul mates."

Her laugh was light and warm in my ear. "Can I ask you something?"

"Does it have to do with Nora?"

"Yes."

I flicked suds out of the tub. "Then ask away."

"I won't pretend I know what you've been through since she and Paris left. But she's so happy you're here. Is there no chance you two could have a relationship again?"

I rose up, getting out of reach of her siren's grip. Facing her across the tub, I propped against the porcelain. "I plan on fucking you for the foreseeable future—"

"So sweet, Cairo." Her foot stroked my pecs.

"—so you might as well understand the truth about Nora now," I continued. "She likes life to be on the right side of perfect. Perfect education. Perfect career. The perfect jet-setting guy she falls in love with during the *perfect* trip to Egypt. All very romantic and shit. You could make a movie about it.

"But wait, the handsome Jack Sharpe isn't so perfect. He hits the bottle a little too hard, has no ambition, and only went to Egypt because he was between jobs and didn't know what else to do with his life. Don't get me wrong, he worshiped the woman. Would've done anything to make her happy, but he just wasn't quite—"

"—perfect," she whispered.

I inclined my head. "She was fucking around with Isaac before I was a thought. It's only by chance Jack's sperm got there first. Nora got it right on the second try, and then she had the hook to make him leave his wife for her. Took a few years but she finally got it." I swept the space. "Big house. Rich husband. Perfect daughter. Unfortunately, there was still me."

"Paris said her father wouldn't agree to custody of you."

"Paris knows Nora's version of the custody battle. Family court is backward and sexist, Rain. Constantly swinging rulings in the mother's favor because of an outdated fantasy that pushing a kid out of your vagina magically transforms you into a nurturing feminine goddess. Those fools never met Nora. If she wanted me, her second husband couldn't say shit about it. It wasn't up to him."

She defied my attempt to put distance between us and rested her chin on my chest. "What's the real version?"

"I was 'a behavior problem.' Acting up at school. Picking fights. Throwing bags of dog shit at Isaac whenever that fucker was in range."

Her eyes bugged. "You what?"

"Got the wettest and rankest just for him."

"Cairo," she cried, giggles leaking through her lips. "You pelted the man with shit?"

"Bet your ass. Got him three times in the same day once."

She howled, shaking on top of me. A beat after I was laughing too. I said this woman was magic.

"Anyway, with all that going on, Nora stood up and told the judge the best thing for me was stability. A new home and stepfather were too much during this time of *upheaval*, and I was better off living with Jack. She'd revisit custody when *I* was ready. In other words, when I was willing to sit down, shut up, and play happy family."

"I'm sorry, Cairo."

She rubbed my chest, trying to seep comfort into my bones. Rain was ten years too late from the time that could've made a difference.

"So what's all of this now? Is it possible she wants to reconcile? It's not about custody anymore. You're a grown man. Nora doesn't have to care for you or be responsible for your actions. She can be a mother to you without... being a mother."

I traced her lips. "You are perceptive, Rain. Hit it right on the head, and now I'm wondering if you already know this story," I said. "Yes, that's exactly why she's playing the role now. Nora isn't a favorite of the Bay Avenue wives. She stole one of their husbands and abandoned her kid like a puppy in a cardboard box.

"Wasn't much she could do about that before since neither one of us wanted me in this house, but I'm twenty-one now. I can be her 'baby' again."

"Oh, my wolf." She kissed me. "I can throw dog shit at her if it'll make you feel better."

I cracked a smile against her lips. "Nah. I'm good. She lives her life, I live mine. Gotta be here right now for Paris, but a few more days and we'll be out of here."

"I'm coming too?" She pecked my mouth, nose, and cheeks.

"You're with me. Always."

She cheesed like I said I loved her. Why should I? She was saying it for me.

"Whatever you say."

"Why weren't you this agreeable in the beginning?" I positioned her over my cock.

"I'm not this agreeable now."

"No? We'll see about that." I lurched forward, catching her bottom lip between my teeth. "Under the water, bitch. Suck my dick."

She slapped me. "Fuck you."

Rain shrieked as I leaped on her, sloshing half the water out of the tub. We wrestled ferociously—stiffening my cock painfully. I needed to be inside this woman like I needed her screams, her tears, her touch, her taste.

I bent her neck back, pressing my dick to her bared teeth.

Maybe this was love.

RAINEY

Roan crouched in front of the door, screwing in the new electronic locks complete with camera. Cairo stuck it out for a week in his mother's house. I endured the frosty dinners—Nora chattering on about work and everyday life while Paris's dad glared daggers at Cairo. He finally voiced his thoughts the night before, whipping out a snide comment about Paris transferring to another university where she couldn't get caught up in Cairo's messes.

"And birds wouldn't fall out of the sky if I pissed rainbows," Cairo replied. "How much other shit I'm not responsible for do you want to drop on me?"

His spoon clattered in his bowl. "You're responsible for this! My daughter is upstairs broken and sobbing because you run around this town acting like the big, tough thug and decent people pay the price."

"Boys, please," Nora cried.

I sank in my seat, holding Cairo's hand under the table.

"I knew it was a mistake to let her near you."

"Real nice, Isaac." An amused twist hung on his lips. "Take shots at me while I'm eating my soup. List your regrets at not doing a better job fucking up my family. After this, you plan on taking your red face and puffed chest to the Crows, and give it back to them ten times worse? No? Because I am."

Cairo punched the table and toppled my wineglass.

"You can come at me for being a shitty older brother, but at least I'm not her sniveling, candy-ass father. I'll make damn sure no one touches her again." He leaned over the table. "And I've got a lesson for you too, next time you get in my face, Stepdaddy."

We were out the next day.

Just as well, because we're all-hands-on-deck installing new security in the Bedlam House, the mayor's house, and Jacques's mother's house. Judge Stone and Mayor Creed both lived alone, and the Crows proved they didn't know their limits.

I padded over to Roan, still wearing the ears from my latest trip to Arsenio's house. He liked doing it there because there was more room to walk his pet.

"What's this?" I picked up the notepad at his feet. Twenty or so names were written down. Jeremy Ellis at the top. "This isn't a hit list, is it?"

"In a way, I'm writing all the people who want me dead. I keep it close for when another name pops in my head."

"Roan, there are a lot of names here. All of these people can't really want to stab you. What did you do to them?"

"Nicolas Everide. He got big and loud about refusing to pay and tried to get everyone on his block to join in. I threatened to tell his firm he was missing a few credits on his transcript, and that law degree in his office is fake. Plus, I fucked his wife."

I pinched the bridge of my nose. "Dare I ask about anyone else on the list?"

"You could. It would help me narrow it down if I got an outside perspective. Which of these people have I pissed off enough to kill me, and which just want to break my legs behind the Roadhouse?"

"Okay, I'll help." I dropped down next to him. "You were stabbed before you betrayed Micah and told the town his brother was screwing him. We can take them off the list."

"I know it wasn't them personally, but it could still be a Crow. We just found out he was stashing more of them in HC."

"That's true," I muttered. "But why would Jeremy have come after you then?"

He flipped through his toolbox. Handy Roan was a sight to see, savor, and lock away for the next go with my vibrator—a gift from Roan.

He tied his wild waves back, letting the world fall into those swimmable pools unobstructed. A torn-sleeve shirt gifted me his muscles rippling as he drove the screws home, and every few seconds he smirked at me as though he was reading my mind.

"I'm an attractive target to take out first, honey lips."

My face heated. It was my second pair of lips that Roan swore tasted like honey.

"I've got access to everyone's records. The Crows included."

"Did they know that at the time?"

He shook his head. "Can't say exactly what they know, but it's too much."

We went through the list together, Roan adding more along the way. I eliminated a few people based on how long ago he wronged them. More than a year seemed a long time to wait to kill someone who walked around unguarded.

"Brooks works in the administration building," I said. "He would've gotten to you before now if he was still upset with you for beating up his brother."

"He was. I heard him shouting about it when the mob came for us."

I paused with the eraser hovering over the name. "Never mind. We need to talk to him."

"What about your psychopath? Any closer to finding out who Blake Jensen is?"

I hesitated. I hated lying to the guys, but I would not walk into another room and find Arsenio, Cairo, Jacques, Legend, or Roan tied to a chair, an arrow aimed at their chest. Everyone I cared about was under attack, it was safer for them that the Letter Man believed they weren't included.

"Maybe," I said. "I found out Cavendish volunteered at Westchester Youth Center. They don't give out information about minors, so that's as far as I got."

"It's a start. I'll see what I can dig up on the kids who went there."

I looked away. "You don't have to. You're trying to find the person who aimed a knife at your heart. That's too important."

"The shit stain who came after me is an opportunistic coward who ran off at the first chance and hasn't had the balls to come for me since." He tipped my chin, bringing me back. "The guy after you is a lot more dangerous. Finding him is most important."

I couldn't argue that.

"Just be careful. He's made it clear I'd regret it if I brought people into our 'game.' This guy does not bluff."

"I take whippings, not worry." Light glanced off his sharpened canine. "Want to drive your warnings home, do it the right way."

I lightly bit his finger, then not so lightly. "Why should you get a treat when you're bad?"

Unsurprisingly, Roan convinced me he did deserve a treat. The locks were installed and we ended up in his room. I literally rode him across the floor, smacking his ass with a riding crop to the tune of his sweet, seductive groans.

My phone went off.

"Leave it."

"The Crows are on a rampage," I said. "I can't ignore calls. What if someone's hurt?"

He grabbed my ankle. "Don't you fucking dare."

I swatted his left cheek. "I thought I give the orders? Let go. Now."

He did, and let me make it all of two steps.

Roan tackled me onto the bed, pulled handcuffs out of nowhere, and secured me to the bedpost. I came screaming into the pillow by the eleventh strike of the crop.

The phone call got lost in my memory after that. We messed around for hours, then passed out. It wasn't until my midnight snack in the kitchen, eating ice cream out of the carton in Roan's sleeveless shirt, did I remember.

It waited for me on the nightstand. I tapped it awake and *Gold* flashed on the screen.

My heartbeat skipped.

Henry said he'd call when he had news. It had been less than forty-eight hours. What did he find so soon?

I went outside to listen to his message.

"Miss de Souza, call me back as soon as you get this. I mean it. Don't worry about the time."

I called him back immediately.

"Hello?"

"Miss de Souza."

"Please, call me Rainey."

"Rainey," he corrected. "It's late and I'm certain you don't need the preamble, so I'll get right to it. You're right about this starting with your grandmother."

I hadn't realized I was still clutching the ice cream till it splattered on my feet. "What? How?"

"I started from the beginning, as you suggested. AgriProspects was the company you knew about because they were up front with their menacing and harassing. Others hid behind paper."

"Hid behind paper?"

"I found multiple suits and claims against Abigail de Souza. Some citing animal cruelty. Some child abuse and neglect. One went so far as to say she was mentally unfit and needed a court-assigned guardian to handle her affairs."

"She what?" I cried. "That's insane."

"It is," he said, voice hard. "This is above and beyond, Rainey. It's obvious someone was gunning for her relentlessly. Half of these accusations would've landed her in jail, and you and your sister in a foster home. Most importantly, it would've gotten you all off the farm."

"But why? It's nothing special," I half shouted, tears welling in my eyes. "It's just a fucking farm!"

"We're not seeing the whole picture yet, but we will. That's why I said to call me back any time. I'm in my office right now, going further up your family tree to the initial land sale. Maybe there's something at the start of this. Another party involved who was cheated."

"And the great-great-great-grandson decided to even the score? This farm's been in my family for six generations. It's ours."

"I don't have the answers right now, but I will," he said calmly. "We'll figure this out."

"The answer is with AgriProspects, isn't it? Were they behind the lawsuits against Gran?" I asked. "And how did we get on their radar? I've always wondered that. Can you look into a connection between the company and someone here in Bedlam?"

"What kind of connection?"

"A law firm. An accounting firm. A CEO who's the long-lost brother of our old neighbor, Silas. There's a reason they came after us and everyone seems to know it but me."

"I'll look into it," he replied. "You said right now the farm is up for sale. Give me the name of the estate agent, and I'll find out if any companies have approached her with an offer."

"I can tell you what Cruella won't. Steven Ellis is buying the farm. We have a contract that he'll transfer ownership to me the day the sale goes through."

"A contract? In exchange for what?"

"I have to do a job for him," I said simply.

"Would you mind faxing me a copy of that contract?"

"I'll do it now. The library is open twenty-four hours for late-night studiers."

"Excellent," he said. "Have you received another letter?"

I checked the mailbox to be sure. "No, nothing yet. I'll call you when the next one comes. I have a terrible feeling about what it'll say."

"You won't be forced to hurt anyone, Rainey. If your stalker is working with someone in the police, there is a way we can do this that doesn't get the local force involved. You just have to trust me, and don't try to do this alone."

"Trust me," I said, thinking of Bella. "I'm done underestimating him."

"I'm standing by for your fax. Goodbye."

"Bye."

Stuffing my phone away, I grabbed the knob to go inside. Movement flickered out of the corner of my eye.

I stopped, peering at the Sigma Kappa house across the street. Their house neighbored a copse of trees and bushes that provided cover for the many parties they threw and the illegal activity going down during them.

I thought I saw...

...someone duck into the trees.

Why would a frat boy do that at one in the morning?

I backed inside, closing and sliding in all the new locks.

I called Gold back.

"Hey. I'll fax you the contract in the morning."

I LEFT EARLY THE NEXT day to head to the library. That left me plenty of time to grab breakfast, find a quiet spot in the student union, and stick in my headphones.

Dante poured in my ears.

"—all heard the news Jonah transferred out of Bedlam U. Should we take this as an admission of guilt or an innocent man fleeing rumors and suspicion? No one likes the question game, so here's your answer: NDAs and hush money couldn't put this secret back in the box, like it did the first time.

"My sources confirm Jonah assaulted that girl, then used Daddy's money to pressure her and her family into settling out of court. It's a good thing he fucked off on his own. He was leaving our town one way or another."

I slurped on my mango banana smoothie, listening with half an ear. Dante didn't need to confirm for me that the Crows were bad news.

Nelson rounded the corner and claimed a seat at a study table three down from mine. I waved but he didn't see.

"—Paris Keller."

I promptly forgot about Nelson.

"Witnesses say six guys in ski masks rolled up on her and Rainey de Souza. It wasn't a fair fight in any way," he said. "It just so happens the Crows added two new guys to their crew recently. But that's just a coincidence, right?

"Jeremy Ellis said it is the other day on the deck. He asked if those witnesses saw crow tattoos. Ellis even floated the accusation that they were framed by a certain group of guys that would do anything to run them out and stop the town from splitting. Rainey is the Bedlam Boys' girl and Paris is Cairo's sister. Maybe the ladies agreed to take a beating for the cause."

My jaw dropped. *Jeremy said what? That two-faced lying dickhead can beat me and Paris in the street, but he can't face up to it in the open.*

"I put a poll on my website asking you guys to chime in on those responsible."

Website? Since when did Dante have a website?

"It's open for three more days on Dante's Den dot com."

I immediately pulled out my laptop and typed it in.

"After voting closes," he continued, "I'll release the poll asking what punishment you feel this attack on our own deserves. Write-ins allowed."

Clicking the top result for the search, black flooded my screen. I squinted at a small spec of white in the middle. I stared at it and it stared at me—the spot growing bigger and its skull eyes finding me through the laptop.

I hit *enter* scrawled across its face, and the curtains drew back, revealing a simple website with a tab for past shows and one to contact him. The home page had nothing to say for itself except for a single question in bold white letters and the poll beneath.

Who attacked Rainey de Souza and Paris Keller?

The Crows: 71%

The Bedlam Boys: 20%

Neither: 9%

Incredible that anyone would believe Cairo would beat and strip his sister. As incredible as the idea she'd volunteer for the privilege to cast doubt on the Crows. It gave me hope that the majority swung one way.

Jeremy had more work to do. Bedlamites weren't fooled.

I shut the laptop and lit on Nelson and his new tablemate. Their back was to me, so I didn't make out anything but the cool mint green of their hoodie. The guy stood up and I caught a flash of something red disappearing inside Nelson's backpack as he stood up to leave too.

"—dear Bedlamites, I report on justice, I don't deliver," Dante said. "As satisfying as it would be to carry out the punishment you vote for, it's not up to me to see the Crows or Bedlam Boys pay for this. But that doesn't mean you should sit by and do nothing, Paris. Rainey."

Cold slid into my bones, freezing me to the spot.

"No one else has the right to hurt you," he slithered into my ear. "If those responsible don't pay for this in the end, ask for help. You still have friends."

Dante went on to say more. An entire thirty-minute segment on the news in Bedlam, and I didn't hear a thing till the kookaburra laughed, ending the show.

I TRUDGED HOME FOLLOWING a long day of classes and sympathetic tuts at my healing bruises.

Arsenio leaned against the banister, waiting for me.

"I assume you heard Dante's latest show."

My backpack slipped off my shoulders. Arsenio let me rest my forehead on his folded arms without comment. Taking a deep breath, I said the only thing that could be true. "Dante is the Letter Man. The mantle of Bedlam's underground voice was taken over by a psychopath."

"No one *else* has the right to hurt you," Arsenio repeated. "He's protective of you. Implied that he's a friend."

"He's a friend like a bullet wound is a boo-boo."

His hand was warm on the back of my head. "He was angry, de Souza. Everyone listening heard it. The Crows jumping you set him off, and considering who he is, he might deliver justice if it's not done for him—even if he says otherwise. He has some kind of attachment to you, Rainey. That doesn't come from nowhere."

I bent to look up into eyes so unique and beautiful from mine. "What are you saying?"

"I'm saying even the most deranged stalker needs a meeting or moment to build their delusions on. They don't pick a name out of a phone book." He shook his head. "All this you're going through to find him. You don't have to, Rainey. I'm ninety-nine percent sure he's someone you know."

My lips parted. To spout a denial. To form an argument. I couldn't decide.

"But I didn't know Cavendish," I finally said. "Never crossed that guy's path once."

"He knew your sister, didn't he? They were at Bedlam U at the same time. Ever pick her up from campus, or drop by to grab lunch?"

"Yes," I admitted. "All the time."

"It's possible you did cross paths with Cavendish and his friend. The meeting was insignificant to you. Not worth remembering. But it wasn't to them."

Not worth remembering.

I gripped his arms, frustration welling hot and fast.

"Of course," I whispered. "He might know me. I could've sipped tea and eaten cookies with him on the deck and never realized. I lost chunks of time after Gran died and Doc Nash put me on a blackout drug cocktail. I couldn't tell you who I met during that time. Or what I did."

The grave at Black Widow Hill.

"But it's possible I did something terrible," I rasped. "So bad I made enemies who are seeing I get what I deserve."

"*Possible, maybe,* and *I don't know* won't help you." He kissed me, scrambling my mind the way only he could. "If there are gaps in your memory, fill them in. Do whatever it takes. Talk to people who were around. Know where to start?"

I nodded. "I have an idea."

Untangling his arms, I wrapped myself in them.

"What about Dante/the Letter Man?" I tucked my head under his chin. He wasn't hugging or nuzzling me back, and neither was he pushing me away. This classified as tender love and affection from a guy like Arsenio. "Did he just whip the town into planning his next hit? What if everyone votes for breaking their kneecaps and tossing them off Chaney Bridge? The thought of him hurting people in my name makes me sick."

"He won't mess with the Crows." Arsenio snaked his arm around my waist, lifting me off my feet. He made for the door.

"There won't be anything left when we're done."

ARSENIO'S VOICE RANG in my head as Jeremy led me on another chase around campus. I found my way to Parking Garage C in time for a red convertible to pull up to the curb. Jeremy glared at me through the window.

"Get in."

"Good afternoon to you too." I hopped in, beaming away. "You look nice. Is that a new jacket?"

"Fuck you."

I laughed in his sour face.

Jeremy looked tempted to punch me again. He slammed the gas instead, turning on the road that led out of campus.

"That car was worth more than your fucking farm!"

I waved that away. "You're rich. Buy a new one."

"You went too far."

"You hurt my friend," I shot back, "and I bitched less about it than you are over a hunk of metal. Are we putting it behind us and moving on or not?"

Jeremy jerked the wheel, hooking a right.

I bounced off the door, gritting my teeth. He didn't have to do that. Jeremy was just testing how far he could push me before I drowned him in a pool.

"Is that a no?"

"No, depends on what you have for me," he replied. "It better be good or the deal is off. Try me."

I rolled my eyes. "You tell me if it's good. I overheard Cairo on the phone telling someone to gather everyone they know and bring them to Buller's Den Saturday night. I asked what was going on and he said the Crows were going to pay for what they did to us. You'd be gone in a week."

"Is that right?" His grin revealed all his teeth. "Saturday night. Buller's Den. Another party to crash."

"Is that a good idea?" I went through my script, though I was already picturing being home with Roan and Legend, tempting them into another threesome. "Did you see Dante's poll numbers? The masses don't buy that you're innocent. Going after the guys with their hands down their wallets was one thing, but everyone likes Paris. She got all the sweetness that skipped her older brother.

"Going after her turned Bedlam against you. If you show up at a meeting to take you down, you may not walk out of there."

Here's hoping.

"Aw, you're worried about me." Jeremy cuffed my chin. "How sweet."

"Don't say I didn't warn you."

"It's not me who needs a warning."

Jeremy slid into the next lane. A U-turn would take us back to campus, and I hoped he was making it. I wanted away from this guy ten minutes ago.

"They'll whip everyone up with stuff they can't prove, then I'll remind them of exactly what you said. They're the ones stealing thousands from Bedlam. This fairy story about them funneling the money back into the town is garbage. Replacement parts for Creed's car were expensive. Sharpe isn't on scholarship and he's not paying tuition on his dad's salary.

"We'll remind them how much the Bedlam Boys have to lose if the town splits and half their weekly profits go with it. They've got an incentive to stir shit up and blame it on the Crows."

"Sounds like you got it all figured out. Pull over here," I said.

"You did good this week." Jeremy slowed the car as requested. "Keep it up and you'll get back in my good graces."

His hand crept up my thigh.

"Let me make this clear." I picked his hand up with two fingers and dropped it on his lap. "This is a business relationship and nothing more. You've threatened and punched me one too many times. Run back to Quinn."

He muttered something as I climbed out. I didn't care what. The slam of the door meant I was done with him. I had more important things to deal with that day.

The library was the cool, pastry-scented paradise I remembered. Little study pockets scattered all over the space. Couches, desks, computers, and even ottomans to put your feet up. I got myself another panini and set up in a nook on the third floor. Food in reach and feet up, I opened my laptop to Scott Cavendish's old social accounts. I clicked through his friends one by one, searching for faces that matched those in the photos.

Assuming these two thought of each other as friends, a voice sounded in my mind. *The first letter I received after Cavendish's death, his supposed friend didn't seem too broken up about his fiery end.*

That I couldn't deny. It begged the question of if sociopaths were capable of forming real relationships.

I stopped on Craig Brown's profile, matching him to one of the young, smiling faces in the photo.

The Letter Man thinks I'm his friend for all that he's angry with me now. There's no understanding what's going on in his mind, but he still could've accepted a friend request.

"—over here."

A couple of students from my bankruptcy class spotted me and tromped over, loaded with backpacks, textbooks, and laptops.

"Hey, Rainey. How are you doing?" Violet asked. She was short and thin, rocking hair the color of her name. "Tased, arrested, and jumped. Talk about a rough semester."

"Thanks for reminding me," I said under my breath. "I'm doing okay. You guys studying for the midterm?"

"Yeah. Want to join us?"

"Sure, just give me a sec to finish this up."

"Cool."

Violet, Darryl, Hannah, and Luciano slid in around the table, leaving a spot between Darryl and Hannah for me.

Moving faster, I clicked through the profiles, scribbling the names of the guys I found.

Craig Brown. Oakley Jackson. Seth Harris. Kashton King.

None of these names were remotely close to Blake Jensen. It was my hope Cavendish used an alias, but even if he didn't and none of these guys were him, I could still ask if there was a Blake or someone their old mentor was close to. These guys would all be college age now. Next, I'd find out if that college is Bedlam U.

"Done." I picked up my stuff and parked it beside Hannah. She slid her book over to share with me.

"I don't know why I signed myself up for his torture," she said. "Everyone told me Professor Stein was a nice guy who was easy on grading and didn't load you up with papers, but not even Chris Hemsworth teaching this bare-chested and oiled up could make this material interesting."

"Damn, I'd sign up twice though."

She laughed. "I hear that. But for real, I zone out the second he opens his mouth. I don't remember anything he said would be on the test."

"Don't worry. I got you."

I fished my binder out of my pack.

No doubt bankruptcy wasn't the most stimulating class. I forced myself to write down his lectures because he forced me to listen to them. Afterward, I highlighted the important bits—including the sections that would be on the test.

"Voilà."

"Bless you," she cried, dropping her head on my shoulder. "You are a blessed saint of the goddess. Let her strike down the assholes who jumped you and Paris."

"If she's taking requests, I'd definitely love a good smiting right about now."

"—not worth it," Violet hissed at Luciano. "You'll be thrown out of school if you get caught."

Rolling his eyes, Luciano stuffed a red card back in his pocket.

"What's going on?" I asked.

Violet looked around. Leaning across the table, she dropped her voice. "Word's going around that someone hacked the system and got the answer keys for over fifty midterms. They're selling them for five hundred bucks a pop."

Darryl whistled. "Someone's about to clean up."

"Someone's about to get caught," Violet snapped. "You stumble on an answer key, you let two or three friends take a peek and then you destroy it and never speak about it again. Spreading word around the school, setting up shop, and giving them to whoever asks is a stupid move. Professors notice when their C students all of a sudden get hundreds. When dozens of C students get a hundred, they shut it down, reissue new exam papers, and go on the hunt for the cheat."

She jabbed a finger at Luciano. "When they do, you're going to wish you tossed that card in the trash."

"Alright, alright." Luciano got up and flung it in the bin. "I wasn't actually going to do it. Someone slipped it to me in the hall and for a minute I got to hold on to the dream of an A. Instead of the B minus I've got coming my way."

"You are getting that A," I said. "I've got all the notes. I marked everything Stein said would be on the test. We're all here. Let's do this over a plate of butterscotch muffins, then make this exam our bitch."

He grinned. "That's what I'm talking about, de Souza. Slide those notes over here."

Three hours, eight muffins, and a practice test later, I waved bye to the guys from the library steps. When they were out of sight, I dialed Gold. He answered on the second ring.

"Hello, this is Gold Investigations."

"It's Rainey."

"Ah, yes." His tone shifted. "I looked over the contract. It's rather generous, isn't it? An expensive land purchase just to get information on the people listed here."

"It is, but I assume Steven Ellis is thinking he trades one patch of land for an entire town."

"Yes, that's possible," he said to himself.

"Is something wrong? I read through the contract myself. Except for the wiggle room of the actual date of sale, it's on the up."

"It is 'on the up' as you say. I can't see anything here that raises the alarm except for my own concerns on how much interest your farm has attracted. This is an extraordinary bribe."

"Believe me, I thought the same. I'd be lying if I said I fully trusted the mysterious Steven Ellis, or his sons."

"Hang on to that caution, Rainey. Trust no one until that deed is in your hands."

"I won't."

"Just one thing… Your sister, Ivy. May I have her number?" he asked. "She's older. It's possible your grandmother shared more with her concerning the farm and what made it a magnet for trouble, since she was most likely to inherit and look after you if anything happened."

I swallowed hard. "They could have had those conversations. I wouldn't know. Ivy and I stopped speaking to each other soon after Gran died. She's not doing anything to look after me or the farm."

"I'm sorry." He truly sounded it. "Would you like me to leave her out of this?"

"No," I said. "This isn't about us. It's about Gran. I'll text the number."

"Thank you. Before you go, I thought you'd like to know that I did find a connection between AgriProspects and Bedlam."

I shoved the phone back to my ear. "You did? Who?"

Scott Cavendish.

"A man named Walker Lewis. Heard of him?"

My brows crowded together. "Yeah. He was our old neighbor, technically. His land bordered ours."

"He and Andrew Clein attended the same business school. Graduated the same year," he explained. "It's thin, and could be just a coincidence."

"I don't believe in coincidence."

"Neither do I. My working theory is that when Clein's company went on the hunt for land to acquire, Clein remembered his old classmate who grew up on a farm. That's what brought him to Bedlam."

"Or Mr. Lewis brought him to Bedlam. Almost every Bedlam farmer has sold up and moved. Lewis decided to give his old friend and his failing company a bone, and the miserable greedy shit looked next door, saw us still standing, and promised he'd get our farm too."

"Just as likely," he said. "That's all I have for now, Rainey. I'll call when I know more."

We said our goodbyes.

I put my phone away as Cairo climbed the stairs. I texted him I was studying in the library, and his possessive self told me not to go anywhere. He was coming to get me.

We were off for another bath where I'd melt my beast with massaged temples, then he'd remind me he couldn't be tamed. Any luck, he'd wear himself out too much to leave me alone in bed while he disappeared into the night.

BULLER'S DEN SOUNDED like the name of a bar with a hidden sex room in the back. What you got in reality was a wide-open clearing in the forest boasting tree stumps, a few boulders, and firepit. All the makings of a good party spot, and the empty red cups scattered around proved I wasn't the first to have that thought.

Zara, Elise, Presley, Amy, Paris, and I found spots to sit on a felled log. We talked while people filed out of the dark, filling the clearing.

"Did you see Dante's poll?" Presley held up her phone. "The write-ins are getting a lot of love. Right now, rack the Crows and use them as target practice are top one and two choices for punishments."

"I also saw that eighty-six percent believe the Crows did it. Ten blame the Bedlam Boys and four don't know. Eighty-six isn't the unanimous vote it should be. The Crows still have people believing their lies."

Paris hardened. "Just tie them up in a room with me and walk away. I'll take care of the rest."

Yep. She's Cairo's blood.

"I take back all that stuff I said about the town and splitting it up," Amy said, rubbing Paris's arm. "Bedlam might be a boring little town with residents as crazy as the name, but we look out for each other. We know what it means to protect our home and our own. If Bedlam is going to change, it'll happen because it's what we all want, and we'll do it on our terms."

Nods went through the group.

"We will also together, as a family, stomp the Crows into dust."

"I love you guys." Paris squeezed me and Amy tight.

Buller's Den was filling up fast. I recognized faces from my classes and around campus.

I wonder if the Letter Man is blending in among these people.

The firepit was lit. It cast undulating light and shadows on the shuffling crowd.

I knew he had to be here. Someone who watched me as closely as I was realizing he did wouldn't miss this chance to delight in my ignorance. Him so near and my gaze skimming right past him. There was also the little matter of *Dante's* determination to bring me justice. The den was the right place to be to see that happen.

A sharp whistle cut through the chatter, bringing silence through the den.

"Sit."

That short, gruff command could only be from one person.

The listeners took up seats on the logs, stumps, rocks, ground, and around the pit. It cleared the way for all to see five cruel princes coming out of the darkness. Arsenio, Legend, Roan, Cairo, and Jacques were larger than normal standing before us.

Cairo caught my eye and jerked his chin. A simple gesture but I knew how to read his grunts, shifts, and tells. You're always on alert for a shift in mood when you live with wolves.

"I'll be back, guys."

I skirted the edge of the den and made for Cairo's side. He tucked me under his arm, casual as can be.

"You know why you're here," Jacques began. "These guys calling themselves the Crows, blew into our town and came for us immediately. It was amusing at first. It isn't now."

"Anyone who isn't a sad sack of shriveled balls would come at us head-on," Cairo continued. "They want a fight, they'd have the decency to take it to us. But they're not looking for a fight. What they want is surrender before the war."

"What does that mean?" someone asked.

"Jeremy and Micah's old man funds a company that's looking to buy up Bedlam and raze it to the ground."

The blowback was immediate.

"What?"

"No!"

"They can't do that."

"They're already doing it," Roan said. "Any of your folks receive a call from a company called Foundry? Checking if they're happy with their home, or would they like it better living in a South Florida condo?

"The first step was getting their hands on the property legitimately. The next was sending in the gangbanger brothers to sell you the dream of a brand-new town... where they own everything."

"All those promises," Arsenio said. "Movie theaters, clubs, restaurants, boulevards, and affordable housing. Did you get any of that shit in writing? Once they've got the vote freeing them from town hall's construction restrictions, they can do whatever the hell they want. And whatever that is, I'm not betting on it bettering the town. You tell me when a random, faceless HC company ever shed a tear for the lives of us Bedlamites."

Uncomfortable looks and whispers passed through the crowd.

"What do we do?" I recognized Nelson as the owner of the voice. "My parents are talking about selling to Foundry. They're giving them enough to retire."

"How generous," Legend said sarcastically. "Big business is known for that, right? Their generosity."

"St. James Whiskey isn't."

Six figures emerged from the shadows. Jeremy and that one-sided grin led the pack.

"But the rest of us aren't as shady as you and Daddy," he finished.

"What's this?" Micah called. "You having a party? Why didn't anyone invite us?"

Cairo's hand stole down my back, landing on my ass. "Excellent job getting them here, Rain," he said under his breath. "Tomorrow we'll come back here for a hunt. Just you and me." He nipped my ear. "I'll bring the crossbow."

I flushed hot in the firelight. What did it say about me that Cairo believed giving me a treat was chasing me through the woods, pouncing, and fucking me where we dropped? What else did it say about me that my panties were damp?

The crowd parted for the Crows.

More like, they pushed and shoved till two sides stood opposite each other. If this was a sign of something to come, I wasn't sure. All I knew was I didn't like the expressions on anyone's face as Jeremy and his guys passed through them.

"I caught part of your speech," Jeremy said. "Hope you don't mind if I make some corrections. Tell them the truth you don't want them to hear."

"Save it." Cairo rushed him.

Jeremy got his knife up quickly. Cairo snatched his arm mid-jab and wrenched it behind his back.

Micah, Gael, Asher, Bentley, and Zeke lurched into action, and found themselves thrown back as the crowd surged, grabbing their arms, shoulders, hair, and legs. The Crows thrashed and shouted in the ten-on-one hold.

"Hey! Get off! Get off me!"

Cairo hauled Jeremy to the firepit. He swept his feet, pitching him forward into the flames.

"Ahh!"

My beast, my god, my love snatched his collar, grabbing him just out of the fire's reach.

"Let me up," Jeremy bellowed. "Pull me back."

Roan and Legend were on him. It wasn't to pull him back.

They picked up both legs, pointing him like an arrow directly above its hungry maw. All they had to do was let go.

I stood transfixed—unable to help him. Unable to look away.

"Ready to tell the truth, Ellis?" Cairo shook him, ratcheting his shouts higher. "Admit what you did to my sister. Admit it!"

"Put me down!"

"Guys," Cairo barked. "I don't think he's warm enough."

They held him closer. On the other side of the pit, Paris stepped out among the audience.

"No, stop! It wasn't me," Jeremy cried. "We didn't touch her. I bet you did it!"

He swiped wildly at Cairo's legs. Not the smartest move since those were two of the legs keeping him out of the fire.

"You won't force me to confess to your shit."

"It was him," Paris said, steady and clear. "All of them. They at-tacked us."

"It's a lie! Can't you see what they're doing?" Jeremy addressed the crowd. "They're turning you against us so they don't lose their walking, talking bank accounts. We're not the ones cheating you, they—"

Cairo let go and caught him just as fast. Jeremy's bellow bounced up the trees.

"Oops," Cairo sang. "My hand slipped. I have a feeling it's going to do that every time a lie comes out of that brother-cock-sucking mouth."

"I didn't do it!"

The other Crows yelled and pleaded for their leader, swearing up and down they weren't responsible. My stomach churned in disgust.

Got to give it to them. Their acting holds up under pressure.

Jacques crossed in front of me. Inexplicably, he drew me to his side—his hand warm on my hip.

"How do we settle this?" Jacques was smooth and calm, speaking over the Crows as his thumb stroked me.

I was neither of those things. My skin prickled as though I was the one held to the fire. I couldn't understand this feeling. I was help-less to save Paris. I couldn't even save myself. Another bully blew into my life and hurt the people I love, and for all that I was named after a force of nature, I wasn't strong enough to stop it.

That fury burned on a slow heat beneath my skin... waiting for this moment.

I wanted something to happen. Someone to pay.

Someone to scream.

The Crows within my reach and their payback on the slip of a grip.

My fist clamped on Jacques's shirt. I held on to him to stop me from massaging my temples and feeding the headache. I pushed the pain down. This had my entire focus.

It was time for the Bedlam Boys to do what they do.

"The Crows say they're innocent. We say they're not. If you ask me, there's only one way to settle this," Jacques said, "and we're in the right place for it."

Someone whispered too low for me to hear. Their phrase was picked up by another, and passed on. Again and again, growing louder till two words ran clear in the night.

"Riot Royale. Riot Royale. Riot Royale."

"Put me down!"

"Gladly," Jacques said. "First, do you agree?"

"Agree to what?!"

He looked to Cairo. "Do you agree?"

"Yes," Cairo said. "If Paris accepts me."

Paris wasn't alone. Amy, Zara, Presley, and Elise were silent pillars of support beside her. They nodded one after the other as she swept over them.

"I accept," she said.

I held my breath, preventing any chance of a word escaping. I'd heard of Riot Royales and Gran had the same policy on those as she did Ruckus Royale: stay away.

This was their plan. This is why they wanted Jeremy brought here to a crowd that well and truly despised them. I gazed at Jacques. *The man is a genius.*

"To the ignorant cattle that forced their way into our home, daring to tell us what we need without bothering to find out who we are," Jacques barked. "Riot Royale is a chance to get everything you want. Right here, right now, Cairo Sharpe and Jeremy Ellis will fight until one of you doesn't get up. If Cairo wins—"

"The Crows get down on their knees and beg my sister for forgiveness." He shook him. "On your knees! Then all of you pack your stuff, get the hell out of our town, and don't come back. Ever."

"Terms stated," Jacques called. "Accepted?"

"Accepted!" the crowd shouted back.

Wide-eyed, I could hardly believe what I was witnessing. Riot Royales were old. The last one was when my father was a kid. We had easier ways of solving our problems these days. But then, this was Bedlam.

"Jeremy," Jacques said. "State your terms."

"What the fuck is going on?!"

Roan and Legend dropped his feet. Cairo hauled Jeremy away from the fire—though his hold on him was firm.

"It's a Riot Royale, bitch." Cairo threw him away. The crowd threw him back. "You're fighting for the Crows against me who represents Paris, the Bedlam Boys, and our girl. You state what you want from us if you win. If the watchers accept, they all agree to hold us to your terms—by any means necessary.

"No one reneges on a Riot Royale," he said. "Think of it like that marked shit they used to do at that school, Evergreen Academy. If you don't put me down, our lovely audience will run you out of town. Slashed tires, break-ins, beating you up on the quad. Whatever it takes to help you pack your bags faster. The same applies to us if I lose, so name your terms, Ellis."

"You can't be serious." Jeremy whipped around, face red, eyes wild. "This is a joke!"

"No joke," Arsenio said. "This is your lucky night."

He threw a rock at his feet. A piece of paper was strapped to it. I didn't have to read it to know what it said.

"Burning cars and cowards in masks weren't going to do it, Ellis. This is the closest you'll ever get to forcing us out of Bedlam, so name your terms."

Teeth bared, he snapped from Arsenio, to the watchers, to Cairo, and finally to me. My expression reflected nothing.

"Yeah, alright." Jeremy ripped off his jacket. "*When* I win, the Bedlam Boys get the hell out of my town—tonight. Your false-accuser sister can kiss my ass literally. And that sweet house you're living in rent-free"—he met my eyes—"becomes mine."

I bristled. The implication was clear to me even if it wasn't to anyone else. The Crows would own the house I told him I traded my freedom to live in. Either I moved in with Jeremy, or it was back to a motel till he got around to giving me that deed.

"Terms stated," Jacques said flatly. "Accepted?"

"Accepted."

The watchers moved on a cue, fanning out to form a circle in the clearing.

Moving into the makeshift arena, Cairo shed his hoodie and shirt.

"Rules are simple," Jacques said. "It's a bare-knuckle fight that does not stop until one of you do. No one is to help or interfere, but do not try to kill your opponent. If you do, the prosecution will have more than enough eyewitnesses at the trial."

He motioned to the people holding Micah and the others. "Let them go. They'll respect the Royale."

Growling, Asher advanced on us the second he was free—his fist balled and rising above his shoulder.

I flashed to the meaty fist heading toward my face. The fist that stripped Paris in the dirt.

It was you.

Neither one of us moved.

"Be warned," Jacques hissed. "I'm the worst one."

Asher stopped dead—huffing and puffing, knuckles whitening inches from Jacques's face. Maybe there was a single working brain cell in that caveman skull. Roaring, he shoved away, returning to the Crows.

"You're not," I whispered. I slipped my hand under his shirt, stroking him the way he did me. "Thank you."

"It's not done yet."

That much was true.

Cairo and Jeremy squared off, practically dancing around the circle, sidestepping in time with each other.

Roan took his place between them. "On my signal," he said, raising his phone. "Fists up... Riot Royale!"

A loud *ding* sounded, and Roan raced out of the way—just in time for them to fly at each other.

Cairo went for his signature throat punch. His fist sailed past Jeremy's ear.

To be fair, he'd be an idiot to be caught out with that hit three times. The quick duck and rebound jab to Cairo's ribs was the expected move. Didn't stop me gasping and clutching tight to Jacques.

Cairo wasn't kidding about the rules of Riot Royale. Most likely why people didn't initiate one nowadays. If he lost, people he's known his whole life will pick up the pitchforks and torches and chase my boys to the border. Paris would suffer further humiliation, and the Crows would have another hold on me.

Everything was riding on this.

The punch doubled Cairo over, wheezing— No. He was laughing.

He popped up, grinning away. "Little Jer-Bear came to play."

"Fuck you!"

Jeremy flew at him. Cairo spun, dropped to his knee, and swept his leg. Jeremy hit the ground with an audible thud, skidding to land at Paris's shoes.

"Finish him," she screamed.

This was a new side of my sweet best friend, and if anyone was going to bring it out of her, it was the Crows.

Cairo seized his shoulders and tossed Jeremy on his back. Down and dazed, he didn't see Cairo's fist flying at his gut till it bent him in two.

Jeremy popped up head and feet, clutching his stomach as he rolled on his side, struggling to stand.

"Get up," Micah shouted. "Come on, bro. Get up!"

The Crow got up on his hands and knees, and Cairo kicked him in the face. His head snapped around, squirting blood as far as three feet away.

"Who exactly are you rooting for?" Jacques asked, raising a brow at my latest gasp.

"You know who I'm rooting for. But Cairo's not pulling his punches. What if he kills him?"

"One," he said. "Don't spare any sympathy for that vermin." His fingers dug into my hip. "Anyone who hurts you doesn't deserve it."

I blinked at him in surprise. An extraordinary statement from someone who belted my ass raw without hesitation. Extraordinary because he meant it, and he was angry.

Jeremy rolled to his feet, head lolling. He shook himself hard. I could almost hear him shouting at himself to get in the fight.

Cairo came at him again. Jeremy hit him with a one-two double punch in the face. Cairo dropped, and Jeremy was on him in an instant—pummeling his skull.

The scream trapped in my throat.

Forget the consequences of Jeremy winning. The torture of watching him hurt Cairo was ripping my heart to shreds all on its own.

Cairo abandoned protecting his face. He reared and grabbed Jeremy's forearms. He flipped and the roles were reversed. Cairo fisted his hair and punched Jeremy once, twice, three, four times in the face.

"Stop," Micah hollered. "He's had enough."

"Not nearly." Standing up, Cairo hoisted the half-conscious man above his head. His roar was only a fraction higher than the baying crowd. Sweat glinted off his muscles in the firelight. "Bedlam now."

"Bedlam forever!"

He threw him.

Jeremy sailed shrieking through the air. I jerked as he hit the ground, my bones jarring with the impact.

That was it. It had to be. No one got up from a hit like that.

Jeremy got his knees under him and stood.

Canine glinting, Cairo waved him over. *Come and get me.*

Jeremy didn't so much run as he did stagger across the circle. He punched wildly, missing Cairo by a mile. Cairo straightened, and his not-quite-right eyes flashed.

"Don't," Micah screamed, knowing exactly what was coming. "He's had enough. Don't!"

Jeremy swung again.

Cairo snatched his fist and wrenched it back. Jeremy roared as his bone crackled like tinder. My love shoved the sobbing gangster to his knees, his wrist secure in his hold. Cairo raised his fist for the final punch. Jeremy would not get up from this.

Bang!

A gunshot shattered the scene.

"Ah!"

Students ran in every direction, stampeding from Buller's Den. Shoving, screaming, limbs flailing, and Jacques lifting me up and running us away from it all. Riot Royale was over.

And there was no winner.

Chapter Six

"It was the Crows. I bet you anything it was one of them," Paris said. She paced the length of the room. "They knew their boy was about to lose, so they shot off a gun to end the fight early."

"How did you get in here?" Cairo mused. "Who let you in?"

Paris picked up the nearest thing and threw it at his head. It happened to be her shoe.

He caught it out of the air and tossed it back. To be fair to him, he and I were just out of the shower and gearing up for round two when she burst in, but I had no problem giving Paris the time she needed. The night before, we were so close to getting rid of the Crows for good. How could she feel safe when they were right down the street and itching for revenge?

"Danny, this is serious," she snapped. "You were going to win. The Royale should've been called in your favor."

"An almost win isn't a win. Jacques can't give it to me, and the watchers wouldn't back me if he did."

"So, we do it again. Another Riot Royale. I'll fight if I have to."

Cairo was shaking his head before she finished. "The Crows won't be tricked into another trip to the den. I can challenge Ellis again head-on, but he's got no reason to agree. He has his own plan to get us out. Why risk another beating when he—?"

"—can beat me instead!"

"That won't happen. Hey." Cairo raised his arm. "Evie, come here."

She climbed onto the bed, stuffing herself under his other arm.

"The Crows will never put their hands on either of you again. That's a promise. I whispered a parting message in Ellis's ear while everyone was running around screaming. Anything that happens to you two within the next eighty years. If you trip and scratch your elbow, I will hold him personally responsible, and I'll kill him."

I swallowed. If Cairo delivered his message in the same tone he used then, Jeremy heard him loud and clear.

He meant it.

"Thank you," Paris said, eyes welling.

There was a time when I thought Paris didn't know the real Cairo. At that moment, my doubt vanished. These siblings were closer than most. They saw each other for exactly who they were.

Paris gave him a wobbly smile. "I knew you loved me."

"Less and less so by the second."

Laughing, she snuggled in, reaching up for the remote.

I popped a kiss on her cheek. Popped one on Cairo's too.

"I have to go. See you in a bit."

He hooked my dress's drawstrings. "Where are you going?"

"To the store. We're running low on a few things. I want to get you an ice pack," I said, tracing the edges of the cut above his eye. "And stuff to make butterscotch muffins. They sell them in the library café and I've been dreaming about them ever since."

"We don't need ice packs or muffins. It's too risky to be out walking alone right now."

"I'll ask Jacques to go with me."

His eyes narrowed.

"You can be there when I ask and watch us leave together, love," I said. "But we do need milk, ice packs, bandages, toilet paper, and food. If the Crows force me to hide in here, too afraid to leave, they're the real winners."

"Subtle manipulation, Rain." He released me. "Jacques goes with you."

I crossed the hall to Jacques's room and let myself in.

"Two," he said without looking up from his laptop. "What do you want?"

I jumped on his bed, earning a three and not caring. I said Legend's room was the secret room behind a bookcase. Well, Jacques's was the library that housed that bookcase. Three walls were nothing but shelves and books. The fourth boasted his television, dresser, and two small bookcases.

"I need to go out for a while," I said, "and I need you to stay here, and say you didn't."

"Why?" he asked simply.

"I can't tell you now, but it's important. I won't be gone long, and I will be safe. I just need to do this alone."

Jacques didn't slow his typing. He might've stopped listening after "I" for all I knew.

I soaked him in.

Jacques Stone was everything I didn't know I liked. Growing up, my crushes were on the rough-and-tumble farm boys, throwing around bales of hay and riding tractors before they rode cars. Brainy dudes with their heads in a book didn't make the cut. And beards?

Before Grandpa passed away, I loved his loud smooches, but I didn't love the scratchy whiskers that came with it.

Yes, a year ago I would've taken one look at Jacques, said he was handsome, but dismissed him as not my type. Like I mentioned before, I didn't know myself very well.

I laid my hand over his. "I'll tell you everything when I get back. All of it, Jacques. No more secrets."

His typing slowed. He flicked down to my hand.

"Go."

"Thank you."

I was downstairs and out the door before he changed his mind. Frankie rolled up to the bus stop at five seventeen on the dot.

"If it isn't my favorite kind of Rainey day."

"Hey, Frankie." I claimed the seat right by her. "How are my favorite godson and goddaughter?"

She laughed. "You got my kids believing you are their godmother. They asked my mom if you're the same as a grandma. Keep this up and you'll have responsibilities if anything happens to me."

"You're not going anywhere. But if anything did happen." The Letter Man's threats were stark in my mind. "I'd always be there for them."

"That means a lot," she said. "Are we off to the farm today?"

"I don't feel safe there after what happened to Bella. I won't feel safe until her killer is caught."

"I was going to say, dear. I'm not comfortable leaving you out there on your own." I felt her sigh in my bones. "Bedlam's not what it used to be."

We tried for lighter topics for the rest of the ride. I waved bye under the street sign for Bay Avenue.

I headed to the only place I could go. I was buzzed in immediately.

The front door hung open.

"Hello?" I called. "Jeremy?"

I stuck my head in, then the rest of me. Tiptoeing down the front hall, a boot came into view, propped on the coffee table.

"Jeremy, I—"

Hands grabbed me.

"Hey!"

Gael threw me on the floor, ricocheting pain up my knees. I gasped as Asher wrenched my head back. His arm circled my throat.

Micah, Bentley, and Zeke stepped off the staircase, joining the silent Jeremy on the couch.

He looked terrible.

Black and blue bloated his nose. One eye swelled shut and the other glared at me through a black ring. Bandaged cuts. Weeping lip. His arm in a sling. Jeremy's own mother wouldn't recognize him.

"Did you know?"

"What... is this?" I croaked. "Let me go."

"Did you know?" he repeated.

"Know what?!"

He waited me out.

"Jeremy!" I punched Asher's thigh, earning his constriction around my throat. "Get... off! I can't—"

I punched him again, desperation sending my strikes wide as black spots crept into my vision.

"Ease up," Jeremy said mildly.

Just like that, the pressure was gone. I sucked in deep lungfuls, gaze burning Asher where he stood.

This fucker is next.

"What is your problem?" I shrieked, thrashing in Gael and Asher's grip. "You said I had to come so we could plan our next move."

"We would," Jeremy clipped, "but I got a notion in my head last night when Sharpe was pounding my face in. Maybe *you* planned *me*. You set a trap for us and we walked right into it."

"No."

"You are in love with those fucks who hit, abuse, and treat you like a dog. And as their faithful bitch, you lured me out there knowing I couldn't turn down the *Riot Royale* unless I wanted all of Bedlam believing I'm a coward. Cairo goes off like the rabid animal he is, and the Crows are nearly forced out of town for good. Just like your owners want."

Leaning forward, I opened my mouth and drew out, "No."

"Stop lying!" he exploded, kicking away the coffee table. "I know it was you!"

It flipped and crashed into the window, shattering two panes. Could have been a scary display if I didn't tempt killers and bruisers to lower their hackles and let me in every day before breakfast.

"Jeremy, listen to me." I tried to get up and was pushed down. "Look me in the eye and tell me if I'm lying. I did *not* know about the Riot Royale. I didn't know people even did those anymore. When Cairo challenged you, I was as surprised as everyone else."

He jabbed a finger at me. "But he did tell you to get me out there, didn't he?!"

"Tell me to—! Are you listening to yourself?" I cried. "Did those punches to your head delete our conversation from your mind? I *told* you, Jeremy. Word for fucking word, I said it wasn't a good idea for you to show up at the den where you'll be outnumbered by people who won't be putting the Crows on their Christmas card list. I said if you did, you may not walk out of there."

I cocked my head. "I believe your response was to cuff my chin and say I was cute for being worried about you. Didn't I warn you, Jeremy? Didn't I?!"

A hundred emotions flashed across his face, and showing stark among them: doubt.

"How was I setting you up when I told you not to come?"

He settled back in his seat, studying me. A thick, oppressive silence blanketed the room. I bore it, holding Jeremy's gaze the whole time.

"Alright," he finally said. "No lie, you did warn me, and I didn't listen. I fucked up."

He nodded at Asher and Gael, who let me go.

"But that went down way too smoothly," Jeremy continued, gesturing for me to sit between him and Micah. "Could the Bedlam Boys know you're working for me? It may not have been an accident you *overheard* him talking about getting people to the den."

Slowly, I squeezed between them, schooling my face to hide the discomfort. "If they thought I was betraying them, I'd be out on my ass. The guys are possessive to put it politely. They don't share. Period.

"But I'm betting they assumed word would get back to you some way. Especially if they told people to spread it around. Did it?" I asked. "Did you hear about the den from someone other than me?"

"I did," Bentley admitted. "A girl I hook up with mentioned something was going down in Buller's Den and we might want to check it out."

"There you go," I said, laying it on a bit too thick. I pulled back. "Anyway, it's over now and a winner wasn't called. Cairo can't pull that again unless you accept."

"Nah." Jeremy absentmindedly rubbed his reset shoulder. "I've got something better in mind for those guys that doesn't involve scrapping in the dirt, or letting a mob run them out for me. I'm going to carry their bodies across the town line myself."

I reeled back. "Jeremy, I'm going to give you more advice that you'll probably ignore. Don't let vengeance cloud your judgment. Whatever is it you and Daddy Ellis want from this town, you won't get it in prison."

To my surprise, he smiled.

"Ah, but then, you don't know what it is we want."

"Why did you call me out here?" I looked away. "Was it just to get your muscle to assault me? Again."

"I'm sorry." He rubbed slow circles on my back. Disgust rippled up my spine. "I apologize to you a lot. I've always been a hothead—doing before thinking, but I recognize if I listened to your warning last time, last night wouldn't have gone down the way it did. So, I'm learning from my mistakes.

"We're planning our next hit together. You'll tell us where to go, how to act, what to watch out for, so this time it's the Bedlam Boys who don't see it coming." His smile hardened around the edges. "A foolproof plan, and if it goes wrong this time, I won't accuse. I'll know exactly who to blame."

Jeremy was looking for a flinch, a wince, a tell. He didn't get it.

"Before we get into all that, and what I think of another dose of your implied threats, I need you to tell me something." I flicked between the six of them. "Was it one of you who brought the gun and shot it off?"

Blank faces looked back at me.

"I won't be a part of killing anyone, Jeremy. Screw the contract, and the farm, if that's what it comes to. Gran wanted it in our family, but she'd never want me to get it back this way. So, if the plan we're making is toward the goal of *peacefully* bringing about the return of Crystal Canyon, then bust out the whiteboards and dry-erase markers.

"If it's a plan to hurt anyone—innocent or Bedlam Boy—I'm out. Understood?"

He put his hand, just the one, up in surrender. "Absolutely. What did you think? We're not planning a hit. I just want to know more about them. Their history, their family, weaknesses, hobbies, friends. And Bedlam's history while we're at it. I got caught out with that Riot Royale thing. That's not going to happen again." Jeremy bore into me. "Unless that's a problem?"

"No problem at all. Where do you want to start?"

JACQUES

Rainey burst into my room.

"Four."

"Jacques." She ducked between me and the desk, blocking the laptop. "The Crows, I think they're going after you next."

I grasped her hips and slid her out of the way. That done, I returned to my essay. Professor Valdez changed his ridiculous midterm topic. We now had twenty pages on a specific instance of society's changing ethics influencing law. I suspect the inflation in pages was an attempt to punish me using his minuscule scrap of authority.

It was another in his long list of failures. I was enjoying myself researching the creation of child labor laws, child abuse protections, and minimum ages for entering into marriage. Essentially, there was a time when young people were essentially seen as small adults. The shift to viewing them as children with innocence to protect was relatively recent. And not a changing standard accepted into the Stone family.

"Have you started his paper yet?" I asked. "I'm curious which topic you chose."

"Did you hear what I said?"

"I heard you say you'd tell everything you've been hiding, de Souza. Including what sent you running out of here and back, shouting about something I've known since Arsenio's car caught fire. Start from the beginning, then I'll decide if it's worth closing my laptop."

Sighing, she settled on the edge of my mattress.

"Jeremy called me out to his house. He's in bad shape," she said. "Looks like he went through a meat grinder, and he's raging about it. I figured you guys wouldn't want me anywhere near him after one of the Crows most likely pulled a gun. None of them admitted to it, by the way."

I hummed, finishing up my last sentence on the marriage section.

"They grilled me, Jacques. They wouldn't let me leave till I told them everything about you guys, from what you eat for breakfast to your favorite cologne. They were specifically interested in you."

"Not a concern seeing as you know very little about me," I said mildly.

"Don't I?"

Rainey curled over my typing fingers. Pointedly, she lifted my hand, clearing the way to swing her leg over and straddle me. The screen blotted out as my vision beheld her soft waves, piercing eyes, and full, chapped, pink lips.

"I know you love chocolate but you're rigid about how much of it you eat. A sweet tooth, but it, like everything else, does not get to control you. I know most people don't understand you, and the effort they put into trying is the effort you give back. You're okay with questions, curiosity, and discussions... but no one asks.

"I know you think your new little cousin is the most fascinating bundle of wonder you've ever seen. That she's proof that no matter how much you know the world, it can still surprise you. I know you like comedies because they're the twenty or forty minutes of the day you can shut your brain off, but you hide that because it wasn't encouraged."

Rainey stroked my stiffening jaw.

"At all times you had to be learning, pushing, striving to be and seen as the best. All those competitions and academic decathlons your parents entered you in when you were young. I dug up the articles. They were years where you did, and won, up to six events in a year. I don't imagine that left you much time running in the park, skinning your knees with the other kids.

"I know your favorite color is blue. You're ambidextrous. You love history, and you don't have sex."

My brow twitched—a half a millisecond movement, but she noticed.

"I'm not saying you won't or never had sex, but"—her fingers trailed along my neck, tickling my collarbone—"even though you clearly enjoy me bare-assed in front of you, rocking back on your fingers as you whip me raw."

My cock hardened—rising, as if seeking her to show just how much he enjoys it.

"You don't take it further or let me return the favor because then I'd see something no one is supposed to see: Jacques Stone lose control." Rainey kissed the corner of my mouth. "How many times after our morning spankings did you retreat to your room to masturbate?"

Every time.

"How many nights did you picture me on my knees, worshiping your cock like I do Legend's? Playing your dirty little whore like I do for Arsenio? Indulging your every socially unapproved fantasy? Or extracting your mind-blowing orgasms on the point of pain?"

I clutched the chair arms to stop their shaking. Didn't work.

Rainey vibrated on top of me, brushing against my dick. She moved slowly up and down, and my lips peeled back.

"I would do all of that and more for you, Jacques Stone, but I can't until I'm someone you trust to see you lose control." She kissed me, snarling and all. "I know that because I know you. So don't tell me I don't."

Breathing hard, I got myself under control. Slowing my pulse. Balling and unballing my fists. Smoothing my expression. Bringing down the mask. When I trusted myself, I spoke.

"I underestimated you, so you punished me," I said, glancing at the erection that would not be tamed as easily. "I apologize, de Souza. You know me—possibly better than anyone."

Surprise flickered in her eyes. She wasn't expecting me to admit it, but it's a vain fool who doesn't recognize he's been bested, or in the presence of his match. As Rainey revealed, I was many things, but a fool was not one of them.

"Now that I know this, it is worth closing my laptop." I brushed my lips over hers, catching her small gasp as melting chocolate on my tongue. "How much of that did you tell Ellis?"

"He wouldn't let me leave until I gave him something."

"Answer the question, de Souza."

Rainey cupped my cheeks. "None of it," she whispered. "I just told you that you won't give yourself to me until I'm someone you trust absolutely. Why would I risk that for the likes of Jeremy Ellis and the Crows?"

"Hmm." She was soft and sweet, peppering me with kisses—claiming my eyes, nose, cheeks, and lips. "I find myself growing attached to you."

I could've been speaking about the weather, and I was. Rain had come into my life, washing away my bullshit to reveal the true man crouching beneath.

"I would not appreciate it if you left," I said.

"Don't."

"I won't, Jacques." She rested in the crook of my neck. "I'm not going anywhere."

We sat there for a long time, saying nothing. Doing nothing to someone looking in from the outside. But Rainey knew what was changing. As did I.

"If they have no usable information," I spoke up, shifting her to the bed. "What has you concerned? They were always coming after me. What's changed?"

"Riot Royale. Someone brought a gun and Crows were all standing there stone-faced when I asked if it was them. That I had to give them something damning, so I told them you barely sleep or eat, and you're hooked on pills to help you stay awake studying," she rushed out.

"I'm sorry. I'm so sorry, but this is one of those 'he said, she said' accusations that can't be proven unless someone drug tests you. Jeremy can't say I lied, and no one else can say... it's... true. I thought this was... the best way..." Rainey trailed off as my guffaws reached deafening.

I clutched my stomach, tears leaking from my eyes—laughing louder than I had in years. "Gave me a pill addiction?" I wheezed. "And he bought it?"

She nodded, eyes wide.

"Guessing you did the s-same for Arsenio, Cairo, Legend, and Roan?"

"Um, yes."

"I gotta hear this."

"Cairo has a foot fetish. Snaps pictures of women's feet when they're not looking. Legend got a girl pregnant and their baby was put up for a closed adoption. Roan picked up a few communicable diseases. Arsenio and his mom are a little *too* close. He calls her mommy when he thinks no one is around."

I stopped breathing, I was laughing so hard.

"So, you're not mad?"

Shaking my head, I wiped my eyes. "Nah. You had to give them something. Might as well be unprovable bullshit."

"That's not it," she continued. "He wanted to know about your parents. The judge, the mayor, the dean, Mr. St. James, the sheriff, and Nora Keller. Jeremy reminded me they were all influential in the community and the main opponents to the new town."

"What did you tell them?"

"There wasn't much to tell. Not more than people already knew. The divorce between Cairo's parents was brutal and the sheriff wasn't fully over it. The mayor doesn't believe a negative word against her son, and Nora wants to rekindle her relationship with Cairo. Mr. St. James is a hard man to do business with and a bit of a cheapskate, but he did pay Gran for deliveries even if he argued about it first.

"For your mom, I told him you didn't talk about her and I never met her, so there wasn't anything to say. By that point, I wasn't comfortable with how many questions they were asking about you."

"I wouldn't be concerned about my mother." I straightened in my seat, regaining my composure. "Even in a small town like Bedlam, she's had no shortages of threats made against her and two attacks on her life. She takes every precaution."

"I have a bad feeling, Jacques. You didn't see the look in his eyes." She drifted over my shoulder. "I'm starting to become familiar with that look."

"He's not going to hurt my mother. My father moved to New York after I turned eighteen and they no longer had to pretend they loved each other for my sake. My cousin and her family live hours away. A rich man's reach is long, so I will warn them to be on alert, but I doubt they will take their vendetta across town lines."

"Okay," she said, though I could tell she wasn't convinced. "In the end, the plan we settled on was inviting your folks and other influential people in the community to a party with his father and other Foundry board members. All this secrecy and double plays in the dark, it doesn't come off well and makes people distrust them right off the rip.

"If they came out in the open and talked about their plans for improving the lives of Bedlamites and bringing out positive change, they could lure people to their side without any more beatings."

"That's a good idea, de Souza. So good, it might work better than we want."

She cringed. "I had to prove I was on their side. Give them an idea that would work on Bedlamites where no one would get hurt. This was the best I could come up with. They want to do it soon. Micah was on the phone to their dad before I left. Next weekend or the weekend after."

"We'll be ready."

She got up to leave.

"You should get ready too," I said, stopping her at the door. "I have a feeling soon I'll lose control."

Rainey spoke without turning around.

"Polygamy," she said. "That's the topic of my paper."

She closed the door softly behind her.

Very, very soon.

RAINEY

I walked into Cairo's room. He tossed me a grin in the middle of his phone conversation.

"She just came in, Mr. Gold. No, thank you." He laughed raucously. "You too. Enjoy the rest of your day."

Cairo held out my phone, his grin curling up. "Dear, the detective you've been cheating on me with is on the phone for you."

I called my feet to move three times. Slowly, I approached and let him place the cell on my palm.

"Hello?"

"Hello, Rainey. Is now a good time?"

"Yes." I turned my back on Cairo. "Is there any news?"

"I'm in that slow period of waiting for contacts to get back to me and searches to turn up information. I got a hold of Andrew Clein's ex-wife, hoping she might give a clue to his current whereabouts. She faxed a list of places he might be, a few of them out of state. Walker Lewis I was able to find," he said. "I asked what his connection was to Andrew Clein. He said he never heard of him and I wasn't to bother him again. He hung up on me mid-sentence."

"That's a little weird, right?"

"Yes. It was oddly abrupt. I'll try again in person," Gold said. "Have him look me in the eye when he says he doesn't know Clein."

"What about Dante?"

"I hired a hacker buddy of mine to track his IP address and location. So far, the source is pinging all over the world. It'll take some time to crack, but she's confident she can."

Hope soared. "That's something. Actually, that's everything. Dante is the Letter Man, Mr. Gold. I'm sure of it."

"Then, we're closer, Rainey. Stay strong, stay safe."

"I will."

"Before you go," he said, stopping me ending the call. "The number you gave me for your sister is disconnected."

My face fell.

"I tried looking her up by name, but it turns out there are a fair number of Ivy de Souzas in Chicago. Do you have any other means of contacting her? Name of her workplace would do."

"No," I said softly. "I can give you her old email address. She hasn't responded to any I sent her, but you may have more luck. I have to go. Bye."

I hung up quick lest he heard the tears clogging my throat. Ivy wanted rid of me so badly, she broke the final straw. I hadn't tried calling her since she told me to get my own life. Now I know there wouldn't have been a point.

"Rain."

"I'm fine," I said, swiping the back of my hand across my eyes. "I left my phone here and you picked up Gold's call."

"Had to know who was calling my girl."

He was damned casual about it too. Leaning back on the headboard—his arms folded behind his head. I climbed on his lap.

"Did he tell you what he's doing for me?"

"He said he was a private investigator. I put two and two together."

"I'm not cheating on you with him. Though that's an interesting way of putting it." I took a deep breath and released it slow. "I got another letter."

He dropped his arms, sitting up. "What? When? Where is it?"

"It's in my backpack. Cairo, he knows what you told the police. About the man in the shiny black shoes. He knows and he put two and two together. I told you about him," I said. "I broke the rules and he was already mad at me. He said I'm going to pay for it. The last time he said that, Bella d-died."

My tenuous hold on control snapped. Wetness gushed down my cheeks. "I won't let you be next, Cairo. Not you, Arsenio, Jacques, Legend, or Roan. I can't do this alone, but I can't do it with you guys either. Please understand."

"I do understand." Cairo grasped my chin between two fingers, drawing my forehead to his lips. My eyes fluttered shut as he kissed me. "I understand, and I'm tempted to count you down myself. Start you at ten instead of one like Jacques."

"What?" I blinked up at him. "Why?"

"How many times I gotta say I can take care of myself? Even if I couldn't, risking myself for you is my choice. What the fuck kind of person am I that I'd sit on my ass doing nothing when my blood wronged yours? Let alone let some sick fuck play games with you when the only sick fuck allowed to do that"—he thumped his chest—"is me."

"Cairo," I whispered.

"Don't make me tell you again. The truth. All of it. Now."

Smile tugging at my lips, I went to the bathroom, splashed water on my face, then went back to him. He didn't interrupt while I told him what Gold found so far and the digging he was doing into the rest. I also told him about the trip to Westchester Youth Center, and Cavendish's mentees.

"Walker Lewis," he repeated. "I'll see if my dad has a file on him."

"Have you found anything in his files so far?"

He shook his head. "That's why I didn't say anything. The old man isn't completely irresponsible. The important case files he brings home are kept locked in a safe. I haven't been able to get the combination out of him—drunk or sober, so every night since you were arrested, I've tried all the combinations I can think of."

"Do you think the file on my grandmother is in there? Maybe the autopsy report?"

"I saw inside once when he had it open and didn't know I was home. There's a lot of old files in there. I don't know if it relates to you or your grandmother, but it's worth a look."

"Absolutely," I said. "I could come with you tonight. Help."

Cairo smirked. "Don't know if I trust you around my old man."

"I'm not going to kill him," I snapped.

"Took a long time to say that, and you only did now that you want something."

I grabbed hold of my temper, reminded it he was risking a lot to help me, and shoved it back down. "Cairo, please. Gran was... everything to me. She was there when Ivy and I had no one. She raised us to be strong and never give up, and in two years and so much pain, I haven't. I won't sit on my ass either. I *need* to be a part of this."

He gave me a long, unreadable look. I didn't know what he would say, but I was willing to fight if I didn't like it.

"Fair enough. I won't sideline you."

My tension ebbed out.

"I'll let you in after he's in bed. You leave before he wakes up. No arguments. Agreed?"

"Yes."

Cairo flipped me over, pulling a squeal from me. My pants and underwear were shortly around my ankles. A soft sigh escaped as two fingers slipped in.

"Where'd you get the money to pay Gold?"

At some point it was decided interrogations would come with orgasms. I was not mad about this.

"Jeremy. I pitched his car in the pool and got six thousand off him. A thousand for Gold and five for the new autopsy."

He paused a second, then resumed his task. "When's it happening?"

"Won't be soon. I have to get a license and arrange transport. Plus find an examiner I can trust. Still, I have the money now. Some paperwork and a car is nothing to how helpless I was trying to raise that kind of money."

"You might have heard Jacques has an in with a judge. Let him know if he can help speed up the process."

"I will," I said, sneaking a hand under his shirt. "I looked up Craig Brown. He goes to Bedlam U and he's on the football team. Tomorrow I'm going to ask him what he knows about Cavendish and Blake Jensen. Want to come?"

"Divide and conquer. You got four names. You meet Craig Brown *in a public place*. Jacques, Arsenio, and I will get the others. Roan and Legend will look up their files."

"Okay— Ah." I spread my legs for easy access. "We're close, Cairo. I can feel it. The Letter Man is out of time."

THE NEXT MORNING, THERE was a black letter in our mailbox.

Legend saw me through the window. Footsteps pounded the floor, then he was there. He tugged me inside, slammed and locked the door. We were both quiet as I opened it.

Hey, Angel.

I said a lot of things in my last letter. What can I say? You betraying me got me a little heated. I was all set to put Paris Keller in this letter. Order you to kill her peacefully, or I'd do it slow.

Choking, I shot up to Legend—eyes huge in horror.

"Keep reading," he said gravely.

Then the Crows jumped you.

I admit, I was still fucking angry, but now it wasn't at you.

No one gets to hurt you but me. This is our show, and I don't like improv. Though, I was impressed with the lengths the Bed-

lam Boys went through to protect your honor. The punishment fit the crime, and although I couldn't allow the Crows to leave Bedlam just yet, I decided the Bedlam Boys deserve a gift and you forgiveness for your error in judgment.

Wednesday morning at eight a.m., stand on the third step outside Bedlam Hall, looking out over Homer Green.

If you're there, I'll know you're ready to put Verlice and Hope behind us, and start over. If not, gifts can always be returned.

Stay psycho.

Love ya, XOXO

Legend broke the silence. "What are you going to do?"

"What would you do?"

He looked me in the eye. "I'd be there Wednesday morning at eight a.m. Homer Green is swarmed by that time. You'll be surrounded by people—one of them me. This doesn't say you have to stand there alone."

"Legend, this guy's idea of a thank-you is—" *Laying me on an unmarked grave surrounded by flowers.*

"Is what?"

"Psychotic," I finished. "Whatever this gift is, the only one who'll like it is him."

"He told you what the alternative is."

I slumped against the door. "I know. He would've ordered me to kill Paris. Who is this guy?!" I burst out. "What does he want from me? Why won't he say? At least Cavendish was clear from the beginning. It was him or Jennifer. This guy's gonna dangle me on his hook till either one of us is dead!"

"Yeah, him," Legend said, "and that's coming soon, Rainey. I can promise you that." He wound his fingers through my hair, soothing me though I didn't want him to. "I'll have Roan post double the security around Homer Green on Wednesday. What do you say?"

Unbidden, my head moved up and down. "I've seen what punishment is. I'd rather take my chances with a gift."

I spent most of the morning in a fog. I walked in and out of class with blank note pages and *wah wah wah* where the memory of the lecture should be.

I didn't take proper note of where I was till I looked up and saw the football field.

Craig Brown.

If there was anything important I had to do that day, this was it.

They practiced on Monday mornings. Dozens of padded-up guys running across the field to practicing cheerleaders and the onlookers who hung around for a taste of the glory.

The field was empty that morning. I headed to the locker room, crossing my fingers that they were gearing up and practice wasn't canceled.

Voices and slammed lockers reached my ears. I found a spot on the wall as guys trickled out, loaded down with gym bags and gear. They weren't in uniform. Didn't look like there was practice that day but—

There he is.

Craig Brown came out laughing, slapping his friend on the back. "—be epic, man. Can't wait. BU!"

"BU," the team shouted.

Looking at him grown up and out of pictures, the gawky young teenager became a handsome, confident man. His coarse teddy-bear-brown hair shaved close to the scalp and an easy grin hung on his lips. I decided then that if Blake Jensen was an alias, it wasn't his.

The Letter Man was dead inside. I had no doubt that when I finally laid eyes on him, the emptiness would shine through too strongly for a fake smile or forced laugh to hide. I would know that man when I saw him.

"Excuse me, Craig."

He slowed down.

"Over here," I called. "Do you have a minute?"

"Uhh. Just one." He peeled away from his friends, loping over to me. "Do I know you?"

"No. I'm Rainey," I said. "We haven't met. I just had a quick question for you. Was Scott Cavendish your mentor at the youth center?"

"Yeah. Why?"

"I'm trying to track down one of his—"

"Craig." His friends stopped at the entrance. "What are you doing? We have to go."

"We have an away game," he explained, taking a step back. "Bus is waiting."

"Real quick. Did you know someone named Blake Jensen? Another one of Cavendish's mentees?"

He brightened. "Yeah, I know Blake. Wasn't with the center though. Just hung around after school and got tight with Scott. We all did. He was a great guy."

Not so much of the great.

"Yo, Craig! Want to walk to New York?"

"I'm coming." He faced me, walking backward. "That it?"

"Last thing." I scrambled to get the photo out of my pack. "Blake. Is he in this photo? Point him out."

"Blake's not—"

"Craig," the coach boomed. "On the bus. Now."

"I really got to go. That's Blake." He jabbed a face in the pic and took off running after his teammates.

I spun it around, scrutinizing them.

Blake Jensen did exist, but he was one of the floaters the coordinator spoke about. Not signed up, but still joined in and got close to Scott Cavendish.

Is he the one I'm looking for? Blond hair, pointed nose, and pimply cheeks. Dye can change the hair and acne cream was doing wonders these days. The other features would've grown with him into a pleasantly attractive young college student who liked to smoke outside farmhouses and snatch women out of crowds.

I didn't recognize that face, or know what to do with Roan's word there wasn't a Blake Jensen enrolled as a student or working at the university. That fact wouldn't trip me up yet. The Letter Man was smart. Concealing his identity on campus clearly wasn't hard by how easily he blended in with the mob.

Fishing out my phone, I called Cairo.

"You don't need to meet up with the other mentees," I said by way of hello. "Craig Brown backed up that there was a Blake and he was tight with Cavendish."

"Know what he looks like?"

"He's in the photo."

"Then bring that ass back here. I need a midmorning fuck to get through the rest of the day."

I rolled my eyes though my feet were already moving. "Something happen?"

"Yes. I've been invited to dinner tonight."

CAIRO KEPT THE DETAILS to himself as he chased me through the house, tackled me on the stairs, and fucked me raw where I fell. He didn't have much to say when he returned that night either.

I sat at his desk, working on my midterm paper for Professor Valdez.

Cairo came in and picked up my backpack for me.

"Bring the laptop," he said. "You'll wait in the car until I come get you."

"Do you want to talk about...?"

His steely expression silenced me.

I followed him out to the car. We were quiet for most of the drive to his father's house—a route I knew well. As the bungalow loomed in the distance, I spoke.

"You'll tell me everything one day," I said. "All your secrets, hopes, fears, and worst sins. You'll pour it all into me, knowing the woman who can handle all that is you, is me. One day, you will, Cairo, and I can wait. But there is something you're going to tell me tonight. Right now. And if you don't, it'll change everything between us."

He killed the engine in the driveway. Cairo pocketed the keys, but didn't get out. He waited.

"My grandmother was harassed, threatened, and ultimately murdered because there's something about my farm that's worth killing for. Is what makes de Souza farm special, the same secret of this town?"

Cairo didn't speak for a long spell.

"Cairo, you understand that if you know why my grandmother was killed and you keep it from me—" My throat tightened. "There's nothing worse you could do."

"I know," he rasped.

"Then don't do this to us. I don't need the details, or the history, or to know who 'she' is. This is about Gran. Why did she have to die?"

Expelling a long breath, for the barest second, the feral light in my beast went out. "I can't be sure about your farm, but if I were to stack the odds, they'd swing heavy one way. The farm's secret is all of Bedlam's secret."

"Wha—?"

He spun on me. "You need to understand something. People have died for knowing this, and others have killed for it. Our grandparents and their grandparents went to their grave with the promise of Bedlam forever being the random dot on the map with the weird name. If anyone knew, all this goes away. And Foundry is doing their best to make that happen.

"You will not repeat what I'm about to tell you to anyone for any reason. As far as we're concerned, as soon as we get out of this car, this conversation didn't happen."

"I understand, baby. Please, just tell me."

He reached for me, stopped short, and dropped his hand.

"There's only one reason someone would come for your grandmother's land as aggressively as AgriProspects did.

"In Bedlam," he began, "the town that used to be Crystal Canyon, there are diamonds."

I sat there long after he left, my sobs the only sound breaking the silence.

Chapter Seven

Cairo came back for me almost an hour later.

The lights were dim in the house. Stepping in, I saw it was because a fair amount were burned out or flickering.

Stale beer hit my nose. Pushing down the urge to cringe was easy since I didn't have the energy to do it.

In Bedlam there are diamonds.

What did this mean?

There were diamonds on my farm? For years, someone or some-ones tried to drive Gran out—get her locked up, and us sent away, for greed.

The whole thing made no sense, and yet, everything was falling into place.

Why Gran was so determined to leave this legacy to me and Ivy. Why people tried to take it from her.

But it wasn't just her. I was supposed to believe our whole town was sitting on a treasure trove and out there was a *she* employing the Bedlam Boys to protect the secret and take out anyone who brings unwanted attention on us?

Cairo led me through the sparse wicker-chairs living room, holding tight to my hand.

"Why—?"

"Don't ask me questions, Rain. I can't answer them."

"But why do you have to collect payments from people if what you said is true?" I plowed on. "It doesn't make any sense."

"We don't get a cut," he hissed.

"Why?"

"Rain—"

"We're alone, Cairo. Why can't—?"

"Because we're not." He whirled on me, then his gaze traveled up. "We're not alone, and when we are, I still won't talk about this. Look at me, Rainey. This is serious. You don't know the danger I put us both in by telling you, so I didn't. You don't know. Nod if you've already forgotten."

Slowly, I nodded.

"Good. Dad keeps his files in the office. Stay close to me," he said, taking off upstairs. "Don't wander off."

"I want to see your room."

"You're having a lot of trouble listening tonight."

I was having trouble with everything that night. Trouble with the thought the place I slopped around in the pigpen and chased chickens might hold riches in its soil. Trouble with my gran becoming a casualty in the battle to keep it in our family, and me taking on the fight clueless and unprepared.

Did she know?

Would she have worked so back-breaking hard her whole life if the option to retire in the French Riviera was beneath her fingertips?

But if she didn't know, how did Andrew Clein and AgriProspects?

It suddenly made sense why a dying business came for us so hard. It was a stroke of luck too late, they didn't get what they were after in the end.

We topped the landing.

A thunderous snore slipped under the first door on the right. A familiar rush of hatred flooded by senses. Cairo was on a hunt for the truth, and of course I wanted it too, but as far as I was concerned, there was nothing we would uncover that would sate my need to watch that man carried out in cuffs. Cairo would get over it.

I stroked his back. *I'm here for him now.*

"In here," he said, ducking into the room at the end of the hall.

We passed a third closed door on the way. I would see inside it eventually—when Cairo wasn't raw and prickly from being more vulnerable than he expected to be that night.

Jack Sharpe's office was a simple space. His desk and computer against the wall, looking out over the window. A liquor cabinet beside it and blown-up pictures of Jack fishing as decor. A few of them with a young Cairo holding his flopping fish for the camera.

Cairo crossed to a photo of him and Jack sitting on the rim of a boat, and swung it open. A green wall safe drew me in.

"Kind of an obvious place to hide this," I spoke up. "Shouldn't a sheriff know to be more creative?"

"There's a world of stupid criminals, Rain, but very few are dumb enough to rob a sheriff. He could leave his money on the hall table. It's not going anywhere."

"Fair point."

I rested my chin on his shoulder, studying him while he studied the lock. "What have you tried?"

"His birthday, his parents' birthday, my birthday, and Paris's. I tried his and Nora's wedding day, and the day they met."

"Did you try their honeymoon?"

"Yeah," he said. "Nothing."

"What about on his phone? I'm not going to lie, I've got a few passwords saved in my notes."

He was shaking his head before I finished.

"His cell is a half-useless brick that he forgets at home or in his office every other day. He'd care a lot more if passwords were on it."

"That's true," I muttered.

I worried my lip, cycling through the options. People were predictable creatures and they liked shortcuts. An important day in your life was easy to remember, and the sentimental liked to link the combination to the precious things inside.

"You said he keeps case files in there. Maybe the combo is related to him being a cop. Have you tried his badge number or the day he joined the force?"

Cairo snapped his fingers. "You're as smart as that pussy is sweet. Stay here."

A smile tugged at me while I leaned against the wall waiting for him. He was getting generous with the compliments and the kisses these days, but a rare breed like Cairo Sharpe didn't bring anything straightforward.

He returned with his father's badge. Cairo twisted the dial, swinging to the last number, and pulled the handle.

Nothing.

"Shit. I don't know the date he joined," Cairo admitted. "I'll ask him in the morning. How long are we doing this tonight?"

"Till the morning."

He dipped his chin. "Give me more, de Souza. What else you got?"

I suggested every possible day in the man's life. I even got Cairo to pull out his yearbook and spin in prom night. All my ideas exhausted, I fished out my phone and we tried the internet for other possible significant moments.

It gave us his first road trip. The day he received his first paycheck. Also, the days he lost people important to him.

We did our best to try them all. Over fifty possible combos, and the safe did not open.

Cairo bundled me in the car the next morning, ignoring my arguing that we had time to try a few more.

"I have to come back and get him up for work," he said, carrying me to the car. "You can't be here when I do. He'll lose his shit if he sees you."

"You have to get him ready for work?"

I stroked his cheek as Cairo placed me on the passenger seat and buckled me in. "Just how much do you do to keep your father going, baby?"

He said nothing—just removed my hand and went around to his side. And I finally understood what Nora Keller did to him.

Nine years old, she abandoned him to be the only support for his broken, drunken father—crushed under responsibility that grown adults would struggle to carry. And when he naturally had a hard time processing this and the loss of his family, she told him it was his fault and chained her grand mansion gates closed in his face.

Yeah, a mother like that would quickly become "Nora" for me too.

"I'm sorry," I said softly.

I wanted to say more, but if I did, I wouldn't stop. Just imagining the pain that sweet little boy in the picture felt for so much of his life broke me.

"I'm sorry too." His voice scraped from his throat. "Your grandmother. Sounds like she was one of the few decent people left in this town. She deserved better."

I laced my fingers through his. "We'll get her justice, won't we?"

A ghost of a smile crossed his lips. He heard what I truly said.

I forgive you.

"We're barely through the list of possible combos," he said. "I've got nothing for the next several nights. I'll pick you up at midnight."

"It's a date."

JACQUES

I woke before the sun Wednesday morning.

A light sleeper, I heard her moving downstairs a floor up and behind closed doors. Flipping over, I read six a.m. on the clock.

In two hours, her presence was required in front of Bedlam Hall to receive a gift. Behind her back, Cairo, Arsenio, Roan, Legend, and I argued ways to get her out of this and the consequences if we did.

Rainey wasn't willing to risk another murder—especially if the Letter Man set Paris in his sights. We were up for another murder—his.

Minutes after Rainey's call to Cairo about Craig Brown, he was on the phone to us confirming Blake Jensen did exist. Rainey didn't know we were tracking him down ourselves. Monday night, Cairo used our dinner invitation with the boss to ask her about black letters and families with the last name Jensen.

"What is the relevance?" she asked, polite tone clashing against the intensity in her gaze. "Is there a problem I'm unaware of?"

"I'm not sure if it's a problem," he said. "I got a black letter in the mail. There were threats made against me and the guys. I assumed at first it was the Crows, but black letters in the mail seem dramatic even for them."

She smiled, though it didn't reach her eyes. "I'm sure it's nothing. Someone being dramatic as you said. The Bedlam Boys have collected their fair share of enemies. If you receive another, bring it to me. I'll decide if the threat is worth acting on and how to proceed if it is."

"Sure," he said. "Thanks."

"How is the name Jensen related?"

"It's not," I answered. "We're looking into possibilities for the new Dante. This guy is bolder and begging to attract the wrong attention by posting revenge polls. Jensen was the last name of a guy who bought sound equipment from the pawnshop on Third. Owner didn't catch a first."

Her lips twisted. "Dante. A thorn in Bedlam's side for a hundred years, and now it seems the mantle was taken over by a silly boy playing a big man behind the microphone. Find him," she ordered. "I cannot think of a Jensen that fits that description off the top of my head. I'll get back to you."

We hoped she'd have more. Wednesday morning dawned and she hadn't called.

Getting up, I slid pants up my bare ass and left my shirt hanging in the closet. I was going down to meet Rainey. I only needed a belt.

Padding downstairs, I paused in the entrance, watching her chop bananas and toss them in the blender.

No one told her she had to make our breakfast. Honestly, it was a task none of us minded doing, and in respect of more honesty, we didn't mind her cooking for us either. Rainey de Souza took care of everyone around her. Even if they didn't deserve it. Even if they were us.

She looked up healthy meals for me. Ran out to get ice packs. Soothed Cairo when he was pissed. Let her ass be stress relief for Legend. Indulged the darkest side of her for Roan. Crossed the razor-thin tightrope of Arsenio's self-control to meet the man on the other side.

I sensed when Cairo told us the name of Cavendish's killer that she'd be dangerous for us. Both innocent and deadly, she'd feed a brutal side of our souls that needed no more encouragement.

I didn't consider at the time what she'd do to the rest of us.

"Breakfast is almost ready," she called. "I'm making your smoothie and a sweet potato breakfast hash for all of us."

"Is this distraction helping you?"

She froze, then continued on, taking the milk out of the fridge. "It's not hurting."

"Would it also help if I went with you?"

"Thank you, but Legend is going to be there. Who knows what'll provoke him, but I can't carry the cost of him changing his mind and opting for punishment because he figured out I told you all about *our game.*"

"We will find out who he is."

She gave me a worn smile. "I know we will. Gold is looking for Dante. I'm looking for Blake Jensen. One of these paths will lead to him."

"Have you considered what you'll do once you unmask him?"

"I'm throwing him at the cops. Let them put that animal in a cage."

"Well then, I'd better get to him before you."

My words hung in the air.

Rainey dropped her forehead on the blender. "Please, Jacques, just tell me everything's going to be okay."

"I can't do that, Rainey."

"Why not?"

"Because I'll do a lot of things, but I won't lie to you."

She barked a mirthless laugh. "That should upset me. It doesn't. There isn't much point of false hope at a time like this. There's just being smart, and one step ahead."

"The latter is my specialty." I unbuckled my belt. "So is providing distractions. Hands and knees. Face the couch."

The stove shut off with a faint click. Rainey came around the island—clad in a see-through negligee and thong.

It was Cairo's idea to toss out her "farm girl" clothes, and Legend's to upgrade her to slinky dresses and lingerie. Mother once asked why I spent time with boys who weren't as clever as me.

I traced the lace pattern on her breast.

Because they were smarter. Bless Legend for the genius he is.

"No."

My hand stilled between the valley of her breasts. "Excuse me?"

"No," she repeated. Her smirk tugged a frown from me. "I won't get down. If you want me on my knees, you'll have to put me there."

"Five."

She caressed my bare chest. "Go ahead and count me up. What number will you hit before you can't take it anymore? Tell me, Jacques." She whispered my name like profanity—forbidden on her tongue. "How high till you lose control?"

"Six."

Rainey brushed her lips along my jaw, licking the small cleft where it met.

"Seven."

If she noticed the croak in my voice, I couldn't tell. But my cock, nothing was small about it straining against my zipper to do what I wasn't. Touching her, seeking her, begging for her.

Of course I didn't have sex. I had complete control of my mind, habits, food, mannerisms, and even my shits. But I had no control over this.

Rainey palmed me through the lining.

It jumped in her hand as I said, "Eight."

Backing away, she trapped my gaze as she pushed one strap, then the other off her shoulder. We moved in sync—the negligee falling in a pile of lace at her feet, and my belt buckle skimming the floor.

"Get on your knees," I growled.

"You first."

"Nine."

Rainey turned and wiggled out of her thong. Holding on to the kitchen counter, she bent and ground her ass on my erection.

Thwack.

"Ah," she cried out, and ground harder.

Thwack.

Thwack.

Blossoming spots of red spread on her ivory cheeks—the world's naughtiest Rorschach test. What do you see?

The last of my control evaporating into smoke.

She reached between her legs and snaked down my waistband.

I broke.

Lifting Rainey off her feet, I gave the woman her wish—dropping Rainey on all fours on the couch. I held her head down, partially muffling her moans in the cushion. My belt fell, gifting those quivering cheeks two more slaps.

The damned infuriating creature hadn't let up through the whole thing.

She tore my zipper, ripping it down. I grabbed her wrist and the other came at me, freeing my weeping cock from my boxers.

Does she fucking have eight hands?!

Rainey stroked me hard and fast—rough, jerky tugs that about punched me in the gut, doubling me over her.

"Yes," she hissed. "More. Give me more."

"N-nine."

"You already said nine, baby."

"That's how high."

I pulled her hand off, hooked Rainey around the thighs, and pushed inside her with one hard thrust. Then another. Then another.

Then another.

A red mist descended on my vision, focusing the world on a single point in time and space.

Rainey de Souza.

I pumped hard and wild. No discernible rhythm or technique. I wasn't half an inch out before I was plowing back in her again. It wasn't entirely clear if I was trying to fuck her, or merge our bodies into one.

"Yes. Yes. Yes!" she screamed. "Harder, Jacques. Don't hold back. Not with me."

The answer to every and all questions in my life were finally answered. This is what I needed. She was what I'd been searching for.

People were cattle, and all my life I'd been my own brand of beast, unwilling to mingle outside my kind. But now, I found her.

Cairo and Legend trotted into the living room. They cast a curious glance to the end of my four-month no-sex streak, then resumed cooking Rainey's breakfast.

Their presence didn't slow her at all.

She grabbed the couch arm, bracing herself to meet me thrust for thrust.

"Ah, ah," she cried. "I'm going to give you a number… for making me wait so long for this."

I laughed—a half-insane sound that was becoming foreign to me.

She tightened around me. I knew her changes in breath, the shifting flush to her skin, the rising pitch of her cries—and I knew what it all meant. Her orgasm was coming in seconds, not minutes.

I rolled her clit under my thumb and angled my thrust to hit—

"Ah!"

Rainey came screaming into the cushion, clamping down so hard around me, I tensed as the punch-in-gut sensation swept me under.

I exploded inside of her.

The last of my strength went with it, and I dropped in her waiting arms. She stroked my damp locks, dropping kisses on my forehead. I felt her smirk in the print of her lips.

No one could argue Rainey won this round. And possibly the next three coming.

"It's almost seven," Legend said, shattering the reprieve. "You should get dressed and eat something. We want to be there early to scope it out."

My head bobbed on her sigh. "Okay. I'm up." She kissed me again. "You're right. You are excellent at distractions."

She wriggled out to leave and I was two steps behind her. That morning, she was sharing her shower with me.

RAINEY

"You alright, de Souza?"

He wasn't talking about the hitch in my step, courtesy of Jacques.

"I'm scared, Legend."

Together, we passed a couple riding bikes and tossing conversation back and forth. You could almost believe we were as carefree. Legend held me close, rubbing slow circles on my throat, and I relaxed my head on his shoulder—drawing in all the comfort he'd give me.

"I'm scared, and it pisses me off. I hate that he has this power over me," I cried. "With a single note, he can tell me to go here or do that. He can take a perfect morning with Jacques and... Well, I don't know *and*... What am I about to walk into?"

"Whatever it is, you're not walking into it alone."

I tilted up to him. "You can be sweet when you want to."

"I thought I saved that for Roan?"

"Hmm. I must be growing on you."

"Don't know about that," he mused. "I'd put my money on your skills around a blow job."

"We'll see who's right."

Our flirting kept up till we came in sight of Homer Green.

Bedlam Hall dominated the quad. Rising higher than its surrounding buildings, it boasted refinement in its spires, history in the molding, and memories in the famed graduation photos that took place on its steps.

Together we climbed those steps. On the third, we stopped in the midst of student traffic and turned toward the green.

"How much time left?" I wiped damp palms on my skirt.

"Twenty minutes."

Legend's gaze was hard, sweeping the expanse for a sign of... anything.

Students stretched out on the grass eating breakfast, doing homework, catching up with friends. It was another normal morning, barring the ten security guards I counted, then counted again.

"What did Roan tell his mom for her to approve more security?"

"He mentioned Jeremy got his ass handed to him the other night and he's not taking it well. There's already been a car fire and two young women beaten in broad daylight. She approved more security for the entire campus."

"Good."

I lit on a blond guy smoking at the bottom of the steps and bore a hole in his skull. He must've felt it because he looked up, saw me staring, and made faces at me. When he saw I wasn't letting up, he loped off.

I didn't look away till he rounded a corner and was gone.

"I haven't met the dean in person yet. What's Roan's mom like?"

"Distraction?"

"Please."

He answered, though neither of us stopped searching.

"She's everything you'd expect of a woman in power. Tough, doesn't take any shit, but also fair and has a wicked sense of humor."

"I can't forget what Roan said. That even he knew not to test his mom."

"I did mention she doesn't take any shit."

I bit my lip, nerves tingling my skin as I physically felt the seconds counting down.

"Should we have told her the whole story?" I burst out. "Or the police? Secrecy isn't worth it if it gets people hurt."

"Hey." His hand slipped into mind. "The truth can cause just as much damage, Rainey. Trust me."

"In Bedlam there are diamonds."

"I do," I said. "That much I trust."

"Plus, we talked about this. All we have is an old photo and a radio host. We can't point the police at anyone. We can't give them details or a target," he said. "All they would do is exactly what security is doing. Keeping an eye out."

"I know you're right, Legend, but I can't relax." My chest constricted. "Because it's eight o'clock."

Legend and I didn't utter another sound. His only move was to stand closer to me, drawing me in as if shielding me from a coming threat. Legend's speech that night in his bedroom came back to me.

"You did indulge your little fantasy that we were your boyfriends. Well, let me be the one to break it to you, this is all there is. We're not waiting for you at the end of it. There won't be grand confessions of love, or sweet speeches about wanting you all along, and now we can finally be together."

I wrapped my arms around his waist, loosening as he held me tighter. *So that's why you tell lies, St. James. You believe the truth is too dangerous. If only your actions were let in on the deception.*

"Do you see anything?" he asked.

"No. Nothing out of the ordinary."

A minute passed.

Two minutes.

Five.

Ten.

"Was this a trick?" I spun around, searching the faces coming out of the hall. "What's the point of making me stand here?"

Legend gripped my arm. "What if he wants you here so that you're not where you should be?"

Panic choked me. "Legend, the Bedlam House! Are Arsenio and Jacques still there?"

"They don't have classes till after noon. There's no reason they wouldn't be."

"We have to—!"

Something flickered in the corner of my eye. In the split second my brain processed the information, a guy dropped his backpack at the foot of the stairs, scattering notes that flew away with the wind.

Shock bleaching his skin, he clutched the arrow sticking out of his chest.

"Ahh! Ahhh!"

Students screamed—shoving, crying, and running in every direction. But the loudest screams were mine.

Legend carried me away as security rushed in, shouting for all to get inside. He ran with me clear across campus to the Bedlam House.

A black letter lay on the welcome mat.

"HOW LONG HAS THIS BEEN going on?"

"Months," Henry replied.

The investigator squeezed my shoulder and Cairo was there in an instant, drawing me out of his reach and moving me between him and Legend.

His automatic possessiveness would've made me smile if that was something I could still do.

"Do you still have the letters?" asked the detective.

Samuel Ribecco, Henry's friend on the force, was an older, weathered man. Gray hair, furrowed brow, and ingrained weariness in his blue eyes gave the look of a man who'd seen and lived through it all.

Henry was the first call I made after Legend rushed me home. The next morning, the three of us drove to his office in Hunter's Crest where the two of them waited for us.

"Yes," I rasped. "Some of them. Here."

I handed over the ones I had left, including his latest.

Don't say I never give you anything.

Someone had to die for your betrayal, but as a gift to the Bedlam Boys who I'm sure are reading over your shoulder right now, I decided that someone didn't have to be Paris or one of them.

At this point, I'm certain we understand each other and we won't have this problem again.

Love ya. XOXO

Ribecco read with a rapidly worsening expression. "I see," he said. "How is the kid who was hit?"

"Critical condition," Legend said. "Though he meant to kill him, his aim was off. Missed his heart. But it's still bad."

Ribecco pierced me through. "You should've gone to the police straight away."

"You don't know how this goes by now, *detective*?" I glared right back. "I didn't forget to put a trip to the station on my to-do list. He threatened me if I told, then he revealed he has friends feeding him details of a murder investigation. I was trying to stop more people from getting hurt, and I'm here now because I obviously failed. So, are you going to help or just sit around banging on about what I should've done?!"

"Easy, Rainey," Mr. Gold said. "Sam didn't mean anything by it. We all want the same thing here." He gave his friend a pointed look. "This madman behind bars. Sam, the letters are no longer being hand-delivered. He's too smart to walk into a post office, so I say we stake out the mail drop boxes in town. See who shows up with a black letter."

"Not a bad idea," Ribecco said, tucking the letters in his coat pocket. "How often does he send you these letters?"

"Once a week. Maybe more."

He bobbed his head, scratching his stubby beard. "A week. Bedlam's a small town. There won't be many boxes for us to cover. Go easier if you could lend some of that fancy surveillance equipment, Henry."

"It's yours."

"Bedlam is a special case," Ribecco told me. "I am allowed to make arrests in that jurisdiction. Even so, the HCPD usually extends the courtesy of a heads-up before we move in on another sheriff's turf."

"It's too dangerous," I said. "The Letter Man doesn't need to kill any more people to prove he's serious. If he finds out I handed these over to you…" I tossed my head. "I don't want to think about what'll happen. Part of me didn't want to come here, but Mr. Gold said I could trust you."

"You can. Henry and I got it from here," he said. "You go home and get some rest. If another letter shows up, contact me immediately. Before you even open it."

"Okay."

Henry led us out.

"Give us a week." He opened the door to a deceptively beautiful morning in a worry-free town. "One week, and we'll have something for you.

"Good luck, Rainey."

TEN DAYS LATER, MY phone hadn't rung.

I broke down and called Gold on the eighth day. I got an answering machine and a recorded voice promising to call me back. Two days and I was still waiting for that call.

"What if something happened?"

Arsenio's hands were cold on my throat, draping the necklace between my collarbone.

"This silence isn't like him. He's never missed a call before. Plus, he promised an update in a week. What if something happened to him?" I stopped Arsenio from reaching for his tie. "What if the Letter Man found out he was looking for him?"

"There's nothing either one of us can do about that tonight." Arsenio shifted me out of the way of the mirror. He was that young boy in the bow tie and suspenders once again, except this boy was all grown up and devastating in a Burberry suit with his curls gelled into a bun. He looked like he walked off a modeling shoot.

"You and Ellis planned this dinner. Least we can do is show up."

I slumped against his dresser. "I can't focus when all I'm doing is waiting for the other shoe to drop."

"Gold is fine, de Souza."

"You're just saying that."

"I'm not," he sliced in. "The crazy fuck you've been going up against is enjoying all this. The game, the chase, the clues in the Dante broadcast, the letters taunting you. If he discovered Gold was onto him, I guarantee you'd have gotten another letter filled with promises to make you pay for it.

"He's not keeping you in the dark, de Souza. He wants the lights on, so you know there's no chance of escape."

The silence stretched long past comfortable.

"So what does that mean?" I asked. "What's stopping Gold from calling me back?"

"You'll find out when you hear from him."

He tugged me back in front of the mirror. Grabbing my jacket off the bed, he helped me into it, laying the fabric over my curves.

The guys bought me a new dress for the night's festivities. A formal dress with a swooping neckline and conservative hem. It was perfect for the dress code I set, in the town hall banquet room I booked, to meet the guests I put on the list.

Jeremy and Micah were all over me the last week and a half pulling things together for the party. Naturally, Daddy Ellis hired an event planner for the fine details, but the person who had to answer her questions, was me.

"Are you nervous?" I asked as he messed with a stray lock of hair that slipped the bobby pins.

"I don't get nervous."

"So, what's all of this?"

He winked. "Can't a guy fuss over his girl before she meets his mother?"

"Well, now I'm nervous." My smile didn't last long. "Jeremy told me all your parents rsvp'd."

"They're as invested in the future of this town as we all are. Especially the woman governing it."

"Steven Ellis will be there. Some of Foundry's board members too," I said. "This dinner could be a good thing. Get what's happening out in the open. Let Steven Ellis come up with excuses to our faces for why his sons are using such extreme methods to push the vote for Crystal Canyon."

"I'm sure those actions will be introduced as dinner topic in the subtle, backhanded way politicians and businesspeople work." Arsenio stepped back to admire me. "Tonight, I'll stick close to Steven Ellis. We can listen to the Crows bluster all day long, but he's the true power behind this. We'll probe him," he said. "Get him to admit what he truly wants to do to this town."

I cast a glance at the door, imagining I saw through to Cairo getting ready in his bedroom across the hall.

"Do we have a chance of stopping this, Arsenio? The Crows haven't done a great job endearing themselves lately. Jeremy is convinced they can't get anywhere without forcing the Bedlam Boys to leave town, and he's making stupid moves because of it. But I've heard what people are saying."

"What would that be?"

"That Bedlam is stuck in the past and eventually the future is going to leave it behind. People aren't interested in getting in bed with the Crows, but they are on board with changing the way things run around here."

"What you're saying is this little dinner of yours may give Foundry exactly what they want."

"When you put it like that, I get the impression you're pissed I came up with this 'little dinner of mine.'"

He laughed. "I'm not. Honestly, I'm not. Foundry has the forum to defend themselves and their actions tonight, but so does Bedlam. Their claims will be challenged. Their promises will have to come with receipts. All of Bay Avenue and the business owners of Bedlam are coming tonight, yes?"

"Yes."

"They're not a bunch of college students dreaming of smoke shops and a Panera Bread. They carry weight in this community, and they won't be so easily convinced."

"But there's something that might end the war for good," I said. "Stop the collections."

"Excuse me?"

I closed the distance between us. "Think about it. I know you've helped a lot of needy families, but has it been enough? Foundry's already bought up a chunk of property in this town. The thing is he can't do anything with it unless the town splits.

"As long as he's under the power of town hall, he's stuck, so it doesn't matter if he buys up every blade of grass. Year after year, we keep the people on our side and ensure they vote no. They'll happily do so if living here didn't come with a separate tax and violent collectors."

"Hmm." Arsenio pulled me close tying my coat's drawstrings. "Under normal circumstances, this would be a sensible, wise suggestion that'd be rewarded with your pussy on my face. But it's not that simple, Rainey. Keeping as much property out of his hands is our first, second, and third priority. Laws are all well and good, but once he has the land, the 'asking for forgiveness instead of permission' route becomes a lot easier to take under cover of darkness. I know you don't understand this." He pressed a soft kiss on my forehead. "But we've done what is necessary. Just as we will tonight, and every day coming."

My eyes fluttered shut.

I did understand. Thanks to Cairo, I understood all too well. Arsenio was right. If they had the land, they could fence it, block it off, chain it up, and who'd know what they were doing till someone finally busted in. By then, Steven Ellis could make off with exactly what he came here for, and after what was done to Paris, it was my life's mission to ensure he didn't get it—no matter how many dinners they made me plan.

Jacques, Cairo, Legend, and Roan waited at the bottom of the stairs for us. We split into two cars, and not a lot of chatter went on in mine.

Legend and Roan rode up front. Arsenio sat next to me, absentmindedly stroking my nipple through the fabric, just to have my mind well and truly scrambled before we arrived.

In the distance, Bedlam Town Hall rose over the horizon.

Our town hall builder stole his design plans from the same blueprints used for others around the nation.

Columns lifted the triangular roof and its sign bearing our name. Two stories of red brick, a meeting room, offices, and banquet hall for seasonal parties and the rare times VIPs dropped onto our patch of land for a visit. It was the simplest of simple spaces—designed for function, not fancy.

Until Palmer Baskin got her hands on the place.

My mouth fell open when I walked in. Ellis's event planner spared no expense. Each white linen-covered table was topped with oversized wineglasses that spilled flowers over the rim. Curtains were brought in to drape along the walls, cutting scarlet lines through the room. On stage, a string quartet serenaded the arriving who's who of Bedlam and Hunter's Crest.

A warm hand fell on my back. "Would you like to meet the woman who bore me?"

"Yes," I said, turning into Roan's arms. "I want to know if there were any early signs after you were born. A six six six on your scalp or maybe horns sticking out of your curls."

He laughed. "I've progressed from an imp to the devil. Loving the promotion, honey lips."

"Please, don't say anything that'll make me blush in front of your mother."

Roan whispered in my ear. "No promises."

Roan was handsome in everything he wore from a suit to a saddle. That said, he gathered his wicked, devilish aura and channeled its power to become the sexy, tight-suited picture before me.

His untamed locks were battled into submission, and swept back from his eyes—gifting all their full intensity. Roan put something on his lips that enhanced their natural pink. His kiss told me it tasted of cherries.

Roan led me off, strolling slow around the tables. "How many of these faces are familiar?"

"Not many," I admitted. "I recognize Legend's mom and dad over by the stage, and who they're talking to—Nora, Jack Sharpe, and Paris's father. Otherwise, it's just a bunch of faces I'd sometimes see when Gran and I came into town for supplies."

"That's all right because there's one face that's more important than the rest." Roan gestured with his chin, drawing my eye two tables over.

He didn't have to tell me his name. One look, and I saw Jeremy in his eyes and Micah in his long, tended locks. Steven Ellis tossed his head back laughing and his hair flipped, catching candlelight in his strands. Small-framed glasses hung on a nose slightly crooked as if from a break.

Steven spoke to a woman whose black hair pulled tight from her face. She did not laugh with him. Actually, she didn't so much as smile, though he was having the time of his life talking to her. She just nodded along, delicately sipping her champagne and looking refined in an empire-waist dress.

"Eileen Stone," Roan said.

"Jacques's mom?"

"Yep. I know what you're thinking, and I've had the same fantasy."

"You do *not* know what I'm thinking, because it most definitely wasn't that I'd like to sleep with my boyfriend's mom."

"Your boyfriend, is he? Damn. Guy has sex with you once and enters into a commitment."

I bumped his shoulder. "Imagine what that means for you."

"There's a storage room at the end of the hall. More than enough room."

Checking to make sure no one was looking, I scraped his lobe between my teeth, biting down. "We can't now," I murmured. "I want to, but I got us into this mess. I can't abandon the guys in it."

"Mother."

I straightened, turning fast to greet the slim, red-haired beauty making her way over to us.

"Darling." She kissed Roan's cheek, and in typical mom move, fussed with his hair. "How are you, dear? You're so close, but you never come to see your mother."

"Don't worry. This bird isn't destined to leave the nest."

Her eyes danced. "Does it make me a bad mom to be the tiniest bit relieved?"

Paris's comment about a mother's blind spot came back to me. There was an entire town who'd like to see my devil love leave the nest. One of them tried to help him along via knife. But Josephine Banks didn't see any of that looking at him.

"Introduce me, Roan."

"Rainey, my carrier. Carrier, this is Rainey."

My dean shook her head, smile playing on her lips. "What happened to the days he called me mommy? Nice to meet you, dear." We shook hands. "Do you go to Bedlam U?"

"Transferred in at the start of the semester."

"What do you think so far?"

"I love it," I said honestly. "I love the library and butterscotch muffins. I love my lectures and having actual classmates. I love sitting out on Homer Green with Paris and an iced latte. That's why these last few weeks... All the stuff that's happened..." I dropped my gaze. "I don't want the bad to be what I remember when I look back on these years."

Dean Banks was gentle pulling me in for a hug. "I don't want that for any of you. It does seem it's been one disaster after another since Ruckus Royale."

An odd note in her tone made me look up.

Josephine was fixed on something over my head. I turned and landed on Jeremy and Micah Ellis—decked out in their finest. They chatted with a couple of the other Crows, knocking back drinks and laughing about a funny thing Gael said.

Jeremy caught me looking and winked.

"But I never imagined there'd be an attempted murder on my campus. From a kidnapping to a brawl, and now poor Mr. Binari, struck down by an unknown assailant while walking into administration," she said. "It was suggested I close the school for the rest of the semester. Though I'm tempted, I can't do it."

"Why, may I ask?"

Josephine leveled a serious look. "We have students from all fifty states, the territories, and other countries. If the owner of that arrow is a student, the last thing they should be given is permission to pack up and fly out of reach. Colton Binari will have justice."

"He will. I can promise you he will."

"I believe this is the right decision, but I can't shake the feeling I should be doing more."

"I noticed there's more security patrolling. Also, you allowed midterms to be pushed to next week. A lot of students are scared and can't focus right now, and we can all see you care about that, Dean Banks."

She squeezed my forearm. "Please, Rainey. Call me Josephine off campus. Which is the last thing I'll say about myself. Tell me about you. Are you and Roan dating?"

"We..." I trailed off, glancing at him for help. How much did his mother know about Legend and their habit of adding a third to the relationship?

"We are," Roan said clearly. "Legend and I fell for her instantly. Like the strike of a match."

"Oh, how sweet," she crooned. "And did you say this was your first time having classmates?"

The three of us talked while the room filled to bursting. It seemed everyone rsvp'd to this dinner.

"Josephine," I began. "What are your thoughts on the town splitting?"

"Ridiculous." She bat the question out of the air. "It's completely ludicrous and not a thought I entertained for a millisecond. We were chanting Bedlam forever since I was in diapers. It'll be our chant long after I'm gone."

She waved over my head.

"Eileen is calling me over," Josephine announced. "You two, enjoy your dinner.

"Bub." She smooched Roan's cheek. "Don't leave without saying goodbye."

He saluted her off.

"She's great," I said. "So sweet and sincere."

Everyone was beginning to find their seats. I assumed the Bedlam Boys would sit together and me with them, but Legend was at a table with his parents. Cairo sat beside his father at a table near the front, which killed the thought I'd be eating with him. While Arsenio and Bedlam's mayor claimed a table with Judge Stone, Jacques, Steven Ellis, and his boys.

The only people smiling at that table were Steven Ellis and Mayor Creed.

"Shall we?" Roan pulled out a chair at an empty table.

I sat, indulging this time alone with him.

"I know what you're asking yourself," he said, dropping next to me. "How did that sweet, sincere woman pop out a guy like him?"

"I wasn't asking myself that. Goodness, you're doing a terrible job reading my mind tonight." I laced our fingers under the table. "The show people put on outside isn't the same one playing behind closed doors.

"Gran was tough as nails—barking at farmhands, getting in the faces of cheats trying to overcharge us on repairs and equipment. But when it was just the three of us, she was the calmest, most patient person you ever met. Only raised her voice to tell Ivy to turn the music down.

"I don't know what made you the man you are today, Roan. All I know is I want to ride that man and be the bread to his threesome sandwich."

"Not tonight, gorgeous." He spoke as an elderly couple joined our table. "Tonight we're spit-roasting you till we pass out."

I crossed and uncrossed my legs, fighting to ignore the pressure building at the mere thought of what Legend and Roan were going to do to me.

"Everyone, may I have your attention?"

A deep, silvery voice echoed out of the speakers.

Steven Ellis found his way to the stage. His smile swept over us, reminding me of the disarming grin on Jeremy's lips when he apologized for hurting me. Again.

"I want to thank everyone for coming out tonight," he began. "I'll have you know this dinner wasn't my idea."

Panic climbed my veins.

"It was my sons who suggested to me and my fellow board members that we come out, meet the good people of Bedlam, and discuss your concerns and hopes as Foundry becomes a partner with your town. All the shop talk comes later, I promise." He paused for polite laughter. "Until then, please eat and enjoy."

The servers—hired by Palmer—brought out the first course. I murmured thank you as he set down a bowl of chilled avocado and prawn soup. I tried a sip, and moaned.

"Dammit, even her menu is delicious. Something about this night has to go wrong."

Roan brushed his lips on my cheek. "Don't worry about tonight, Steven Ellis, or the Crows. More ruthless than them have regretted underestimating Bedlam."

We worked our way through the rest of the meal. Roast chicken, potatoes, and carrots. For dessert, my new best friend, Server Brooks, brought out chocolate clementine tarts. I asked him to marry me and he laughed till Roan told him to fuck off.

"So, the possessive streak is one you all share," I said.

"Thought you knew that by now, babe."

Steven Ellis cleared his throat into the speaker, bringing an end to the scattered conversations.

"Once again, good evening," he said. "Now seems like a good time to give my spiel. While you're all still smiling from the delicious food.

"My intention is for tonight to be a discussion— No, a conversation. We're here to get to know you, and for you to meet our Foundry family. To start off, let me share our vision of Bedlam with you."

Ellis launched into a fairy tale of shopping centers, affordable housing, more daycares, entertainment, and a new student bar that'll funnel its proceeds toward improving security around campus.

I stifled a snort. *That's rich seeing as your spawn is one of the biggest threats to security.*

"But that's enough of me," he said with a laugh. "I'm going to walk around, the music will play, and feel free to talk to me, or my partners with your ideas of how we can grow together. Thank you."

Applause followed him to his seat—louder than I'd like.

The guests got up to continue their mingling. Most of them circled Steven Ellis, waiting for their chance to speak to him. Arsenio caught my eye and gestured for me to join them.

"Excuse me." I kissed Roan, then drifted over to Arsenio, Jacques, their mothers, Steven, and his sons. They formed a little semicircle that allowed some to come in and out, but neither of them went far.

"Good evening." Steven kissed the back of my hand. "It's great to have you here, Miss...?"

"De Souza," I finished.

"Miss De Souza, lovely to meet you. I'm especially interested in your thoughts about the future of Bedlam, because you are the future of Bedlam."

Does this guy always talk like he's running a political campaign?

"Where would you like to see your town in ten years?"

Marjorie's and Eileen's eyes were on me. Did they know about my relationship with their sons? And was I about to torpedo their first impression of me?

"To be honest, I lived most of my life on the outskirts of Bedlam," I said. "I grew up on a farm with my grandmother and older sister. Living the way I had—working together, seeing my efforts take root, learning to care for other creatures better than myself. It's shaped what I want for the future, and that I want it to be more like the past."

Ellis's grin twitched. "How so?"

"Gran would tell me of the parades they'd throw when she was a girl. People from every corner of the town came out to celebrate. On Thanksgiving, her family and the neighboring families set up a table that stretched across the field, they'd fill it up with food, and everyone was welcome to join.

"They stopped doing all of that by the time Ivy and I were old enough to miss it. Maybe we grew up more isolated than we had to be because we lost our Bedlam family, and became another family of three."

Heat crawled up my neck. Couldn't remember the last time I was stared at for this long.

"This is my long-winded way of saying that what always made Bedlam great is how we band together when times are tough. We're family," I stated. "As long as we don't lose that, Bedlam has a bright future."

Steven, Mayor Creed, Arsenio, and Judge Stone clapped.

"Well said, Miss de Souza." Steven shook my hand enthusiastically.

Glad you liked it, asshole. Just for you, a non-answer saying a whole lot, but not really committing to anything at all.

"The future you dream of is the future we see. Many small towns are losing that small-town feel. No one knows each other anymore. They don't talk to their neighbors. They're not gathering to celebrate together or one another. In the town we're building, your family will be bigger than three."

Brooks came over holding a tray of champagne. We each took one—Judge Stone the last to step forward and claim hers.

"I was also moved by what you said, Miss de Souza."

I don't know what I expected of Jacques's mom, but the low, smoky voice of a smooth jazz radio host wasn't it. Neither was the smile as she patted my shoulder.

"I remember those days too. My father would put me on his shoulders during the Westchester parade, and I'd collect so many balloons as we danced through the streets, I thought we'd float away."

She stroked Jacques's cheek. "I want that same sense of family and community for my son and his children. I don't deny that we've lost a bit of it over the years, but I have to ask, Mr. Ellis—"

Eileen turned the stern, joyless gaze of countless life sentences and more to come on the smiling man.

"How does tearing our home in two, razing all that makes it unique and charming, then filling it with yuppie newlyweds checking off their bucket list *buy vacation home where the locals say y'all*, help us get back to the family we used to be?"

She sipped her champagne, waiting for the answer.

All eyes turned on him.

"That's a great question," Steven said, refusing to lose that smile. "And I believe my son, Jeremy, is the best person to answer. Jeremy, you've lived here for months. What's your perspective?"

"It's like this, Judge Stone."

Jeremy was slick all over from the gelled hair, shiny shoes, and shit-eating grin. An incredible feat seeing as his arm was still in a sling, and his bruises were healing.

"I go to school with Rainey and the other students planning to leave this town two minutes after they graduate. They're only stopping to kiss Mom and Dad goodbye on the way. The fact is Bedlam can't get where it wants to be because the way it is now is driving people away. Rainey."

I started at being addressed.

"You said you have a sister," Jeremy said. "Where is she now?"

My teeth ground, sensing where this was going.

"She lives in Chicago."

Jeremy held out his hands like that proved everything.

"See? Families are breaking up and people moving out, because Bedlam celebrates all the wrong things of its past, and ignores the good. There are no more balloon and dancing parades, but Ruckus Royale is held every year. I can't buy coffee from national chains, but I can get beaten up and dumped in the woods because I'm the new guy."

I stopped myself kissing my teeth. This guy can twist history to suit himself better than anyone I've ever seen.

Arsenio tucked me under his arm. I felt him headed for my nipple and quickly held his fingers, lacing them through as he chuckled under his breath.

I thought Roan was the one I had to look out for.

"Bedlam needs to be shaken up. Foundry is going to tear down, but then it'll rebuild in her vision," he said, gesturing to me. "A safe, modern town where everyone in it is family."

Steven threw an arm around his son. "I could not have said it better."

Eileen's expression didn't let up. "Jeremy, I'm truly sorry to hear you've experienced violence in this town." She coughed, cleared her throat, and continued. "If you can identify your attackers, I encourage you to step forward. We don't tolerate b-bullying in any f-form."

Jacques grinned at Jeremy over her shoulder. His smile tightened.

"I'm fine, but what I went through is what a lot of students are going through," he said. "Intimidation and bullying. In the new town, everyone will feel safe."

"You speak as though... it's a forgone conclusion—" Eileen burst into a coughing fit.

"Excuse me," she wheezed. "Sorry, I just—"

"Mother?" Jacques held her shoulders as she bent over. "What's wrong?"

"I— I can't—"

Her champagne glass slipped through her fingers. Eileen followed its path.

"Mom!"

Jacques caught her before she hit the floor.

"Rainey, call Doctor Nash!"

"Oh no. Are you okay, Judge Stone?" Jeremy asked.

Her chest heaved, breaths laboring as she struggled for each one.

"Let me help—" The Crow grasped her arm.

"Don't fucking touch her, you son of a bitch!" Jacques flew at him, punching Jeremy across the face. "You did this!"

"Hey!"

Micah, Steven, Arsenio, Mayor Creed, and three townspeople pried them apart.

"You'll regret this!"

My insides curdled under the rage and loathing Jacques spewed at the Ellises. I'd never seen him, or anyone, like this.

"If anything happens to her, I swear you'll find out how we got our name!"

"Hello?" The doctor sounded in my ear.

Suddenly Cairo was there. He took the phone from me. "Jacques, enough! It'll be quicker if we take her to him. Get her in my truck. Now!"

The two ran out with Eileen, friends and the guys' families on their tail.

"Oh, dear. I hope she's okay." Steven clicked his tongue, his arms slung around Jeremy and Micah. Jeremy cracked his jaw but otherwise would live.

"But this is the sort of thing we're talking about," Steven said to his growing audience. "Violence, menacing, accusations. My son tried to offer a hand, and that boy punched and threatened him. If I'm not mistaken, he's the same boy who's a part of the group that has so many of us concerned. I can assure you in the new Crystal Canyon, no one will fear their neighbor. All are welcome. All are safe."

I drifted to Jeremy, meeting his eyes.

He winked.

I turned and walked out.

I'd catch a ride to the doc's. I'd walk if I had to. All I knew was I wouldn't spend another second in a Crow's presence, and the next time I saw one, it'd be me they'd have to drag off.

Chapter Eight

I put my hand on Jacques's shoulder, gently shaking him. He accepted the water I held out, downing it in one go. His head fell back in his hands.

He and I were in Doc's waiting room. It pushed two in the morning.

Jacques sent the other guys home an hour ago, but I refused to leave. No one should sit alone in the dark waiting to hear if someone they loved was alive. I knew that better than anyone.

"It was Ellis," he rasped. The first sentence Jacques spoke since I arrived. "Wasn't it?"

"Judging by the wink he tossed me on the way out the door, that's a safe bet."

His fists balled.

"But how?" I asked. "She was fine and then all of a sudden—"

"She went into anaphylactic shock." Doc Nash came out of the exam room. "Very severe. You did well to get her here in time."

Doc Nash was a pleasant man with a wide smile and bushy eyebrows that he wriggled to make his young patients laugh.

I looked away.

All I saw in Doc Nash was the man who witnessed me at my lowest.

"Any idea how this happened?" he asked Jacques.

"We were having dinner in the hall."

"Ah, yes. I received the invitation to that as well. What did you have to eat? As you know, your mother is allergic to sesame seeds. Could she have ingested...?"

He trailed off as Jacques roughly shook his head.

"Nothing we ate had sesame seeds. Mother even had the server check with the chef to be sure. She was talking to Jeremy Ellis and his father, drinking champagne, when she collapsed."

"What kind of champagne? Was there anything in it?"

"It was ordinary champagne from what I tasted," I spoke up. "And we each grabbed our own from the tray."

Jacques shoved off the seat. "Is she going to be okay?"

"She'll be fine," Nash said. "I gave her something to temper the reaction and help with her breathing. She's sleeping now. Would you like to stay?"

He motioned toward the hall. "I keep pillows and blankets in the closet. You're welcome to sleep on the couch. Just you, Jacques. Rainey, I'll drive you home."

I tensed.

"I'll drive her home," Jacques said, "and come back. Leave the key under the mat for me."

"Giving it to you works just as well."

Doc Nash tossed over his entire key ring. He truly was a nice guy, even if I could hardly remember our time as doctor/patient.

"Let's go," Jacques said.

I didn't speak till we were in Cairo's truck. He left it for us to ride back.

"What are you going to do?" I whispered.

"Nothing."

I blinked. *I couldn't have heard that right.*

"Nothing? The Crows did it, Jacques. I don't know how but I'm sure of it. To make it worse, Steven used your explosion as further proof Bedlam is lost to a bad element, and the town needs to break off and start new. They both punished and used you, and worst of all, it worked. They won more support tonight, Jacques. I saw it."

"All of this I know, de Souza."

"Then, why won't you do anything?"

"Else," he hissed. "I won't do anything else. Even though I'd like to drive this truck through the gates, and mow down every Crow that comes running, they haven't done it yet."

"Done what?"

"Committed the act that turns all of Bedlam against Foundry for good. No chance of winning back favor. No forgiveness to be bought with overpriced dinners."

His death grip on the wheel eased. Jacques leaned back in the seat, calm smoothing out his features. He was stone in name and personality once again.

"We almost had him after he hurt you and Paris, but the slippery bastard got away courtesy of the Letter Man, as you call him."

"I still don't understand that. He said he can't allow the Crows to leave Bedlam yet. Why if he was so pissed at them for beating me?"

"We can't understand his motives. All we know is the result gave the Crows a chance to get away and spread the lie we arranged the beating and then Riot Royale to get rid of them. They were innocent the entire time. Me punching him in the middle of *helping* my mother added to the victim image."

"That wasn't your fault. Anyone would've punched that smirk in."

Jacques didn't seem to hear me.

"They haven't done it yet, Rainey, but I will. I'll push them the final leg, cutting the Crows out of Bedlam for good. We're not waiting anymore."

I laid my hand over his. "Just tell me what you need me to do."

"MOM AND I VISITED EILEEN yesterday," Paris said.

It had become routine for us to walk with each other to and from classes. Neither one of us wanted to be caught out alone with Legend and Roan still on the Crows' hit list, and them showing no signs of stopping.

"How is she doing?"

"Rattled. She knows someone must've slipped her something, but she can't think how or when."

"Not someone."

We shared a look.

"Judge Stone is used to people threatening her life. She's not used to them nearly succeeding, or smiling at her as she goes down."

"This whole thing has gotten way out of control. None of this makes sense anymore." I snorted. "What am I saying? It didn't make sense at any point. No one asked Foundry or the Crows to come in and fuck with our town. They're playing our saviors while they escalate the violence."

"It's not going to work, Rainey. Deep down, people see who they really are."

We kissed cheeks outside Lecture Hall Three.

"Good luck," I said. "Kick that Modern Ideologies midterm's ass."

"It's going to be *kissing* my ass. I'm not walking out of here with less than an A." She waved, heading in with the other students. "Good luck with Bankruptcy."

"Thanks."

I left the poli-sci building and passed the quad heading for mine.

Nelson was in his usual seat one down from mine when I rolled in with the other sleep-deprived, coffee-hungover law students trying to survive the next hurdle into law school.

"Hey, Rainey."

"Sup, Nelson. Ready?"

He blew out a breath. "Ready as I'll ever be. You?"

"It's been a rough semester. I heard this morning that Colton's still touch and go. Hard to cram facts about bankruptcy laws in your head when it's already stuffed."

"Sucks for sure. I knew Colton, he's a nice guy. But a bad one still doesn't deserve that."

No one deserves the Letter Man, and despite what I may or may not have done to the person buried in Black Widow Hill, I don't deserve it either.

No drug would've made me hurt an innocent person. The only time in my life I harmed someone human or animal, was when they killed my grandmother.

I wasn't saying I shouldn't be punished if the truth came out that it was me who killed that person. But it was *me* who should be punished. Bella and Colton didn't hurt a soul, and whatever vengeance the Letter Man was enacting, I'd see to it that the one who faced the punishment, was him.

"Morning, students." Professor Stein strolled inside, carrying his briefcase. He held it up as he faced us. "Before we begin, I have a simple and straightforward message to anyone who bought a copy of this midterm—"

Nelson's head shot up.

"How dare you," Stein snapped. "How dare you betray this institution, your integrity, and yourself. The investigation into who bought these tests is ongoing, and when you're found, you can expect your expulsion to follow. As for this morning, I have in this case a new test that hasn't been seen by anyone—including my teaching assistant.

"You have an hour and a half to complete it. Turn it in and leave when you're done."

He opened the briefcase, handed half the tests to the TA, and began giving them out—giving each person a disappointed glare as he passed.

It had never been so quiet during an exam.

No one so much as coughed.

Afterward, I handed in my test and went out to the arboretum to hang out till my next exam. We got the same speech and modified test paper in Land Transfer.

It was official. The cheating ring was exposed before it could do a single one of the buyers any good. I hoped for their sakes they attempted to cram some studying in between whipping out their credit cards. Going by Nelson covering his sobs beside me, I'd guess not.

I dotted my last period. Gathering my things, I carried my test to the professor, catching him mid-conversation with a security guard.

"This is her," she said. "Rainey, you need to go with Mr. Reynolds. The dean would like to see you."

"Me? Why?"

"She'll explain," said Reynolds. He swept out his hand for me to go ahead of him.

I contemplated arguing and decided against it. I'd find out what was going on soon enough.

I trailed the guard outside and across campus to the administration building.

This was the quietest part of campus excluding the library. A broad staircase took us away from the hall of closed doors, all leading to a different office, and none of them letting a sound through.

At the top, Reynolds gestured for me to continue ahead. The dean's office loomed at the end of the hall. I went inside—

"That's a lie!"

Jeremy's shout blew me back out. Dean Banks didn't flinch.

"Mr. Ellis, I have told you for the last time to stop shouting and take your seat." She flicked over his shoulder. "Rainey is here. Let's hope she can clear this matter up."

He spun on me. "Rainey, thank fuck. Get over here and back me up."

I came into the room slowly, gazing around the grand space like something might pop out from behind the fern, or the wall of bookshelves would open up.

"You wanted to see me, Dean Banks?"

"Yes. Please, sit down."

I claimed the chair next to Jeremy, darting between both of them for a clue to why I was here.

Dean Banks folded her hands atop a stack of folders.

"Rainey, as I'm sure you've heard by now, the school suffered a massive security breach and the midterms exams for multiple classes were stolen and sold. We had no idea this happened until the thief attempted to do it again. They tried to get into the room where we hold copies of the test, not knowing we went through a massive system overhaul after we discovered the arrow that almost killed Colton Binari was shot from the roof."

"The roof?" I repeated, leaning in.

"Yes. Roof access is restricted to those with a code. Of course, I trust my staff completely, so the only explanation is an outsider got their hands on it. Hence why all were changed and the system upgraded."

"Okay," I drew out. "Then, why am I here?"

"Because while I don't suspect Mr. Ellis of sneaking onto the roof with a bow and arrow, I do have reason to believe he and his friends stole and sold the midterms."

"We didn't do it!" Jeremy was up and out of his seat again. "How many times do I have to tell you we didn't even know this shit was going on?"

"We reviewed the security cameras and noted multiple instances of a person with a Crow tattoo on their neck giving a red card to students. We questioned one such student and got them to hand it over. When I called the number on the card, they asked for my email and PayPal address. An hour later I had the answer key to the Chemistry II midterm."

"We had nothing to do with it," Jeremy gritted.

"My security team tracked down the number and it comes up as registered to a Jeremy Ellis."

"Someone bought a phone in my name. That's not proof."

"We've also identified there were six people of differing heights and builds handing out red cards," the dean plowed on. "They were careful not to look directly into a camera, but dear me, six people on this campus refer to themselves as Crows and have such a tattoo on their neck. Can you name them for me?"

I almost whistled. *Damn, this lady does not play.*

"I don't give a shit what was on their necks. Anyone can slap on a crow sticker and hand out cards, but this time I can tell you exactly who they were. Your precious boy and his buddies. And Rainey can back me up." He bent over me. "Tell her who really stole those tests."

"Excuse me?"

Dean Banks took something out of her desk. "This is the clearest photo of the person who broke into administration. Mr. Ellis believes you can identify them."

She held up a photo of a broad figure, half a face, and a baseball cap pulled low. A blur of black ink covered his neck. The resemblance struck me immediately.

"See," Jeremy cried out. "She knows it's him. Rainey, tell her that's Stone. The Bedlam Boys set us up!"

"I—"

"That's him. You know that's him."

"But I—"

"Tell her!"

"He doesn't have a beard," I shrieked, shoving the guy out of my face. "Yes, he looks like Jacques, but I've eaten breakfast across the guy every day for the last two months and I've yet to see his chin. This dude is as smooth as a baby's butt."

"That," Josephine said slowly, "is what I said. This man is clean-shaven. Jacques Stone, who I also see regularly, is not. Want to know who does look very much like this man in the photo? Gael Stoll."

"And you want to know who looks very much like Gael Stoll," Jeremy mimicked. "Jacques Stone. Come on, he shaved! Obviously. That guy isn't the well-behaved Poindexter he's got everyone believing. He pops pills to keep those grades. I don't put stealing tests past him. The Bedlam Boys printed up a bunch of red cards and posed as us. They've been coming after us since we got into this town. Now they're trying to get us expelled.

"I'm not lying down this time, Dean. The Bedlam Boys have gone too far." Spittle showered her desk. "Stealing and selling tests on our record? Expulsion? No other university will accept us. We'll be lucky to get into a trade school. This'll ruin our lives."

"You should've thought of that before."

"Before what? Before nothing. We didn't steal those tests. Jacques shaved!"

"Do you have proof Jacques or anyone else is involved?"

"Rainey." Jeremy bore into me. "You live with them. Tell her they set us up. They had it in for us since the start."

I opened my mouth.

"Do not say a word, Miss de Souza." She rose from her seat. "Mr. Ellis, I will not have you put accusations in this young woman's mouth. The number is registered to you. The men in this photo have tattoos matching yours. I've found my culprits."

"What is this? Why did you call her up here if you already made up your mind?" His eyes narrowed to slits. "Oh, I see."

"See what exactly?"

"You're with them. You know we didn't do this," he said, jabbing a finger at her. "You and the Bedlam Boys set us up. Roan trumps up an offense, and you have all the excuse you need to expel us. You and that spawn of yours do this often? How many other innocent people have you expelled?"

Shaking my head, I pinched the bridge of my nose. *Oh, Jeremy. You do not help yourself.*

"I beg your pardon." Josephine's voice was a low, dangerous hiss. "I will not have my integrity questioned. No one is targeting you, Mr. Ellis. You are here because the facts lead to you."

"Just like you planned it, bitch."

"Jeremy," I cried. "Stop."

"You first," he said to Josephine. "Toss out your fake evidence, apologize, and let me get back to my test. If you do, I won't have to fly in a team of fifty New York lawyers to sue your ass for everything I can think of."

Face unreadable, Josephine took her purse out of the desk and pulled out a business card. She held it out to him. "A hotel suggestion for those fifty New York lawyers. The Magnolia has a great continental breakfast."

I was so very far from the door, or I'd have snuck out a long time ago.

"Mr. Ellis, you are expelled from Bedlam University. Security will escort you from the grounds."

"Fuck this!"

Jeremy slammed out of the office. The peaceful admission building woke up to his shouts and rants going straight down the hall.

Josephine and I looked at each other as his noise faded.

"Is there something you want to tell me, Rainey?"

"I don't know anything about this," I said honestly. "I don't mess around with cheaters. You cut corners on a farm, and you're begging to lose a limb or your livestock."

She sighed, easing onto her seat. "If only everyone felt that way. This is the first time I can recall being disappointed in my students. Mr. Ellis should not have been expelled, because no one should've taken him up on his goods."

"What's going to happen to the rest of them?"

"Expulsion. There'll be no more Crows at Bedlam University."

JEREMY GRABBED ME COMING out of the building.

"You did nothing in there!"

I grabbed his wrist, stumbling back as his hold on my neck forced me against the wall.

"She expelled us! Expelled!"

I was calm—face neutral in his burning glare. "Let me go."

"You are on their side! You—"

"You're a fucking idiot," I snapped. "You called me up to convince the guy's second mom that some beardless dude in a baseball cap was him. Genius. Her son's best friend. The son of *her* close friend, Judge Stone. She wasn't going to believe that was Jacques without a hell of a lot more evidence.

"After you stormed out, I tried to sell her on you having enemies all over the school and any of them could've framed you, because the Crows wouldn't do this. Unsurprisingly, she couldn't hear me over you calling her a bitch."

A dozen emotions warred on his face.

"If she and Roan were in this together, did you really think shouting in her face was going to appeal to her? Like you said, her mind was made up. There was nothing either one of us could've said.

"You've got a real problem with your temper, Jeremy, and you need to get a handle on it. You swing from smart to stupid too fast."

He growled, tightening on my neck.

"Like right now," I forced. "I'm the only ally you have, and I might've cozied up to the Bedlam Boys, got them to say on a recording that they forced the Crows out and how. Proof it was them would've gotten you a lot farther than pissing that woman off. But I don't think I will now, because *your hand is still on my throat.*"

Jeremy released me.

"Do it."

"Why should I?"

He balled his fists, looking like he wanted nothing more than to strangle me again. Proving that he did possess a sliver of self-control, Jeremy shook out his hands and sucked in a deep breath.

"Rainey. Sweet, beautiful Rainey," he mocked. "I apologize for putting my hands on you. I'm a little heated from, you know, getting framed, expelled, and watching my future go down in flames all in one afternoon. I thank you that in your all-knowing wisdom, you have once again given me great advice. The Bedlam Boys will admit for the world to see that they're responsible."

"I can try to record—"

"No," he said. "I've got it from here."

His smile curdled my blood.

"Jeremy, what are you going to do?"

"Nothing stupid. It's past time the Crows and Bedlam Boys talked this out. Settled it like gentlemen. And if I record them saying they're responsible for the stolen midterms, even better."

Two security guards came out and put their hands on Jeremy.

"Time to go, son."

"Don't look so worried," Jeremy called over his shoulder, that smirk hanging on his mouth. "Everything's going to be fine. The crows are always the last one standing on the battlefield."

"YOU HAVE TO BE CAREFUL."

I snuggled between Roan and Jacques, tracing patterns on Legend's chest with Roan molded to my back.

"You're the last two he hasn't gotten to yet, and he's said more than once he's got worse in store for you, Roan."

"I don't doubt that he does," Roan said.

"You're not worried?"

"They've been going after family. My dad took off when I was six. If I can't find him, they sure as hell won't. That leaves Josephine. Even if they get through her security, they'll be the top suspects as the guys she just expelled. Their asses would end up in jail, and that would hardly prove their innocence. There's no upside, Rainey. That route to revenge will not leave them satisfied."

"Your mom isn't the only person you care about," I reminded.

"You mean me," Legend said. "Yeah, most likely the Crows are coming for me."

"Do you have to say that so casually?"

He laughed. "I'm no easy target, Rainey. They can try, and I know they will, but they're not getting me anywhere alone. A head-on assault's not going to work either. I can afford twice as many lawyers as Daddy Ellis. Lawyers who'll see to it that every charge from emotional distress to attempted murder sticks if they so much as spit on my shoe. If I'm honest, I've been waiting for them to try.

"That's the last straw, Rainey. The mistake they can't come back from. Going up against me," he said. "It'll be the last thing they do."

I rested my head on his chest. "As hot as you are right now, you're not reassuring me. You didn't see the look on Jeremy's face as he was led away. The only word that comes to mind is unhinged."

"Course he is. Jacques just pulled a trigger on the long con that booted his ass from Bedlam University. I wonder if Foundry hires losers expelled for cheating."

I shot up. "So it was Jacques. Was that him in the photo coming out of administration?"

"Nah." Grinning, Roan pushed himself up on his elbows. "The guy is good but not even he can make his beard grow back that fast. Lookalikes, honey lips. Jacques and I hit up HC's talent agency saying we were testing the school's security and laying a trap for a cheating ring working out of the school.

"Found six guys with a striking resemblance to Jeremy, Micah, Gael, Bentley, Asher, and Zeke. Then, we told them we had to draw a crow on their necks, so we could tell who was actor, and who were the real thieves. Five hundred bucks each just to walk around handing out cards, we had more volunteers than we knew what to do with.

"The guy we hired for Stoll was a great double. But Stoll also happens to look like Jacques without the beard. Yeah, the Crows are right to pin this on us, but they're not going to get anywhere picking people out of photographs or chasing after the test-buyers to say who they got it from. They're done."

"Wow, that's—that's nicely done," I said. "Except like you said, they're pinning this on you. I'm going to be very upset with both of you if you're caught and hurt by the Crows. You better be careful."

"Oh?" Roan trailed his finger between my breasts. "What happens when you're upset with us?"

"My blow jobs decrease in frequency and creativity. Your sexual frustration increases."

"Damn. What do we think of that, Legend?"

"Can't have it, Roan. Guess we better watch our backs."

Roan hummed. "I'll start with watching my front. Let's get a taste of what we'll be missing out on."

Legend positioned himself behind me so he could get a taste of something else.

I shivered as he brought out the paddles. Palming Roan's cock, I raised my ass up high.

THE NEXT FEW DAYS BLURRING into a week, passed without incident.

Word spread on the Crows' expulsion. The whispers mostly agreed that they deserved the sentence, but were split on who did it. Did they steal and sell the midterms, or were they framed by the Bedlam Boys? Obviously, the people who actually bought the tests from the lookalikes, weren't coming forward to admit anything and get handed their own expulsion.

I wanted to stick to Legend like glue. Conflicting schedules and his repeated assurances no one was going to touch him, made that difficult.

Jacques and I were in the kitchen making breakfast Friday morning, when his phone rang.

He paused in chopping up bananas and stuck the cell in the crook of his neck.

"Hello? Yes, Ellis."

My chopping ceased too.

"Don't know what you're talking about," Jacques said. "I'm sorry to hear that."

I moved closer, straining to make sense of the murmurs on the other end.

"That's not going to happen. No," Jacques replied, tone even. "This has nothing to do with fearing you—a laughable concept—and everything to do with distrusting you. If we meet you out at Westchester Drumlins, logic suggests it'll be a trap."

I tossed my head, mouthing no though Jacques refused. That was a trap up, down, and sideways. No matter what Jeremy said, the last thing he wanted to do was talk things out like gentlemen. A guy who manhandled me on every explosion of his short fuse, did not know the meaning of the word.

"The Roadhouse," Jacques said. "Why should we? What's in it for us?"

He paused to listen.

"Ridiculous. We never took your little threats and pranks seriously. Why would we care if you stop? As far as the Bedlam Boys are concerned, you haven't started."

A bold claim.

The Crows beat up me and Cairo's sister. Set the last memory of Arsenio's father up in flames. Poisoned and nearly killed Judge Stone, and Jacques yawns and says "What else you got?"

Why was I the only one who did not want to find out?

"I see. Interesting. We'll be there."

He hung up.

"Well?" I asked. "What did he say?"

Jacques resumed making his smoothie. "Ellis and his Crows want to meet us at the Roadhouse this afternoon. In exchange for helping them reverse the expulsion, they'll transfer to another university and leave Bedlam for good."

"Help them how? They can't think you're about to go to the dean and tell her you hired actors to set them up."

"He said something about convincing our girl to be Stoll's alibi for the time someone broke into administration. He wants you there too."

"Will you go?"

"I see no reason why not."

"This could still be a trap is enough of a reason."

"The Roadhouse is packed on a Friday night. If they're going to pull something, they'll do it in front of witnesses, and there goes the innocent victim act."

"I don't know, Jacques. You said you would force them to commit the act they couldn't come back from. You didn't see Jeremy going off on Dean Banks. You weren't there when he went off on me. The Bedlam Boys branded him a thief and cheater. You got him kicked out and the dean is getting the sheriff involved. You just forced someone who's never known consequences to eat it in a big way. He's not sitting down anywhere just to *talk*."

"I'm aware of this, de Souza. The Crows will strike, and we'll be ready."

THAT NIGHT, THE SIX of us pulled up to the Roadhouse.

The establishment was the kind of place you picture when you heard the name. Dim lighting, old-fashioned décor, neon signs, wood paneling everywhere, and a simple menu of fried chicken tenders, wings, and cheap beer.

It was the main bar for Bedlam U students thanks to it sitting a ten-minute walk away. A fact that meant two dozen bar-goers fell silent as we made for the Crows' booth in the back. They all knew the beef, and they were all watching.

"Gentlemen and lady," Jeremy greeted. "Join us."

Jeremy, Micah, Asher, Gael, Bentley, and Zeke moved down the booth, making room for the rest of us. The beer and bowls of chicken wings on the table said they made use of their time while waiting.

"What do you want?" Cairo dropped.

"Wait," Micah said. His eyes were on Roan. "Before we get down to business, let's order more food and drinks. Hang out. Relax. Get to know each other like we should've from the start."

"You stalling, Ellis?" He dumped a bowl of wings on the floor. "Got a reason you don't want to get to the fucking point?"

"What? No."

"Then, get on with it."

"Fine. Whatever you want."

Gael leaned over. "It's like this. I know I'm not the guy on the security tape, and *you* know I'm not the guy on the security tape." He stuck a glance through Jacques. "We're not all rich. Some of us got families depending on us getting a degree and good jobs. This ain't about no vote or frickin' Crystal Canyon. I need these stolen tests off my record. That's the beginning of a mutually beneficial agreement between us."

"Interesting," Legend said. "But that does bring up a question for me. What was in it for you before? You say now getting Crystal Canyon isn't important, but you were willing to come up here and fuck with us in the first place. Did the Ellises provide *incentive*, or were you taking orders till the water got too hot?"

There was nothing to read on the Crows' faces, and I was paying attention. That was all I was doing. Jeremy accused me every chance he got of not being on his side. Saying too much against or for the Crows in this situation wouldn't get me anywhere good.

"What does it matter?" Gael flung. "The point is we're willing to give it up."

"It matters." Legend stroked my thigh under the table. "Let's say you were offered shares in Foundry and a cut of their profits for carving up our town. That's a potentially lucrative deal."

If they dig up diamonds, hell yes, it is.

"Thousands in the bank would turn your life around just as well as a good job. Let's say we clear your name, and you drag your feet leaving town for another six months. Six months is the earliest the vote can be called for Crystal Canyon. You get everything you want, and we're left with no guarantees."

"We'll leave," Jeremy said. "We swear."

Cairo shone those eerie green pools on him. Jeremy was first to look away.

"Just like you swore you didn't beat on my sister or our girl?"

No response.

"Your word is shit," Arsenio confirmed. "After we give you an alibi, you'll have gotten what you want and therefore no reason to hold up your end."

"Alright, we get it," Jeremy forced through clenched teeth. "Promising to leave isn't enough. What do you want?"

Roan's phone chimed.

He read the text, then stood up.

"I've got to go," he said, climbing over me and Legend.

"Is everything okay?" I asked.

"All good. My carrier needs to speak to me." Roan kissed me. "Call me if you wrap this up first."

Micah saw the kiss. He trailed Roan till he was gone, then he flicked back to me, staring till it got uncomfortable for both of us.

Legend may have had a point when he said people love and loathe Roan in equal measure. The man could rip your chest open and eat your heart with a spoon, and the next day you're crying because he didn't call you back.

"—it's going to go," Cairo said. "We'll stick to the original terms. Rain discovers the time this went down and swears Gael was with her. In exchange, you transfer out and we never see your faces in Bedlam again. If you're slow packing your bags"—Cairo plucked a photo from his pocket and slid it across the table—"we pay this woman a visit."

Jeremy looked at it and paled. He snatched the photo off the table as the others leaned in.

"Where did you get this? How?!"

Cairo heaved a sigh. "You still don't understand who you're dealing with, do you? My father's the sheriff, dumbass. I can look up the background of just about anyone, just about any time. Should I tell everyone about Miss—?"

"That's enough," he barked. "We get it."

"No, I don't think you do." Cairo flung photos at all of them. "Because now that the winds shifted, Mercury's in retrograde, or maybe because I fucking feel like it, I just changed the terms. You leave my town and convince your father and his company to go with you, or everything that happened to Paris, Arsenio, and Judge Stone will happen to the people in those photographs. Twice."

Asher and Zeke jumped out of their seats. Micah and Gael had to wrestle them down.

"You won't do it," Jeremy cried. "They're innocent."

"Paris was innocent. Rain was innocent. Eileen Stone was—"

Jeremy swiped the chicken tenders off the table. "No one connected to you is innocent! You're all one gangland family, running Bedlam like it's your turf. No one— *No one* believes your family doesn't know exactly what you do, and helps you get away with doing it. 'Sorry you experienced violence in our town' my ass," he spat.

This was going downhill fast.

"Sheriff Dad refused to arrest you. Judge Stone-Faced Bitch doesn't let a single charge with your name in it go to trial." He smiled nastily at Jacques. "Hey, how is she, by the way? I heard a server accidentally dropped some sesame oil in her food. Tsk, tsk. What an oversight."

Jacques blinked slowly. "This attempt to upset me is both sad and futile. We have an agreement, or we don't?"

"The company's already invested millions in this project. Dad couldn't pull Foundry out if he wanted to," Micah said. "He answers to other people."

"That's too bad," Cairo crooned. "Oh, well, you can keep those photos. We know what they look like."

Legend tugged me up. It was time to go.

"Wait," Jeremy called.

We kept walking.

"Wait! Alright, we'll do it."

That brought us back.

"I'll convince my father to let go of Foundry. Tell him there's no chance of the vote going our way. We'll need time though."

Cairo shrugged. "Take all the time you need. Rain will have amnesia till the last development sign is gone."

"No, she comes clean first. It's the same deal. We need assurances you'll hold up your end too."

They hashed it out back and forth—me the silent figure in the corner while they decided my life, and while Legend had his fun messing around under my skirt. The man had magnet fingers. If we were in the same room, they were attaching themselves to my body.

"I won't let you fuck with her, so you know I'll come through," said Jeremy. "Rainey walks into the dean's office on Monday. The sooner she clears our name, the sooner everyone gets to move on."

Arsenio got a notepad and pen from the barkeep. "Write it. Sign it."

Jeremy hesitated. "Write what?"

"That the six of you will leave and take Foundry with you."

"I don't work for Foundry. This won't hold up if I can't convince my dad—which I will."

Jacques's smile didn't reach his eyes. "Let me worry about the legalities. Sign it."

After a beat, he took the pen.

Jeremy wrote down their agreement, scribbled his signature at the bottom, then passed it to Micah to do the same. They went down the booth till Asher handed it back.

"Pleasure doing business with you."

Jacques ignored his outstretched hand.

We got up and the Crows did too. The crowd parted to let us out.

I glanced back at Jeremy as we spilled out on the parking lot. He tapped on his phone, nodded at Micah, then caught my eye.

Smiling, he tossed me a wink.

"I'm glad we could get this settled," Jeremy said.

Two sides faced each other on the pavement.

"You should know we didn't want it to come to this," he continued. "If your precious mom mayor hadn't turned down our construction requests, and then Judge Stone-Face backed her up in court, none of this would have happened. They forced the board to take extreme measures, and your charming selves didn't know when to back down."

Cairo turned his back on them. "Y'all have a safe trip out of my town. Don't skid off the road and die in a fiery crash, or anything like that. We'd be inconsolable."

Jeremy laughed. "I'm gonna miss your sense of humor most of all, Sharpe. Just a second, St. James."

He grasped my arm and pulled us both up short. Legend was holding my hand.

"This is for you," Jeremy said, handing him an envelope. You guys have a good time."

Jeremy and the Crows headed for their cars.

Legend watched them go, eyes narrowed as he held the envelope.

"What's it say?" I asked.

Ripping it open, he took out the note and read.

Legend shot after Jeremy.

"Hey! Come back! Stop, you filthy little shit!"

Honking and laughing raucously, Jeremy swerved around the human obstruction and peeled out of the parking lot. "Good luck."

"Legend?" I cried. "Legend, what's wrong?"

We followed him out into the street. It was me who caught him, stopping his futile chase after the disappearing taillights.

"What does the note say?"

He just handed it to me.

You're about to find out that you're missing something. Something you can't live without. And when you do, you'll crawl to me sobbing and licking my fucking boots, dripping apologies.

I suggest you make them good.

It was nearly word for word what Legend said to Jeremy before he took Micah.

"Oh no." Air punched from my lungs.

"Roan."

Chapter Nine

Legend broke every traffic law speeding to the dean's house.

Dean Banks lived on Bay Avenue in a home provided by the university. Roan hadn't gotten around to inviting me inside, but I knew the English cottage-style mansion near the end was his, along with the car parked outside with the engine still running.

"Roan?"

We piled out, checking in, around, and under his car for any sign of him.

"Roan!" Legend shouted.

He ran to the call box and jammed the button for Josephine.

Arsenio, Cairo, and Jacques ran up the curb, squealing in behind us. Arsenio and Jacques raced to me. Cairo hit the pavement and kept going.

"I don't understand," I said. I dialed Roan's number for the twelfth time. "Where is he? How could they have gotten to him?"

"How doesn't matter. We need to know where. Where is he?!"

Beep. Beep. Legend jammed the button. *Beep, beep, beep, beep, beep.*

"Jo, come on. Answer!"

"Hello?" Josephine's voice poured out the speakers. "What on earth is going on? Who is this?"

"Jo, it's me, Legend. Is Roan there?"

"Roan? No, why?"

"Didn't you call and ask him to swing by tonight?"

There was a pause.

"No, I did not," she replied. "I haven't spoken to my son since yesterday. What's going on?"

"He was taken by the Crows," Legend dropped without hesitation. "He got a text from you saying you need to talk to him, and left the Roadhouse. His car is in front of your gate with the keys still in the ignition."

She gasped. "I'm calling the sheriff."

Cairo came running back. He slapped his hands on the hood, breathing hard. "No lights on in the Crow house. No cars in the drive."

"They wouldn't take him there," Jacques said. "The sheriff would have stormed the place and cuffed them for kidnapping in ten minutes. They've taken him somewhere private."

I choked on a sob.

"I thought it was going to be me." Legend kicked the fence. "It was supposed to be me!"

"We'll find him," Jacques said. "Ellis can't hide. Not in our town."

"What if he's not in Bedlam?" Arsenio spoke up. "He could be on the road to HC right now."

Legend made for his car. "I'm going after them."

"Legend, stop. The Crows grew up in HC," Jacques said. "They know where to go for privacy. We don't. We'd end up driving around aimlessly for hours."

"I don't care!"

"Legend, he's right." The voice that spoke was mine. "Getting lost in HC doesn't help Roan. Besides, I don't think they've got him stashed an hour away."

He advanced on me. "Do you know something?"

"I know what we all know about Jeremy and his friends. They like a spectacle. An audience. Those guys burned Arsenio's car for all of Greek Row to enjoy. They poisoned Jacques's mom at a party full of people, and they jumped me and Paris in broad daylight on campus. They need everyone to see your punishment." My heart squeezed. "I can only assume it'll be the same for Roan."

Cairo turned me toward him. "When he was dropping his hints, did he give a clue what that punishment might be?"

I shook my head.

"You can't think I'm going to sit around waiting to get the call he's been hung from a flagpole!" Legend shouted more tonight than he had in the weeks I'd known him. "There's gotta be a way to track them down. Rainey," he cried. "Call Ellis. Make up whatever bullshit you have to. Say you want to be there when they teach him a lesson. Just get him to tell you where they are."

I was dialing before he finished the sentence.

"Legend, are you still there?" Josephine asked.

"We're here."

"I'm buzzing you in. Wait for the sheriff with me."

"I can't, I—"

"I know what you're going to do, and I won't have it. We're doing this the right way and allowing Sheriff Jack to do his job."

"Jo!"

"I'm scared too," she shrieked. "But Jack has the man- and firepower to get him back safely. All you four could possibly do right now is aggravate the situation worse than you already have. I want my son back safe and sound. If Jeremy Ellis and his ilk did this, I will not risk the consequences of you feeding into their hands.

"Inside. Now."

I flicked between the guys, wondering what they would do. The dial tone rang and rang in my ear.

Jerkily, Legend swung open the gate and went inside. The others followed after, leaving me the only one standing on the sidewalk.

The call picked up.

"Hello," I croaked.

"Rainey." Jeremy was smooth and light. "What's wrong, darling? You sound upset."

I straightened, summoning calm I did not feel. "I'm not upset. I'm curious."

"Where we are? I'm afraid we can't tell you that."

"No, I'm curious if Legend was right. You blew up the deal that was going to get you guys back into Bedlam U. You've gone from arson, assault, poisoning, and now to kidnapping. As embarrassed as you were by Roan's little video, this revenge has officially reached disproportionate."

"*In Bedlam, there are diamonds.*"

"Not to mention the Crows willing to back you into a life sentence."

"Is there a question?" Jeremy drawled.

"What is it about Bedlam that you need so badly? The six of you must have something big coming your way that makes all this worth it, and I'd like to know what."

"Told you more than once I don't know anything. Dad asked me to make sure the vote went our way. That's what I'm doing."

"You're doing more than that, and you're fooling me about as much as you're fooling Bedlamites. Here's some advice from the good angel on your shoulder: ask your brother about the hold Roan has over people. Someone tried to kill the guy and people will still riot if anything happens to him.

"I'm telling you now, whatever you're thinking of doing—don't. You will destroy any chance of getting the town to vote for Foundry. I can't let you blow this," I said. "Because if you do, I won't get my cut of what I strongly suspect is a whole lot of stinkin' money. My farm is going to need some repairs. Plus, I'm thinking of a complete kitchen/living room renovation."

"What is this? Blackmail?"

"How am I blackmailing you, Jeremy? I don't have anything to hold over your head. No, this is me trying to save you from making a mistake. Again. Stop and think. You know I'm right."

He hummed. "Thank you for the advice. I'll take it under advisement."

"Where are you?" I asked, because I had to.

"You'll find out soon enough."

"Jer—"

Click.

I stood there, pain and frustration battling. Despite what we said, I wanted to tear both towns apart looking for him. There was no way to know if what I said got through to Jeremy. The bitter, petty man stored hatred for Roan since the video, and it's been brewing for weeks.

This was his chance to let all that rage out.

"Rain."

Cairo stepped out from behind the gate, and took my hand. I let him lead me inside.

"Anything?" he asked.

"No. Jeremy wouldn't tell me where they are."

"He doesn't trust you."

"No," I whispered. "I'm the first he blames when something goes wrong. He's looking for a reason. If I keep calling and begging him to tell me, he'll know who I truly care about. But still that's all I want to do."

"Begging doesn't appeal to a man like Jeremy Ellis. Bragging does. He'll tell us all on his own."

By then it'll be too late, went unsaid.

Cairo took me through a charming home that reeked class in the molding, and family in the dozens of photos of her and Roan spanning the hallway. He was making faces in most of them, completely ruining the pictures with up-closes of his nostril hairs and his tongue hanging out of his mouth.

My giggles quickly turned to sobs. I didn't have to ask anyone about the hold Roan had over people. He hooked me with the first flash of his grin.

The guys waited in the library with Josephine. Roan's mom paced the carpet in her bathrobe, flicking to the phone every five seconds and willing it to ring.

A buzzer rang and she ran to the door panel.

"Jo." Sheriff Jack came through the call box. "We're outside. You got my boy in there?"

"He's here. They're all here."

I wasn't.

I got up and excused myself to the bathroom. I hadn't progressed to the point I could be in the same room as Jack Sharpe and not try to claw his eyes out. Cairo was right to keep an eye on me the nights we tried to crack his safe.

In the bathroom, I splashed water on my face.

I was half a second away from crawling out of my skin and swirling down the drain. I couldn't wait any longer. I had to call Jeremy.

My phone chimed as I fished it out. I checked the screen.

Number Blocked.

Thumb moving of its own power, I tapped open, allowing the video to play.

The blackness bled on the screen. Spinning to make me dizzy, I caught a flash of light, then the cameraman settled on three masked faces, and Roan.

I clapped my hand over my mouth, smothering my scream.

Roan's nose, mouth, and forehead leaked gore on the ground. Two of the masked men held him upright. One by the hair so everyone could see.

"Welcome, all, to a time-honored Bedlam tradition."

Muffled as it was by the mask, I could not mistake that voice.

"Jeremy," I hissed.

"It's the one, the only, Riot Royale!"

More figures filtered in and out of the shot, hooting and hollering. There was nothing on their necks, but I figured out their little tricks with makeup a long time ago.

"Legend," I screamed. "Legend!"

I bolted out of the bathroom and ran into the library, startling Davidson into reaching for his gun.

"Look. This video was just sent to me."

Legend shoved Davidson aside rushing to me.

"—my terms," said the masked Jeremy. "If I win, Banks admits he's behind the cheating scandal and that the Crows selling tests is as made-up as that little video he screened at the party. After his apology and confession tour, he'll drop out of Bedlam U, unlatch from Mommy's teat, and start over at minimum a thousand fucking miles from here. Accepted?"

"Accepted!"

"If you win, Roan, what are your terms?"

Jeremy grabbed his chin, bending his head back. Roan mumbled something.

"What was that? You'll have to speak up."

"Go... to hell," he croaked, "brother-fucker."

Jeremy punched him in the gut, ripping a scream out of Josephine.

"Who sent you this video? Jack? Jack," she cried. "Look, they have Roan. Can you see where they are? It looks like the woods."

Jack reached for my phone. "Let me see—"

Chimes, beeps, and ringtones went up around the room.

Legend pulled up the message from *number blocked*. A video was attached.

"I'll state Banks's terms. If he wins, he doesn't get his ass beat. Too badly. Accepted?"

"Accepted."

"Ready?" That could only be Micah. "Riot Royale!"

The guys released Roan. Wobbling, he caught himself—his fists beginning to lift.

Jeremy spun and kicked him in the face.

Roan hit the ground and didn't get up. I lit on a shape behind him.

"That tree," I blurted. "We sat on that tree. Buller's Den, Legend. They're at Buller's Den."

Legend grabbed me and was out the door.

"Wait," Sheriff Sharpe bellowed. Loud footfalls chased us out. "Stay here. Let us handle this!"

If Legend heard him, he gave no sign.

The two of us flew out of the door and into his car. I glued to the video the entire time, though it was horrible to watch.

Unsteady from their pre-fight beating, Roan was slow to get his hands up, block his shots, or return any of his own.

Jeremy kicked his chest and sent him flying.

"What?" Legend asked, hearing me cry out. "What's happening?"

"It's bad. He's going to kill him. We have to get there now."

He slammed the gas.

On the screen, Jeremy dragged Roan up by the hair and hauled him around. Roan snapped back, catching him in the mouth with a punch that spurted blood clear on camera.

Dropping him, Jeremy tripped over his feet and fell on his bad arm. He wasn't wearing his sling for a half-assed attempt to swear later that it wasn't him in the video and no one could prove otherwise.

My Roan used this unwise decision to his advantage. Jumping on Ellis, he pummeled his bad shoulder over and over, raining punches that ratcheted his shouts to sobs.

Jeremy's roar rang through the speakers.

"Is that Roan?" Legend jerked the car around someone not going fast enough. "Is he okay?"

"That was Jeremy. Roan's doing okay. He might win—"

Figures shot across the screen and grabbed Roan. They threw him onto the fallen log, bouncing his skull off the bark. They were on him before he recovered.

"No!"

Asher and Zeke, by their hulking masses, stomped him into the ground.

"They can't do this," I screeched. "Riot Royale is one on one."

These disgusting, loathsome Crows hadn't made time for the history lesson. They dragged Roan barely conscious to the middle of the den, where Jeremy waited. They had to hold Roan up to keep him on his knees.

"No," I breathed. "No, please."

"This is for, and to, everyone you've hurt, deceived, and cheated." Jeremy reached for something off-screen. "There's a new law in this town. The Bedlam Boy Dynasty is broken. Your oligarchy—judge, sheriff, mayor, dean, and St. James Whiskey—is over. You can be gotten to anytime, and anywhere."

A raised his fist and a flash of silver glinted in the moonlight.

"Noooo—!"

He and his silver knuckles struck Roan across the temple.

"Let this be a lesson to all of you."

The screen went black.

Legend sped the whole way to the closest entrance into the forest. Tumbling out, we shouted Roan's name, our calls echoing back to the cries of hooting owls and creatures fleeing at our presence. They seemed to be warning *go back, you shouldn't see what lies ahead.*

A firepit peeked through the trees. We skidded into the den.

The Crows were gone. Even the sounds of them running away had long faded. And Roan...

He lay facedown in the dirt—silent and unmoving.

Roan didn't stir at our screams. He didn't wake when we lifted and carried him away.

All the way to the hospital we begged for him to wake up.

Roan didn't hear us where he'd gone.

"EVERYTHING'S GOING to be okay," Josephine whispered. She felt for my hand and held it tight. "He'll be okay."

I rubbed her shoulder, tears welling when I noticed the smear of blood on my palm.

Want to know when you can say everything's going to be okay and when you can only wish it? It's after you rush your unconscious boyfriend to the town doctor, and he takes one look and shouts to get him in the car. We had to rush him to Hunter's Crest Hospital.

It was a small operation and only two nurses were hanging around the station when we busted in. They rushed Roan in the back, bobbing their heads at Nash's barked orders.

That was an hour ago. In that time, no one had come to see us nor did Doc Nash return. But I had plenty of time to count the ducks decorating the hospital chairs, and time the hum of the air-conditioning till it turned off and started again.

"Josephine."

Sheriff Jack came in with two cups of coffee. He peeled her fingers off mine and wrapped them around the warmth.

"I'm sorry to do this now, but every second spent toward finding these guys is a second sooner that they're caught," he began. "My son says Roan got a text from you and then left. You say you didn't send it?"

"No," she rasped. "My phone is missing. I got home and it wasn't in my purse. I assumed I left it at the office and planned to go back for it in the morning."

Jack Sharpe turned to me. "You were at the Roadhouse during that time, correct?"

I glared at him.

"Miss de Souza, please," he said, rubbing the bridge of his nose. "This is not about you or me at the moment. It's about Roan."

My eyes narrowed to slits.

"Yes, we were at the Roadhouse," Arsenio spoke up. "Roan left and we stayed about another half an hour. In the parking lot, Jeremy Ellis gave Legend that note."

Legend passed it over. It was snatched by Josephine.

"Something you can't live without... Sobbing and licking my boots," she read. "This is horrible. All because I expelled him?"

"No," I said quickly. "Mrs. Banks, please, don't blame yourself. Jeremy and the Crows were stewing in their hatred for a long time, promising they'd make Roan pay for outing their secrets. They weren't waiting for a reason, they were waiting for an opening."

"It's true, Jo," Cairo said. "The Crows went down the line coming after us. We thought they would hit Legend next to hurt Roan. Instead, they went straight to hurting Roan."

Josephine swung to the sheriff. "Arrest them, Jack. Now. They'll see morning through bars!"

"This note is certainly enough for me to bring in and hold them for questioning. I suspect they'll use the timeline issues as a defense, but it won't be enough. The town has been singing one name since these attacks started. They will be held to task."

"Timeline issues?" Legend repeated.

"Roan was grabbed while we were in the Roadhouse, serving as the Crows' alibi," Cairo explained. "That's why they called us in for that bogus sit-down. Everyone at the Roadhouse saw Roan leave alone, and the Crows stay put on their ass. On top of the masks, covering their tattoos, and that Roan's name isn't in the note, they're setting up to bleat innocence again."

"Jack," Josephine cried. "Tell me that's not going to work. Just because they didn't do the snatching doesn't mean they weren't responsible. Even I recognize the voice. Jeremy Ellis did this."

I sat up straight, a thought crossing my mind.

"No, he didn't," I said slowly.

"Rainey, how can you say that?"

"No, Jeremy did, but he didn't take Roan. Josephine, have any students or former students visited your office since you expelled the Crows?"

"Yes, one. Why?"

"Did you leave them alone at any point?"

She nodded. "It was this morning. Miss Cunningham interrupted the meeting. She said there was a discrepancy in the athletic fund. I told her to take the matter to Coach Higgins right away. I stuck my head out of the door for a minute. Maybe less."

"That was all they needed. Jeremy saw where you keep your purse, remember? He told his buddy to snatch your phone out of the desk, and grab his seat before you turned around."

Josephine clapped her hand over her mouth. I could see her mind working to deny she was so easily fooled, and then accepting it was the only explanation.

"When the truth came out about Jonah, Jeremy sent him away and had Asher and Zeke up here two seconds later," I said. "I never got around to asking him just how many Crows there are, but at this point, it's clear they're more gang than they are friends. Jeremy Ellis is the leader ordering them to beat on innocent women, or disguise as a server and drizzle something on a certain dessert."

Jacques's jaw clenched.

"My point is we have been underestimating Foundry and the Elises this whole time. We thought we were dealing with spoiled rich boys and oily businessmen. Not a gang leader who strikes brutally and without remorse, claiming territory and stomping out disrespect." I rubbed my now healed eye. "Explains why even though he can protect himself further by farming out the beatings, Jeremy likes to do those himself. He enjoys hurting people."

"Chilling observations," Jack said, tucking away his notepad. "If they're correct, it changes the tenor of this investigation. I'll have to contact HCPD and find out what they know about the Crows, their gang affiliation, and their size.

"You can leave this in my hands, Josephine. Roan will have justice."

The sheriff walked out as Doc Nash came in. We were out of our seats and across the room in the time it took him to peel off his mask.

"Josephine, would you like to speak in private?"

"No, you can say what you need to in front of them."

Sighing, Doc Nash aged ten years in front of me. "Roan was beaten severely. It's hard not to believe they attempted to kill him, because that's certainly what they nearly did."

Josephine choked on a sob.

"Broken ribs, bruised kidney, concussion, and there's some internal bleeding. It took a while for us to find and repair the tear, but we've stitched him up. Roan is out of surgery—"

"Will he be okay?" I interrupted.

"The next few days are up to Roan. We've given him something to sleep," he said. "If he pulls through in the next twenty-four hours, it'll give us hope he'll recover. You can't..."

His voice faded, and so did I—shrinking away from the group.

A strange calm gripped me. Chilling, but peaceful.

It told me exactly what to do.

Taking out my phone, I tapped on a single name.

Me: The police are looking for you. They're not buying the supposed alibi or the makeup over your tattoos. Hide out on my farm. They won't think to look for you there.

The response came back quick.

Jeremy: Not necessary. We've got a place.

Me: I hope it's in Bedlam because the sheriff blocked the roads.

I motioned Cairo over and showed him the messages.

"I'll take care of it," he said, striding off.

A minute passed.

Then five.

I was screwed if Jeremy and the Crows were already out of Bedlam. Eventually, I'd find an excuse to get close to him, or Jeremy would summon me. But it would not be that night.

If Roan had to spend that night trapped in darkness and pain, his life an uncertainty, so did they.

Jacques moved to my side. He faced the wall, shielding that look in his eyes for only me to see.

"They finally did it, didn't they? Committed the unforgivable act."

"Yes."

"Was this what we were waiting for?" I spat the question.

"No one was waiting for this, de Souza. I knew the expulsion wasn't the end, but I did not see this coming. I did not want it."

My cell chimed.

Jeremy: Isn't your farm abandoned? We need food, water, toilets and shit.

I typed off my message and hit send.

"None of us saw this coming and we should've. Tonight, we make it right."

Arsenio wandered over, catching the tail end of our conversation. "That was always the plan, de Souza. I told you, this ends in fire."

I DROVE CAIRO'S TRUCK up the lane I hadn't walked in weeks.

Gran. Ivy. Bella. The Letter Man.

There were endless terrible memories attached to my home. Part of me had to ask what I was fighting so hard for. Could diamonds in the soil ever satisfy when they're stained with blood?

I carried the takeout, blankets, and water bottles to the barn. Jeremy made me wait eight minutes after I knocked, though I heard them inside whispering.

The door opened a crack.

"You alone?"

"Obviously."

"Asher," Jeremy called. "Check."

He came out and Jeremy let me in. Jonah hopped off a hay bale to take their food.

I was right. Jeremy did call in reinforcements.

They all looked plenty cozy stretching out on the hay, poking in the stalls, and playing with my bows and arrows.

"Hey! Put those down."

Zeke scoffed. He lined up a compound bow, aiming it at me. "Why should I?"

"That was a gift from my grandmother. It's important to me. As the woman currently hiding your ass from the police, you can at least show respect for my things."

"Put it back, Zeke," Jeremy ordered. "The lady's right. She's going out of her way to make our stay comfortable. We're not disrespecting her hospitality."

Zeke grumbled under his breath, but he put it back.

The longer I'm around these guys, the more certain I am they are a gang.

Zeke came down from the loft. He grabbed a carton of chicken fried rice and leaned against the stall door, chatting with Micah and Jonah.

Jeremy tugged me in the opposite direction.

"We almost hit the roadblock on the other side of Chaney Bridge. How'd they get that organized so fast?"

"You have to ask?"

"Cairo."

I shrugged. "They know it's you and they know you've got every reason to book it to HC and hide out for the next few weeks."

"They don't know it's me. Not one hundred percent, and the cops will need a hundred and ten to make a charge stick. My lawyers will make sure of it."

I studied him through my lashes.

This guy freely rained terror on the streets of Hunter's Crest and Bedlam while Daddy paid to make it all go away. No wonder he didn't know consequences.

"You." Jeremy flipped his knife on his palm. "Why are you helping us? It's not in your *contract*."

"I told you, Ellis. You're going to cut me in for the real prize."

"Hmm. I didn't think you cared about money, de Souza." He glanced around. "With how hard you fought to be a farmer slopping in pig shit again."

"This is my home. This is my land. Nothing mysterious about wanting to get back what's mine. That said, I do like being a farmer, so fuck you."

Chuckling, he put up his hands. "Fine, fine. Does beg the question why you're hitting me up? And what happens if I refuse?"

My expression remained blank. "I'm not going to give you away, if that's what you're thinking. That doesn't benefit me when you still have my farm to hold over my head. Part of me was hoping you'd cut me in for the bigger deal all on your own. I've done as much work as your buddies at this point. I've warned you off, fed you information, and traded in the jail cell you were driving straight toward for a warm night in my barn.

"But if all that isn't enough, consider how much help I can be going forward? Keep you updated on the investigation, let you know if the Bedlam Boys are getting close, and when the time is right, I can drive you right out of Bedlam in Cairo's truck. No one is going to stop me if I say I'm going out on an errand for the sheriff and his son."

"Huh. Interesting." Jeremy propped the knife handle under my chin. He clearly found this amusing. "No doubt all of those would be helpful, but why wouldn't I force you to do them for free by holding this very farm over your head like you said?"

"Because I don't like when people play games with me. When they do, I get what my gran used to call 'stormy.' And when I'm stormy, I do what all natural disasters do and blaze over everything in my path," I said flatly.

"What that looks like for you, *Jeremy*, is I start getting curious about what makes Bedlam so special that you're willing to go to these lengths to get a piece of it. Then, I'll start thinking twice about your too generous bribe, buying me a six-hundred-thousand-dollar farm— But oh, wait, you're dragging your heels on giving me the keys and now I'm wondering if there's a reason."

His grin melted away.

"Maybe I start thinking you're buying all this land and just sitting on it, because you're waiting for your moment. So, now that I'm curious, and stormy, and fed the fuck up with you, I bring in assessors, crews, maybe even drilling teams and make sure I'm not sitting on oil or something."

Jeremy's sockets were two smoldering pits. "Watch yourself."

"Why? Because I'm getting close."

"Because you're too stupid to know what you're dealing with. Do— Do you know?"

"Do I know what?"

Jeremy probed me, searching my eyes for a trace of deception. He got nothing in return.

"You tell me not to play games, de Souza, but I don't know anyone who plays them better than you. I ask again, what do you want the money for?"

"Ivy won't come back to an old farmhouse and five a.m. wake-up calls. She'll come back to her dream house, hired help, and start-up money to build her own marketing firm. I want what's left of my family back together. You can appreciate that."

He grunted. "The Crows were each offered a flat rate for their services. It's generous, but it does not total the six-hundred-thousand worth we gave you. Plus an extra six thousand, and my car. Sell your sob story to someone else. Better yet, let your sister live her own life. She's better off out of this shit hole."

Jeremy, you're making this so much easier for me.

"You're not getting any more money." He cuffed my chin. "As for your services, they are to continue as required, along with the additional help you laid out. We're not having this conversation again. Say you understand this, or you'll come back tomorrow and find out what I did to Granny's bows."

Raising my chin, I said, "I understand."

"Hey," Micah spoke up. "Where's Asher?"

"I'll find him." I snatched Jeremy's knife out of the air. "Just in case."

He didn't have a chance to stop me slipping out the door.

Arsenio, Cairo, Jacques, and Legend streamed out of the darkness, running past me.

"Hey!"

"Jeremy!"

"Agh!"

I strode over to the tied-up, gagged Crow thrashing in the bed of Cairo's truck.

"Oh, look. I found him."

Chapter Ten

"Why the sudden urge to treat me to dinner, dear friend?" Paris waggled her eyebrows at me.

"Does everything I do have to have a hidden sexual meaning?"

"You are a hidden sexual meaning."

"I have no idea what to do with that."

We laughed.

"Seriously," I said. "Cairo texted me earlier saying we should go out. *Antonio's* by the square, and it's on him."

"Hmm. Suspicious."

I delayed answering by taking a bite of my pappardelle. "What's suspicious?"

"My dear brother doesn't get charitable out of the goodness of his heart. Wonder why he really told you to take me out. Have you seen him? I've called, but he's not answering."

"No, haven't seen him." *For two days.*

The guys busted into my barn, tied and gagged the Crows, tossed them in the back of Cairo's truck, then told me to drive myself home in Legend's car. I couldn't be a part of what was coming next.

I fought them of course. Argued that this was for Roan, and they weren't pulling that Bedlam Boy-only garbage. We stopped pretending I wasn't one of them since Axel Verlice.

"You can't come with us, Rain," Cairo told me. "There are other people involved now. Those show-off fucks sent that video to half the town."

"They what?" I cried.

"She's seen it, and she's authorized dramatic action."

I swallowed. "You're going to kill them?"

"Would you shed a tear if we did?"

My gaze flicked to them kicking and yelling on the bed.

"I'll shed tears, but they'll only be for Roan."

Cairo stroked my lips. "If she shows up while we're taking care of this, you can't be there. No one's supposed to know about what we do for her, or Bedlam."

"I understand."

I said I understood, but when's that ever been true in regard to the Bedlam Boys? All I knew was I'd been sleeping in their beds alone.

"Sorry about Mom," Paris said under her breath. "Ever since that video hit my phone and the Crows went on the run, she's super momma-bear protective. I've got to check her every time she tries to follow me to the bathroom."

Speak of the Nora.

Nora joined our table on the terrace, resplendent in a cream pantsuit and diamond earrings. I arrived to pick Paris up for dinner and Nora was dressed like this, though I surprised her at home. She volunteered to join us for dinner, and I couldn't think of a reason why she shouldn't.

"How are we doing, ladies? Room for dessert?"

"I love their melon sorbet," Paris said. "Rainey?"

"I don't get out of bed for less than chocolate profiteroles."

Nora's laugh chimed like bells. "Rainey, you're such a character. I'm glad my baby has you to put a smile on her face."

Paris fondly rolled her eyes. "She's my friend, Mom, not my comic relief. And as your friend," she said, turning on me. "I can't let you stay in that house alone while all of this is going on. I'll sleep over tonight. We can make a whole thing of it and invite Amy, Zara, and the girls."

"Sleep over?" Nora repeated. "Paris, why would you stay there when Rainey is more than welcome at our home any time?"

"Because Cairo's got a killer movie selection stashed in his closet."

"Nonsense. That's not a good reason for you not to sleep at home where you're safe."

"I don't need a good reason. I'm nineteen, not nine."

I rose half out of my seat, squinting at a strange light coming from the square.

"What is that?" I asked. "Is there an event tonight?"

"I didn't hear about anything," Paris said.

As she spoke, someone came running from that direction and stopped to speak to a couple strolling up the sidewalk. She said something to them, hands waving, then all three took off running.

"Something is going on."

Paris and I shared a look, then got up.

"Wait, girls. Girls," Nora cried. "Come back."

More people were running through the square, directing others to see what was ahead. I grabbed Paris's hand automatically, sensing what was coming before we rounded the fountain. Heat blasted us in the face.

Lips parting, the sound I meant to utter was stolen by the wind.

A ring of fire stretched to the sky, and defied its lack of reach by bending the air and sending its smoke high.

The burning well circled nearly the entire patch of lawn once used for family picnics. The people that occupied it now weren't there for that purpose.

Jeremy, Micah, Zeke, Asher, Jonah, Bentley, and Gael strapped to seven wooden stakes reminiscent of Ruckus Royale. Where it differed was no sand pooled at their feet, it was blood.

"Help," Jeremy bleated. "Please, h-help. Get us down."

His face was a ruin.

Nose broken and weeping, eyes half swollen shut, and blood matting his hair. That was only from the neck up.

I looked down, and hissed.

In the middle of their chests, a blistering brand scorched permanently on their chests.

Bedlam Forever

"Bedlam forever," Paris whispered.

I could only stare.

The beating Jeremy took at Riot Royale looked like love taps compared to the battered man before me, and the other Crows were not better treated.

Paris and I got as close as the flames allowed us—which seemed to be the point.

No one was to get to them, cut them down, or answer Jeremy's pleas. The Crows would suffer the public spectacle they were happy to give Roan until emergency services did only what they were required by law.

"Paris."

Nora gathered her daughter in her arms, tucking Paris's head under her chin.

Turning to look at them, I noticed the growing crowd, and the familiar faces within.

Judge Stone fell in step with Dean Banks, saying nothing of the blatant crime before her. Nearest Jonah's post, Mayor Creed blankly watched the spectacle. And across the flames, Arsenio, Legend, Jacques, and Cairo pushed through the crowd—lining up as a silent, dark force.

Bedlam's protectors.

"Please, help! Get us down from here." Jeremy was near tears. "The Bedlam Boys did this t-to us. They're insane! Monsters!"

His sobs did not move me, nor anyone else.

The video spread through town. Roan's hold on our bodies, minds, and souls held. Paris's innocence tugged at our hearts.

No one would help these men. Their pleas fell on uncaring ears.

The Crows chose the wrong town to terrorize. Didn't they know the blood of revolters ran in our veins?

I gave them my back, facing Paris in time to see Nora look across the flames and meet Cairo's gaze.

Expression hard, fire danced in her eyes, and for a second, I saw the barren, frozen wasteland that defied their brilliant pools of green.

Nora looked at her son, and nodded in approval.

She.

"Come on, sweetie," Nora said, rubbing Paris's back. "This is too much. Let's get those profiteroles and sorbet to go. Rainey, are you coming?"

"Yes," I said as sirens sounded in the distance. "I'm right behind you."

I cast one last look at my guys.

"Bedlam now," they bellowed.

"Bedlam forever!"

"YEAH. YEAH, OKAY," Cairo said into the phone. "Got it. I understand."

He hung up and set his phone on the porch steps between us.

The night before, the Crows suffered in a ring of fire. This morning, the sun rose on a cloudless day, a magpie hopped across our lawn, and a stillness settled in my bones as I watched him.

It was just the two of us on the porch.

Legend left for the hospital early. Arsenio and Jacques were out dealing with the aftermath. I was at Paris's house until an hour before. Cairo brought me home and we made it this far.

"That was my dad," Cairo said. "The Crows are handcuffed to hospital beds in HC. They're keeping them in to treat the burns and injuries, but Steven Ellis and the lawyers Jeremy kept boasting about are all over Dad. They're demanding our arrest though we have a dozen witnesses swearing we were with them when the Crows disappeared, and when they reappeared in the square."

"Witnesses," I said, smile tugging at my lips. "I take back what I said. Bedlam is a family. We look out for our own."

"Ellis should've listened to you." He tsked. "Stupid sap is going to regret that for a long time."

"How long? Will they see jail time for what they did to Roan?"

Cairo dropped his head back on the post. "Jeremy is saying they have witnesses too. They were at the Roadhouse when Roan was taken. As for Jonah, Dean Banks confirmed he was the one who came to her office that morning, but they didn't find her phone on him and he's not saying anything. Hasn't spoken a damn word since they cut him down."

"Traumatized?"

"Better be," Cairo hissed.

"All of this is sounding like they might get away with it."

He shook his head. "Roan will wake up and identify his attackers. Jonah snatched him when he got out to put in the gate code. The Crows met up with them in Buller's Den and beat him. What happens after is courtroom drama, but even if there's someone left with the slightest doubt the Crows got what they deserved last night, they won't after he speaks up."

Cairo inclined his head. "Though I won't lie to you. From what my dad's saying, they're setting this up to look like we're two groups with a long-standing beef, lying to get the other in trouble. Basically, the police can't believe the accusations we make against each other."

I scoffed. "As long as his lawyer includes Jeremy and Micah among the liars. I still can't believe how far these guys are willing to go. They're already rich."

"I've never met a rich man who had enough."

I left the beautiful bird to his hunt for breakfast, and gazed at my beautiful wolf. The nod between mother and son played in a loop in my mind. Try as I might, I couldn't see it as innocent.

"Cairo," I began.

"Rain."

I was done asking to ask. The question came easily.

"Is your mother the one who gave you this job?"

He stilled.

"Did she tell the Bedlam Boys to kill Axel Verlice?"

Cairo slowly dropped his head and peered into my eyes. As the silence stretched, I accepted he wouldn't answer.

"The job wasn't mine," Cairo said. "It was my father's."

I frowned, but otherwise did not say a thing or make a move.

"Jack Sharpe was elected sheriff for a reason. She needed some-one in law enforcement that could make certain cases... go away. But my father, deep down, is a good man. A moral one. He couldn't bring himself to play judge, jury, and executioner on the streets. So for a long time, he found other ways to handle the problem without pulling the trigger.

"Until one day, Dad got a call. A couple of supposed vacationers came up to rent out Jubilee Farm for the season. Harmless guys pos-ing as husbands. They wanted to sip tea on the porch while watching the sunset. Nothing to worry about, except the owners of one of the neighboring farms saw something strange.

"Men with tools cut through the forest bordering his land, head-ing for the farm. Obvious that they didn't want to be noticed," Cairo said. "So, he goes out to check what's going on and they say they don't know what he's talking about. There are no men. No tools. No reason for him to interrupt their afternoon. As he's leaving, he notices a mound of dirt under a tarp and a structure that wasn't there before.

"A couple days later, Mark Jubilee's daughter called asking the neighbor if he's heard from her parents. She's been calling for weeks and neither one called her back. He tells her they took off on vacation. She replied, no they didn't."

Goose bumps rippled down my flesh. I did not like where this story was going.

"The neighbor called the sheriff immediately. When *she* got word of what was going on, she ordered him to handle it off the books. There was no doubt that those men knew, and they must've done something horrible to the Jubilees."

Cairo's eyes glazed. "I was thirteen. It was soon after the divorce, and I— I didn't trust the guy by himself," he said softly. "I didn't know what he'd do. So, when he got a call in the middle of the night that made him slump against the wall, pleading with the person on the other end, I assumed it was Nora.

"Dad eventually got himself up and told me he was going out. He wouldn't be long, and I was to finish my dinner and go to sleep. But I *knew* he was dragging himself back to Nora for another kicking. If that soulless woman got her hands on him again, destroyed any more of his dignity, my dad would swallow his gun. I couldn't let that happen."

"What did you do?"

"I climbed in the back of the truck when he wasn't looking. Together we drove out to Jubilee Farm."

My chest tightened. No, this story would not have a happy ending.

"I heard them arguing," Cairo said. "Crashing, shouting, and then pleas for help. I didn't think, Rain. I grabbed the spare shotgun my dad kept under the seat, and came in through the back door.

"The kitchen was a mess, but Dad had them both on their knees—gun trained on them. Man, they were bleating their innocence. One bawled his eyes out. The other spun a story of a shady guy that offered them fifty percent of their haul if they lured the Jubilees out and hid their excavating. They didn't hurt anyone, and they promised to leave and never come back."

I blew out a long breath. "Your father wanted to believe them. He couldn't stomach executing two men in cold blood."

"That's why he lowered his gun, Rain. Told them to leave immediately, and if they ever returned, it'd be a different story. He turned his back on them, and the bawler shot up, snatching a cleaver off the block. He swung for my dad's head, and I fired. Two shots in the back without hesitation. His friend ran at me and I killed him too."

Holding his hand, I dropped kisses on his knuckles, willing warmth into his body.

"Dad vomited. He screeched and bawled and hugged me so tight it hurt. He was a mess, so I took charge. Made him bury the bodies in that hole they were digging. Then we searched the house to find and remove any trace they were there. Dad found the Jubilees in the basement freezer."

"Oh no. That poor family." I stroked his cheek. "And my Cairo. You were only thirteen."

"The old man said that a lot in the months following. 'You're only thirteen. This will mess you up for the rest of your life. Sorry. Forgive me. I'll be a better father.' On and on it went till he and the shrinks realized I was fine. Too fine.

"There wasn't a change in my sleep or eating. I wasn't pissing my bed or sobbing into my breakfast. And more than once, Dad would try to leave in the middle of the night and catch me sneaking in the truck bed to go with him."

A mirthless smile stretched his lips. "Everyone asks what's wrong with my eyes, Rain, and the answer was always simple. They scare people... because they're empty. Like me, you look inside of them and can't find warmth or love or happiness. You can't find anything at all."

"That's not true—"

"That's why I was the most logical person to take on the job," he carried on like I hadn't spoken. "Dad didn't have the stomach for it. If he tried, it would've destroyed the little left of my father."

I swallowed through needles. "So she... your mother... gave kill orders to her thirteen-year-old son?"

The smile remained as he tangled in my hair.

"No, Rain. When Nora found out, she went off on him. A killer for a son hardly fit into her perfect life. She hardly cared if he got caught and went down for it, but if I'm hauled away in cuffs, everyone will look at the mother who abandoned me as the first blow that warped my mind."

"Or maybe it's because she does love you deep down. She doesn't want that life for you."

His laugh was a harsh sound. "No, that's not it."

I couldn't argue with him. Nora was a stranger to me. I could trust her son knew her a lot better.

"What you need to understand is that *she* is not one person. She is multiple people. The guys and I don't need to use names. They're all basically one entity, taking orders from the same person. Nora is one of the people working with her. She convinced Jack to take on the job when they were married, and expected him to continue after.

"For years after what went down at Jubilee Farm, I knew something more was going on with him, but Jack kept me out of it. He refused to answer my questions and made sure I wasn't following him when he went out at night. During that time, his drinking got worse."

"How did we get here?" I asked. "Now you are doing your father's job. The five of you. If Nora didn't want you involved, what changed?"

"I didn't give up. When I was old enough to drive, I started tailing my old man. Noting who he met, looking up the numbers he called, paying attention the nights he left his badge in the office. Jacques helped me put the pieces together. They led to Arsenio, Legend, and Roan in different ways. The boss has multiple people working for her, doing different jobs around town.

"We were already the Bedlam Boys by the time she made another call to Dad, and I answered the phone. I told her Dad's not in that business anymore. She was dealing with me now. At first, she was hesitant, then I mentioned I'd been doing the job anyway. Cleaning up after my drunk father's messy crime scenes, and pouring him into his uniform the next morning to continue the charade at work.

"Officially, our job is collections and keeping shits like the Crows in line. Unofficially, we're the town's cleanup crew. This serves her well since it keeps Nora off her back and the job still gets done. She calls Jack to give him a name, knowing I'll get it out of him."

"Goodness," I breathed. "I truly don't know anything about the home I've lived in for almost twenty years."

"You'd be surprised how very few people do."

"You're not, you know." I kissed him soft and light. "Empty. An empty person wouldn't go to the lengths you have to protect your father. He wouldn't care for his sister. And we wouldn't be as connected as we are.

"I've known empty men," I said, Cavendish floating through my mind. "They need to hurt others because they can't feel pain themselves. While you've known pain, heartache, abandonment, and loss, Cairo Sharpe. That's why you bleed it from me. You know what I need to breathe."

He bent his neck, our mouths closing the distance.

"Morning."

The mailman bounded up the path, waving to us like it was just another sunny day.

For everyone else, it got to be.

"Don't have much for you today." He climbed past us, heading for the box. "Can I say, people don't send letters much these days. Especially not black ones."

We shot off the steps, startling the poor man into jumping back.

"You two have a good day," he said, hurrying off.

Cairo looked over my shoulder as I tore the black letter open, tearing out the note.

Well, well, well.

Did you hear my voice as you read that? Of course not. Stupid bitch, you don't remember me, so you got the cops out here looking for me.

The thing about living in a small town is you know everyone's face. You for sure recognize the strangers suddenly camped around drop boxes in town.

Clever plan, but ultimately, a waste of time. If you wanted to meet me, Angel, you didn't have to go through all this trouble.

I'm arranging a little meeting for us as you read this.

I suddenly came into some good news and I want to share it with you.

If you're lucky, we'll both get what we want.

You'll get answers.

And I'll get you.

Stay psycho.

Love you, XOXO.

"Arranging a meeting for us?" I repeated. "What does that mean?"

"I don't think there's a hidden meaning, Rain."

"But why would he?" I spun on him. "He said he'd meet me last time because I did what he wanted and killed Verlice. He found out that was a lie, and you know what I walked in on. This time I haven't done anything for this guy. Plus, he knows the police are onto him. If there's a meeting planned, it won't be for beers at the Roadhouse."

"That's why we do this smart. Get Gold and Ribecco on the phone. Let them know he's onto them. Those two will have to come up with a much better plan for when we ambush this guy."

"I'm supposed to go along with this meeting thing like it could possibly be real?"

Cairo bundled me inside, closing and bolting the door behind us.

"If the letter comes with a time and place, we pass it on is what I'm saying. Let him walk in on a surprise."

"What if he ambushes me again? He's snatched me in the middle of a crowd before."

Cairo cocked a brow. "Won't be a problem because the allowable distance between us just got a lot shorter. Between me, Arsenio, Jacques, and Legend, there'll always be one of us available to walk with on campus. As much as I hate to say this." His lips peeled back from his teeth. "Nora's cool to let you stay with her. I like her security cameras, gates, guard, and home alarm patched into the station, a lot better than I like our frat house with a few new locks."

"You want me to stay over Paris's without you guys?"

"Just at night," he replied. "Even we have to sleep."

I hugged myself, wishing like hell this wasn't happening.

"Paris's house is safer, but it's not impenetrable. And it'd have to be for me to consider putting my best friend in danger. The Letter Man isn't above shooting Esteban in the guard box, hitting *open* himself, and strolling inside. I've put so many people in danger since this started. First, Jennifer Wilson, and now Colton who is still in the hospital. I won't put Paris at risk. There has to be somewhere else I can lie low for the night."

"That has as much security?" A strange look came over his face. "Know what? There is a place."

Cairo backed toward the stairs. "Get your stuff. I've got to talk to the sheriff, and you're not staying here alone. I'll drop you at the hospital. Meantime, get Gold on the phone."

I wasn't about to turn down a trip to see Roan.

"Let's stop by Gold on the way," I said while my fingers were dialing. "I'm starting to worry there's a reason he hasn't returned my calls."

I PEERED THROUGH THE glass door.

The lights were off. The closed sign hung in the window. Gold's desk was visible, neat, and missing its owner.

"No one's here," I called over my shoulder. "I don't know where he lives and he's not answering his phone. What now?"

"He's got friends like Ribecco on the force." Cairo leaned on the car hood. "Call the station and tell them you haven't heard from him in a while. They can do a wellness check on his place. Make sure nothing happened."

"Good idea."

I hopped back in the car and Cairo drove me to the hospital. On the way, I put a call in to the HC police and told them I hired Gold to work a dangerous investigation, and was beginning to get worried that I hadn't heard from him in two weeks. They promised to look into the matter and I had to let that be enough.

Please be okay. I sent the thought out into the universe. *You've been so kind to me. You've helped me get answers I've searched a long time for. I couldn't stand it if getting tangled up with me got you hurt.*

Cairo dropped me off to be with Roan and Legend.

Roan woke on his own the day before. They had him on two different kinds of drugs that made him drowsy. The result was I held his hand and filled him in on the details while he lay there sleeping. Afterward, Legend drove me back to Bedlam.

"Yeah? That's not a bad idea," he said on the phone. "They're not using the place, so why shouldn't we? Cool. Be there in twenty."

"Who was that?" I asked.

"Cairo. He's got the keys to the Crow house. They paid rent to the end of the month and the cops cleared it as a crime scene, so it's sitting empty. It's got way better security. Figured this was a good compromise."

"We're not worried about Jeremy or one of them coming back?"

"They're in HC. On top of that, they're all under arrest. After they're discharged, the Crows are moving to a cell."

"Huh. This is a good compromise. All the security and no one to put in danger. The downside is I've got to spend more time in the place that filth lived and breathed."

"Now he can do the first good deed in his worthless life and provide a safe place for you." Legend punched the gas. "No one else is fucking with what's mine."

Twenty minutes later, we pulled up to the Crow house gates.

Cairo, Jacques, or Arsenio buzzed us in. The three of them stretched out on the couch, soccer game playing, and bags of Greek takeout on the coffee table. They made themselves right at home.

"Rain, eat something," Cairo said.

"Don't mind if I do."

I helped myself to a couple of chicken kebabs, lemon potatoes, and Greek salad. Moving aside the soup, I spotted my recent note from the Letter Man.

"We've been talking options," Arsenio explained. "Has the investigator or his cop friend gotten back to you?"

I shook my head.

"Then, we need our own plan for taking down this guy when he sets the meeting."

"I still say he's going to see that coming. By now, he knows I told you guys and the police. I'm not making it easy for him. He won't make it easy for me."

The doorbell chimed. Cairo got up to check it out.

"It's Davidson," he called back. "I told him to get the alarm codes from the owner, and info on how to change them. We'll be outside."

I shifted to Jacques. "What do you think? Isn't your genius mind screaming that the same person who thought giving me a gift was attempting to kill an innocent person, only has worse for me planned down the line?"

"Yes," Jacques replied. "To meet him anywhere, at any time, is a bad idea if *he* controls the situation. We simply ensure that we do."

"But how—?"

My phone went off. I checked it and shot off the couch.

"Guys, it's Gold. Give me a sec."

I went into the dining room, turning my back on the guys.

"Gold? Are you okay?"

"It's me. I am fine," he said. "The police stopped by my place this afternoon to check on me because you were worried. I'm sincerely sorry I put you through that. I can only imagine what went through your head."

"I thought he killed you," I said bluntly. "I got another letter from him today, and he knows the police have been watching the drop boxes."

"That's unfortunate." He sounded like he was speaking to himself. "I'll have to call off Ribecco."

"What's going on? Why haven't I heard from you?"

A deep, weary sigh gusted through the phone.

"I'm very sorry. I believe I'll say this to you often during our conversation. The fact is I came across some information during the investigation that I simply did not know how to tell you."

I slowly lowered myself on a dining room chair.

"I've taken this long to get back to you, because I've checked, rechecked, then checked again. I owe it to you to be one hundred percent certain."

"About what?" I croaked.

"I'm hired to give hard truths. I've done so for years without hesitation, but to tell this to you after how much you've already suffered. It's the first time in my career I thought I was doing something... wrong."

"Mr. Gold, you're scaring me. Please, just say it."

"I'm sorry, Rainey."

That made three.

"It's about your sister, Ivy. How much do you know about where she's been and what she's done in the past two years?"

"Ivy?" I echoed. "I spoke to her a little while ago—before she hung up on me. She's in Chicago with her boyfriend, loving her new life."

"I see."

"See what?"

"There's something you need to know about Ivy," Gold began. "She is—"

Pain exploded in my skull.

I pitched forward, head hurtling for the table edge. I ricocheted off and toppled out of my chair.

"Rainey? Hello, Rainey, can you hear me?"

The world spun.

Wetness dribbled down my face and neck. I touched them and my fingers came away covered in blood. Trying to make sense of the sight, I hardly registered the boots coming down beside my head.

Eyes fluttering shut, I drifted away.

Chapter Eleven

"Wake up. Hellloooo."

Pain lit my cheek.

"I said, get up."

I slowly came to, descending into agony.

My head ached. Temples throbbed. Cheek stung. Wrists burned.

The final realization pushed back on the grogginess. Why did my wrists burn?

Blinking, my vision blurred on a face.

"Finally," a voice said. "I was a minute away from starting the party without you."

Blonde hair came into focus, and little by little, the brown eyes became clear. A round nose. Thin lips.

And a name.

"Zoey?"

My former orientation tour guide beamed. "Look at that. There is intelligent life on this planet. I was worried those knocks to the head rung your bell for the final time, you crazy bitch."

I bristled. Why the hell was this woman talking to me like that? And where was I?

Drifting up, I peered through crisscrossing metal to the clear night sky.

We were outside and on Chaney Bridge by the looks of it.

"Hmm."

What am I doing here? What was I doing before?

"Hmm! Hmm!"

What's that—?

Zoey stepped out of the way, and I fell on Arsenio, Cairo, Jacques, and Legend—wrists bound and suspended from ropes tied overhead. They balanced on a ledge on the balls of their feet. Gags stretched their mouths open.

"Guys!" I raced to them and made it three steps.

My bound hands yanked me off my feet and smashed me against the rail.

Zoey laughed herself sick.

She was dressed in a bright yellow sundress with a matching bow keeping her bangs out of her face. You'd have thought she was going out to a picnic, if not for the crossbow held in her gloved hands.

I squinted. *My crossbow.*

"Where are you running off to? The fun just started."

"What the fuck are you doing?!" I screamed. "Let us go."

"Now why would I do that... Angel?"

Cold dread climbed my spine. "What did you say?"

"Need me to spell it out," she sang. "I promised I was arranging a meeting for us and here we are. I'd have thought you'd be happy, seeing as you put so much effort into finding me."

"You?" I scurried back as she closed the distance. "But— But how? Why?"

"How and why you already know. But you *forgot*." Zoey rolled her eyes. "How convenient."

"You're the Letter Man," I sliced in.

"Woman. Thank you very much."

"But you... Blake Jensen..."

My conversation with Craig came roaring back.

"Blake. Is he in this photo? Point him out."

"Blake's not—"

"A guy," I whispered. "He was going to say that Blake isn't a guy. The face he pointed out!"

I snapped up to her. In my mind, I moved past the person I thought Craig pointed at, to the girl I dismissed outright.

Her hair was brunette. The round nose was pointed, but the resemblance couldn't be denied.

"You're Blake Jensen."

"Correction: I was Blake Jensen."

"And Dante? How did you...?" I trailed off, my mind struggling under the new information.

"Oh, I'm not Dante. But the new guy is a friend," she said. "He kindly made a few changes to the show, and added lines to his script when I asked. I have friends, Angel. Everywhere."

"You're not Dante, but you are Blake."

She gestured with my crossbow. "I changed my name to Zoey Mariner the second I hit eighteen. Ugh. You don't know the hell I went through. My parents thought it'd be cool and revolutionary to give me a guy's name. Instead, I was bullied relentlessly. They called me a man. Stole my tampons, saying that guys didn't need them. It was awful."

"Boo hoo. I don't give a fuck about your sob story." I strained in my binds. "You shot Colton. You killed Bella! And the guys. Get them down from there right now."

Zoey aimed the bow at Legend and fired.

"No!"

He jerked out of the way and the arrow sailed past, missing him so narrowly I heard his jacket tear.

"You're not in a position to make demands, so don't do it again. You are, however, lucky that I'm in a sharing mood. Go on," she sang. "Ask me all about my dastardly plan. *Why did you do it? How did you get away with it?* I love this part."

I spat at her feet.

She heaved a sigh. "You always were stubborn."

"You don't know me."

"Au contraire. If you want to get technical, I'd say I'm the only one who knows the real you. Come on. Haven't you put it together yet?"

"We met during that blurred-out year of my life while I was on the meds. I get it," I mocked. "But if you think that drugged-up robot is the real me, you don't understand how blackouts work. Anything I did"—I thought of the body at Black Widow Hill—"or didn't do. It wasn't a choice."

Giving me her back, Zoey shot at the ropes keeping Arsenio out of the water below.

"Hmm!"

"Stop!"

"Here's how this goes," she said. "I couldn't have you driving the Crows out of town too early, because they hadn't accepted my price yet. You see, you're not the only one I've sent letters to. But I bet you thought you were special. Aww."

My teeth clenched. I had this person pegged before I knew her.

She's enjoying this.

"Now that Cavendish is dead and the leash is off, I'm offering my services to the highest bidder," she explained. "I sent a few letters to Jeremy Ellis telling him that when he eventually failed against the Bedlam Boys, and he was meant to fail, I'd kill them for fifty grand."

Zoey dropped that like a McDonald's order.

"He kept up that he could handle this himself. That's until the light show in the square. He hired me the second he woke up in the hospital. Only ten grand each. A bargain. Though I am missing one," she muttered. "Should've waited, but we've waited so long to do this."

My heart shot in my throat. One sentence penetrated.

"Kill them?" Tears stung as I took in the ropes, and the death she chose for them. "Don't do this. You said you wouldn't."

"Well, when I said that, I didn't have twenty-five grand in the bank. Keep up."

Tears ran down my cheeks. Behind my back, I wriggled my wrists, working to get free.

"That said, I didn't bring you out here to watch them die. If you do, that will be your choice."

"What does that mean?"

"It means that in honor of our past friendship, I'm willing to let you go in their place." She motioned to the ledge above my head. "Jump and I let the Bedlam Boys go free."

The guys shouted through their gag.

"Refuse, and I keep shooting these arrows till they're either full of holes. Or, I get lucky with my aim, catch the rope, and it snaps—gifting them a cold, watery death. Because you broke the rules again, Rainey. You told the police about me even though I've warned you over and over again. I treat you as a friend, but you haven't done the same for me. It's time I stopped giving you chances. You won't talk me out of the decision coming your way. But you can delay it by indulging me and dragging the conversation out as long as you can. So."

Zoey leaned over me and sliced my binds just like that. She backed up and leveled my bow on the guys.

"What's it going to be?"

Straightening, I gripped the railing—cold metal biting my skin.

There were two trucks on either end of the bridge, blocking the opening. One was Cairo's, and the other I saw in the police station parking lot most mornings.

Davidson.

I pushed the name away, focusing solely on Zoey and the healthy stash of arrows in her quiver.

If I keep her talking long enough, I can delay until someone tries to drive across the bridge and sees what's happening here.

"How do I know you won't hurt them anyway? I kill myself and then you loose those ropes, collecting another twenty-five grand."

"If there's anything I honor, Angel, it's a sacrifice." She said that with a seriousness she hadn't used before. "If you give your life for them, they will be spared."

"Okay," I said clearly. "You win. How did you go from that sweet kid smiling with her friends, to a killer?"

"Ah, now that's an interesting story," she mused, pointing my bow at Cairo, Arsenio, Cairo, then Arsenio. She laughed as they shouted at her.

"I met Scott while he was working the youth center, and he saw something in me. By then, the bullies were harassing me just because they could. It stopped being about my name a long way back.

"Scott took me under his wing. He told me about my legacy and that the people I came from didn't take shit from anybody. Then, he taught me how to make anyone who hurt me scream." She winked. "He was a good friend to me. To us. But the guy was paranoid and locked under too many rules. He would not have approved of the little deal I made with the Crows.

"Last year, I made one mistake and he came down on me. Hard. It was no small relief when he got that death wish and ordered you to kill him. Now I'm free to do what I want."

Scott Cavendish was her mentor and supposed friend, and she cheered his fiery death. That answered the question of if sociopaths could make friends they gave a real care about.

No.

"Why do you think we know each other?" I asked. I took a step closer.

"That's far enough." Zoey swung the bow on me. "Hands on the ledge at all times. If you let go"—she flashed and loosed an arrow that struck Arsenio's thigh—"so do I."

"Arsenio!"

His muffled cries shredded my heart in two.

"Stop it," I screamed. "You said you wouldn't if we talked."

She shrugged. "I'm just demonstrating the consequences. I noticed that when I do, I never have to repeat myself."

"You don't." I strangled the metal. "You don't have to *demonstrate*. I'm listening to you. I'm giving you what you want.

"Hold on, Arsenio." I poured my pleas and comfort into my gaze. "I'll get you down from there."

"Ugh. Enough about him. We're in the middle of a conversation, bitch. Don't be rude."

You're going to see who's the fucking bitch when I'm done.

"How do we know each other?" I forced through gritted teeth.

"Oh, that's easy." She beamed. "We hooked up after your grandma got herself killed."

I reeled back.

"Yeah. You were pretty messed up over it. Wanted revenge like no one I've ever seen," she said. "Scott came to you through work. He did the farm's accounts for free. A favor for your grandmother because she brought his mom free produce when she was laid up with cancer and couldn't get out of bed."

"Oh my gosh," I breathed. "Gran was the connection. Not Walker Lewis. How did I not know this? Why didn't I remember him?"

"You didn't meet till after she was killed. Why would you? I don't know who the fuck my parents' accountant is." She shrugged. "Anyway, Scott got close to you, and you started talking a lot of crazy, violent stuff. He sent you the letters first—checking to make sure you were receptive to the help he was willing to offer. When you didn't go running to the police, he told you who he was, and that he'd gladly help you sacrifice Andrew Clein in the name of your grandmother."

"No," I cried. "No!"

Pain pounded my temples.

I dropped to my knees, eyes squeezing shut as I cried out—from which pain, I couldn't guess.

"You're lying!"

"How would I know this if I was lying?" Zoey laughed. "The three—five—seven of us— I won't tell you exactly how many of us there are. Because all that matters is you, me, and Cavendish had our own thing going on. You and I became friends."

Temper leaked into her voice. "You taught me how to shoot an arrow. Not as good as you, but good enough. I taught you how to break a man's arm in a single twist. That's what you did to Andrew Clein first," she hissed. "Broke his arm."

"Stop it!"

Flashes bombarded my mind. Blurred faces, places, scenes that moved too quickly for me to grab one and make it real.

"We got so close, we started watching that time travel show you like. Every Saturday with a bowl of popcorn and homemade tacos. I called you Angel because the Weeping Angels are your favorite monster in the show. That's who you were to me. My favorite monster."

"No," I sobbed. "It's not true. None of this is true."

"It is true!" she roared. "Snap out of this boring mental breakdown and wake up! We were friends. You know it. You remember."

"No!"

But I did.

Fragmented pieces formed a picture of me and a brunette Blake Jensen, laughing and joking while doing target practice on a hay bale. Who would I let touch my precious bows and arrows from Gran, other than a friend?

"There it is," she hissed. Zoey was suddenly in my face, bending my neck back by the hair. "See? I knew you were still in there, Angel."

"Stop. P-please."

"Oh, now you beg? *We* begged." She dug the arrow tip in my neck, breaking the skin. "Scott asked you to sacrifice one worthless guy to further our cause, and you refused. Said you didn't get into this to hurt innocent people. We tried to make you see!"

My head shook in her grip.

"No one is innocent, but everyone is honored in sacrifice."

"No."

The pressure in my skull was unbearable. Each horrid word from her snarling lips drove the spike deeper, unleashing a flood of memories that couldn't be true!

"The sheriff had something we needed. All of a sudden, the stubborn oaf grew a backbone. Refused to give Scott what he asked, so he ordered you to sacrifice the sheriff's son."

Eyes huge, Cairo stopped struggling.

"But oh no," Zoey carried on. "*Cairo was innocent. Just a teenager. There had to be another way.* Blah, blah, blah. Scott said you had two days to gut the guy, or you'd watch while I did it. You walked into the sheriff's station that day and told Davidson everything."

"No," I whispered.

Yes.

I remembered the station bell chiming. Recalled Davidson's smile as he said the sheriff was out, but he'd be happy to help me.

Zoey tsked. "Such a shame. If only Andres was on shift that day. We'd be in prison, and none of what came next would've happened."

"Oh no," I breathed, folding onto the pavement.

My hands came off the ledge and Zoey didn't care. Glee twisted her smile as the spike pried loose the final memory.

"Yes, Angel." Her voice neared a soft coo. "You remember how we punished you. The night we busted into the farmhouse, catching you making a cup of tea like all your troubles were over. What did we do, bitch?"

I tossed my head, shaking roughly. But the vision would not stop unfolding.

The body in the barn. Broken, twisted, and beyond help.

"What did we do to you?"

The woman—for now I knew she was a woman—that I buried at Black Widow Hill, did not answer my calls then, nor did she in the memory.

I heard the name I called her. I saw her face when I flipped her over.

"What did we do?"

"You killed me," I whispered, pain fading as it all came back. "I died that night."

"Yes." Zoey released my hair and stroked my cheek. "That's it. Remember."

"I forgot about dying."

My voice was small. Pleading.

"How could I forget?"

"It's okay." Zoey kissed my forehead. Standing up, she backed away, aiming my bow at my now silent boys. "You were special, Angel. Only you could live on after death. Even so, you must pay for what you've done. Give back the time that wasn't yours."

I rose on shaky knees.

"Scott believed we could bring you back through blood, clues, and letters. But he should have known." Zoey lined the shot at Cairo's heart. The expert marksman I was, I knew this time she wouldn't miss.

"The dead only return through sacrifice."

I looked down below at the black, icy waters.

"Now it's time to make your choice," she barked. "You? Or the Bedlam—"

I climbed onto the ledge and jumped off.

If you'd like to read the next book in the series, Chaos Crown, click here.[1]

1. *http://mybook.to/ChaosCrown*

Keep In Touch

Join Ruby's mailing list for news, teasers, and more:
https://www.subscribepage.com/rubyvincentpage
Join Ruby's Facebook Reader Group:
https://bit.ly/3bNuCOq

ABOUT THE AUTHOR

Ruby Vincent is a published author with many novels under her belt but after taking a fun foray into contemporary romance, she found her love of saucy heroines, bold alpha males, and weaving a tale where both get their happy ever after.